NAKED FLAMES

NAKED FLAMES

Graham Ison

This first world edition published 2019
in Great Britain and the USA by
SEVERN HOUSE PUBLISHERS LTD of
Eardley House, 4 Uxbridge Street, London W8 7SY.
Trade paperback edition first published
in Great Britain and the USA 2020 by
SEVERN HOUSE PUBLISHERS LTD.

British Library Cataloguing in Publication Data
A CIP catalogue record for this title is available from the British Library.

ISBN-13: 978-0-7278-8963-8 (cased)
ISBN-13: 978-1-78029-622-7 (trade paper)
ISBN-13: 978-1-4483-0238-3 (e-book)

All Severn House titles are printed on acid-free paper.

Severn House Publishers support the Forest Stewardship Council™ [FSC™],
the leading international forest certification organisation. All our titles that
are printed on FSC certified paper carry the FSC logo.

Typeset by Palimpsest Book Production Ltd.,
Falkirk, Stirlingshire, Scotland.
Printed and bound in Great Britain by
TJ International, Padstow, Cornwall.

ONE

For days I'd been looking forward to spending the weekend with Lydia Maxwell, an attractive and wealthy, buxom, right-side-of-forty widow. We'd met when I was investigating a murder at an apartment block in North Sheen. Callous though it may sound, once a murder enquiry has been brought to a successful conclusion, I banish it from my mind, usually because I'm dealing with another one.

Lydia's late husband Geoffrey had been what is euphemistically called 'something in the City'. I've never quite discovered what that involves, but he had made a lot of money doing it, sufficient to buy a yacht for half a million pounds and a top-of-the-range Aston Martin that he always drove much too fast. Ironically, it was those two obsessions that, indirectly, were responsible for his death. Lydia had hated sailing and eventually prevailed upon her husband to sell the yacht, which he kept in a marina at Lowestoft, but on his way home after the sale he was killed in a high-speed crash on the A12 the other side of Colchester.

Geoffrey Maxwell had died a rich man and his substantial fortune passed to Lydia. However, I had the impression that she was not too upset by the tragedy, the implication being that her marriage had been unravelling for some time prior to her husband's death. I said she disliked sailing and it most likely had something to with that – she confessed to suffering badly from seasickness – and the drive from North Sheen to Suffolk almost every weekend didn't help. Added to which was her husband's insistence that 'you'll soon get used to it, old girl', a term she disliked given that he had first used it when she was in her teens.

However, apart from my meeting Lydia, the North Sheen murder was memorable for a far less agreeable reason. It had resulted in a second murder, that of one of my own officers, a young married detective constable named John

Appleby who had been gunned down while attempting to arrest the killer. And that is something you remember for the rest of your life.

Lydia had been unwilling to remain living in a flat opposite one that had been the scene of two murders, and had moved to a large house on a gated estate in Esher in Surrey. Being a keen swimmer, she'd made sure that the house possessed its own swimming pool, which she'd had enclosed in an attractive cedarwood chalet, thus ensuring privacy and the luxury of being able to swim in mid-winter.

Quite by coincidence, Lydia's new house turned out to be next door to the one owned by Bill and Charlotte Hunter, and the three of them had quickly become friends. Bill, a very successful financial speculator, and Charlie, as she was invariably known, had been friends of my ex, Gail Sutton. Gail and Charlie Hunter were actresses but Gail had been attracted, like a moth to a flame, to the bright lights of Hollywood by a mind-blowing amount of money for a part in a glossy American soap opera. I had waved goodbye to her at Heathrow Airport knowing, but trying to think I was wrong, that it would be the last I ever saw of her.

I'm pleased to say, however, that my relationship with Lydia seems to be showing all the signs of permanency and Gail is gradually becoming a distant memory.

Late on the Saturday afternoon, she and I were lazing by her pool and, as an added delight, I was relishing the thought of another of her masterclass dinners later that evening.

From time to time, we took a dip in the pool to cool off from what was proving to be one of the hottest days of the year. I was enjoying one such dip and waiting for Lydia to join me when I noticed she was speaking to someone on the phone. I swam to the side of the pool and saw that it was my mobile she was holding. I'd not heard its distinctive ring tone from the pool and Lydia had answered it.

'It's the office for you, Harry, darling,' she said in the husky voice that had immediately attracted me when first we'd met.

I clambered out and took the phone, in a bad temper even before I'd answered the damned thing. I knew exactly why it had rung on a Saturday afternoon and so did Lydia. She'd known me long enough to have learned what such a call usually meant. All that remained was to be told the location.

'Brock!'

'It's Gavin Creasey, sir.'

'What is it, Gavin?' I listened in disbelief as Detective Sergeant Creasey, the relief incident room manager, gave me the details of the death to which I'd been assigned. 'You've got to be kidding me, Gavin,' I eventually managed to say. 'Well, tell them to make sure they've put some clothes on before I get there. And organize a car for me.'

'Dave Poole is on his way to pick you up as I speak, guv'nor.'

'I'm at Esher, not Surbiton, Gavin.' I gave him Lydia's address.

'I'll get him on the radio and divert him, guv.'

'What was that all about, darling?' Lydia asked as I finished the call. The expression on her face was a mixture of amusement and disappointment. 'Why did you ask them to put clothes on?'

'I've been assigned to the suspicious death of a nudist in a fire at a bloody naturist club somewhere near Harrow, would you believe?'

Lydia started to chuckle but eventually became convulsed with laughter and almost collapsed on to one of the poolside loungers. Eventually she managed to speak. 'You can go as you are, then,' she said. In between fits of uncontrollable giggles, she gestured at my nudity.

My sergeant, Dave Poole, got me to the venue of the nudist's death – some thirty or so miles from Esher – in commendably good time. Since the swingeing budget cuts that the government had inflicted upon the police, the usual mode of transport to take me quickly to the scene of a murder had been a traffic unit car. But such luxury had now been vetoed by authority, the reasoning being that if the victim was already dead, there was no hurry. Such are the thought processes of those supreme beings set over us who have no detective experience. They did, however, authorize the fitting of a sat-nav to our cars, which sometimes introduced me to parts of Greater London that I didn't know existed.

I was met at the entrance to the naturist club by a uniformed inspector flourishing a clipboard. I'd long ago concluded that without clipboards, the Metropolitan Police would grind to a standstill. I knew what he was going to ask and forestalled his question.

'DCI Harry Brock and DS David Poole, HMCC West.'

I should perhaps explain that Dave and I are attached to Homicide and Major Crime Command. The addition of the word 'West' indicates that we're responsible for murders, manslaughters and other assorted major mayhem in an area that stretches from Westminster out through Hammersmith to Barnet. Unfortunately, it also includes the Harrow area.

'Thank you, sir.' The inspector carefully recorded this information. 'DI Mansfield is in there somewhere,' he said, and waved at the entrance. A discreet sign stated that this was the Pretext Club. There were open high metal gates designed to look as if they were much older than they were, but access was controlled by an automated barrier a little further inside. There was a CCTV camera mounted on a short post, positioned so that it could read car number plates but, as we later learned, could not see who was in the vehicle. And that turned out to be unfortunate.

The fire brigade was still in attendance when we arrived, although the fire crews had started to pack away their equipment. I spotted the woman who was supervising. She could have been slim, but it was difficult to tell as she was clad in a firefighter's protective gear and wore a white helmet with a single black band around it indicating that she was a station manager. I presumed that she was in charge of the incident.

'Good evening, I'm Detective Chief Inspector Harry Brock and this is Detective Sergeant Dave Poole.'

'Hi!' Taking off her helmet, the woman ran a hand through her damp hair and wiped perspiration from her smoke-begrimed face with a small towel.

'What can you tell me about the fire?'

'I won't weary you with all the details that are on record, like the time we got the call and the time we arrived, and all that sort of stuff.' She sat down on the step of the pump appliance. 'We got a shout to a fire in that chalet,' she said, indicating with a wave of the hand. 'It was well alight by the time we arrived, but it was brought under control very quickly.'

'What caused you to think it was suspicious?'

'Apart from everyone roaming around in the nude, I think you guys call it copper's nose,' said the fire chief. 'You know when something's not quite right, but you can't put your finger on it, so you dig a bit deeper.' Taking a bottle of water from one of her crew with a word of thanks, she took a long drink. 'Well, it's the same with us. Call it a sixth sense, if you like, and there was something not quite right with this one. I think the thing that made me doubtful was that the corpse, what was left of it, was still on the bed, which to me implied that he'd been dead before the fire. In view of my doubts, I've arranged for a fire investigator to examine the scene and I expect you'll want your people to have a look at it.'

'Thanks very much. I hope the rest of your shift stays quiet for you,' I said, and turned to go.

'So do I, Chief,' she said. 'Thanks.'

I crossed to where Jane Mansfield was chatting to a uniformed constable. Mansfield was what we call a HAT DI, an acronym that has nothing to do with headgear, but indicates that she is part of a Homicide Assessment Team. Members of these teams decide if a suspicious death is a murder, and if so, whether it's one likely to involve a protracted enquiry. Mansfield had obviously decided that this particular homicide qualified on both counts, hence my presence.

'What's the SP, Jane?' I asked, borrowing a bit of racing jargon that CID officers use as shorthand for getting the basic details of the story so far. 'Incidentally, I've already spoken to the fire brigade station manager.'

'It's going to be a tricky one, guv.' Jane was just over five-six in height, with short brown hair. She also had a cheerful smile that was now very much in evidence. 'Half of them in there are strolling around stark naked,' she said, cocking a thumb over her shoulder.

'So the fire chief told me, but I instructed the incident room sergeant to ensure they were dressed.'

'So I understand, but apparently they take the view that if

the textiles – that's us – want to come in, we'll have to take them as they are. And that's just the staff.'

'Witnesses?' I asked despondently. I was becoming more depressed by the minute.

'If there are any. Some of them have gone home.' Jane's cheerful smile reappeared. 'I said it was tricky because Saturday midday is when quite a few of the members leave, presumably because they're going back to work on Monday. Gives them time to find some clothes, I suppose,' she added impishly. 'Another lot will arrive today and tomorrow which just about gives the staff time to clean the vacated huts, or chalets as they call them, as well as the rooms in the main block, and to get the laundry under way. But there are quite a few others, pensioners for the most part, who turn up for a week or two, maybe from midweek to midweek, or for just as long as the mood takes them.'

'You're really cheering me up, Jane. Do go on.'

'Anyway, to get back to the incident. The staff started collecting bed linen and towels from the vacated accommodation at about half past three this afternoon when one of the chalet maids, as they call them, spotted that there was a fire in one of the huts. As you know, there's a standard procedure at places like this, and the brigade was called. It was the firefighters who found the corpse.'

'How the hell did he manage to lie there and get burnt to death?' I mused aloud, echoing what the fire chief had said.

'The only thing that springs immediately to mind is that he was dead before the fire started,' said Jane. 'Hence the reservations expressed by the fire brigade.'

'Wonderful! Are the scientists here yet, Jane?'

'Yes, guv. Linda Mitchell and her team arrived about ten minutes before you did, and Dr Mortlock is here, too.'

'Already? I bet he's happy.'

'Happy is not a word I'd have used to describe his mood,' said Jane. 'He was muttering something about a bloody fire death getting in the way of his being able to watch the Open Golf Championship from Carnoustie on television. By the way, your Australian DI is here somewhere.'

'You mean Kate Ebdon?'

'Yes, that's the one.' As she did every time she mentioned Kate, Mansfield pretended that she couldn't remember her name. I knew who she meant, but for some reason I'd never discovered – and didn't really want to know – an element of animosity existed between the two. It could be that Jane Mansfield had been educated at a public fee-paying school and then university, before entering the Force by way of the direct entry scheme.

Kate, on the other hand, had a fairly rough upbringing in Port Douglas in Queensland, her birthplace, and openly boasted about skinny dipping in the Coral Sea. Following a spell in advertising and hospital administration, she finally settled for the Metropolitan Police and started her career by walking a beat in Hoxton for two years. As a detective she'd excelled as a thief-taker in London's East End before graduating to the Flying Squad as a sergeant. Somewhere along the way she'd acquired a black belt in judo, and I'd once seen her put a six-foot villain on his back with little apparent effort. Now in her early thirties and a detective inspector, she had become a great asset to the team. She was also very outspoken about the shortcomings of the direct entry scheme, which was probably what riled Mansfield.

Mansfield may have skinny dipped at university where, I believe, it's considered to be very daring, but it wasn't the sort of thing she'd mention. The other noticeable difference between the two DIs was that Mansfield's usual attire was a rather conservative trouser suit, whereas Kate always dressed teasingly in a man's white shirt and tight-fitting jeans.

'Thanks very much, Jane. I'd better get on with it, I suppose.'

'Better start with the bare facts, then, guv,' said Dave.

'Shut up, Poole.' I could visualize an unending stream of jokes about investigating a murder at a naturist club.

Dave Poole is my black bag carrier, but I should explain that it is Dave who is black, not the bag. In fact, there is no bag. The days of taking a murder bag to the scene of a homicide are long past; we now have a team of forensic scientists. However, the term bag carrier has stayed and is used to describe the senior investigating officer's assistant. Dave's grandfather, a medical doctor, came over from Jamaica in the 1950s and set up a practice in Bethnal Green. His son, Dave's father, became a chartered accountant, but Dave, after getting a good English degree at London University, 'went mad', to put it in his own words, and joined the Metropolitan Police. Impishly describing himself as the black sheep of the family for not pursuing a professional career, he has proved to be one of the best sergeants I've ever had working with me.

'Hello, Harry.' Linda Mitchell and her team of forensic scientists were standing outside the chalet that was the centre of police attention.

'What have we got, Linda?' It was the standard opening question to the crime-scene manager, and what she had to say very often put me on the right track to solving a murder or, rather, prevented me from wasting time by going in the wrong direction.

'The victim is Robert Sharp. He's reckoned to be in his thirties and had joined the club about a year ago. He wasn't due to check out and, according to one of the staff, he came fairly regularly and usually stayed for just a few days. This time he hadn't committed himself to a specific period.'

At that point, Dr Henry Mortlock, the Home Office pathologist, joined us. 'This is a grave disruption of my social life, you know, Harry. I was looking forward to watching the Open on television.'

'You can always see it on catch-up, Doctor,' suggested Dave.

Mortlock took off his pince-nez and polished them with his top-pocket handkerchief while giving Dave the sort of silent withering glare he usually reserved for incompetents who failed to follow his opinion of the cause of death. It was not unusual for Mortlock to display a short temper despite having the outward appearance of a rather overweight, cuddly family doctor in whom one could confide. Dave once described him as going up like a can of petrol in a thunderstorm. It was an oddly contradictory analogy from someone with a degree in the English language.

'What's your verdict, Henry?' I asked, before Dave dug himself deeper.

'Come with me, Harry. I think you'll find it's fairly obvious.'

I followed Mortlock as far as the crime-scene tapes

surrounding the chalet occupied by the late Robert Sharp. The badly charred body of the victim was lying on its back.

'Before you ask, Harry, I haven't the faintest idea when he died, and right now, I don't know the cause of death. I would surmise that he was either very heavily drugged to the extent that he was in a coma, or he was already dead. Personally, I favour the latter. If I can get his remains to my mortuary without bits of him falling off, I may be able to tell you more.'

'Is it all right for Linda to start a crime-scene examination, Henry?' I asked.

'I'll have to wait until the fire-scene investigator has done his bit, Harry,' said Linda. 'But I'll be here when he does.'

'This is all very inconvenient, you know, Chief Inspector.'

'Particularly for the late Mr Sharp,' I said. I had at last found a member of staff who told me where the general manager had his office. The small brick-built structure overlooked the floodlit pool in which there were one or two people swimming, even at this late hour, having been given the all-clear by the fire brigade to return. Presumably as an acknowledgment to our presence, the general manager had put a red towel around his waist, which was just as well. Lydia once said that some men look more sexually attractive in evening dress than they do when naked. I'm not sure that this balding, pot-bellied individual would have looked good whatever he was or was not wearing. His preposterous appearance was not improved by the cast he had in one eye. Heavy horn-rimmed spectacles suspended on a gilt chain around his neck must have created an even more bizarre figure when trying to visualize him without his towel.

'Yes, yes, of course, very sad, very sad, but how long are the police likely to be here?' he demanded.

'Who *are* you?' asked Dave, pocketbook at the ready.

'I'm the general manager.' The man pushed out his chest and for one awful moment I was worried that this physical contortion might cause his towel to fall off.

'I know,' said Dave. 'It says that on the door. But what's your name?'

'Mr Cotton,' said the general manager pompously, clutching at his towel just in time.

'First name?'

'Cyril.'

'Well, Mr Cyril Cotton, I'm afraid we'll be here for as long as it takes,' said Dave. 'One of your members has died in suspicious circumstances and it's our job to find out who was responsible or to satisfy ourselves that it was an accidental death.'

'This is all very inconvenient,' mumbled Cotton again, shaking his head. 'And we have more members arriving tomorrow.'

'Well, that's something to look forward to.' Dave put his pocket book away. 'As a matter of interest, why is this club called the Pretext Club? What is the real reason behind the name?'

'It's a play on words,' said Cotton. 'Pre-textile, or pretext for short, is the state you're in when you're born and before you start wearing textiles. And we enjoy being in that state.'

'Good grief,' said Dave, who hated people who messed about with the English language. 'Now, to start with, I want a list of all the people who were here today, including those who have already left.'

'*What?*' For a moment it appeared that Cotton was on the verge of having an apoplectic fit; his eyes certainly bulged a little more. 'Out of the question. Our list is confidential. It's the Data Protection Act, you see. Anyway, I doubt if our members would want their neighbours to know that they were practising naturists.'

'I don't see why they should be ashamed of it, but in any case, we're not going to call on their neighbours and tell them,' said Dave with, for him, commendable restraint. 'That said, I can assure you that we will get a Crown Court warrant to search this place from top to bottom and, knowing my chief inspector, he's probably already considering arresting you for obstructing him in the execution of his duty. I'm sure you don't want to go to the police station dressed like that.' He waved nonchalantly at the general manager's red towel. 'And the Health and Safety Executive will certainly want to see the list,' he added.

Under threat of arrest and a visit from the HSE, Cotton

yielded immediately, but his sort always did. It saved us the time it would take to obtain a Crown Court judge's warrant, which would certainly be granted. 'I'll get on to it straight away,' he said. 'But I must ask you to be discreet.'

'We are discretion personified,' said Dave, holding out his hand. 'The list?'

'And we'd like a copy of your staff list together with their home addresses,' I said.

Cotton's jaw dropped. 'Surely you don't think that one of our people had anything to do with this terrible tragedy. It was just a fire, surely?'

'Not *just* a fire. A man died. The question is, therefore, are you prepared to swear on oath that none of them was involved?'

'Well, no, I suppose not,' Cotton admitted reluctantly.

'A copy of the staff list, then.'

Within minutes, the general manager had booted up his computer and printed off details of all the club's members, and the members of staff who, surprisingly, amounted to nearly forty.

'Perhaps you would put a cross next to those members who were not here after, say, nine o'clock this morning.' I knew the time the fire brigade had been called but decided that I would cover at least six hours before that.

Cotton spent a few minutes comparing his list with another, which I presumed showed those who had been here before that time.

'There we are, Chief Inspector,' said Cotton, handing me the list. 'Of those who were here, eleven went earlier today, but thirteen are still here. As far as the staff are concerned, I've crossed off those who were not on duty today.'

'Well, you can put them back on,' I said. 'I shall want to talk to all of them, even if they weren't here today.' I ran my eye quickly down the names. As Cotton had said, thirteen club members were still here and had been here at the time of the fire. That figure included the deceased Robert Sharp.

'D'you know if Mr Sharp arrived with anyone, Mr Cotton? I see that he'd been here for five days.'

'I don't know. Rosemary is my deputy and she takes

care of the reception duties. She welcomes the members and allocates them their accommodation. She knows most of them by sight.'

'In that case, I need to have a word with her. Perhaps you would ask her to join us.'

Cotton tapped out a three-digit number on his phone. 'Rosemary, love, would you come over to the office. The police would like a word.'

TWO

The woman who arrived a few minutes later was wearing a white towelling dressing gown, flip-flops and an excessive amount of make-up. She was heavily built and middle-aged, and the expression on her face made her appear ready to start an argument.

'I'm Rosemary,' she said, glaring at me.

'That would be Mrs Rosemary Crane, would it?' asked Dave, having glanced at the staff list.

'Yes, that's my name. How did you know?' she demanded, in a hostile tone of voice.

'I had to give the police a list of the staff, Rosemary, love,' said Cotton in an apologetically whining voice. 'They insisted. They also wanted the membership list.'

'But that's confidential, Cyril,' protested Rosemary, turning her hostile gaze on Cotton.

'Not when we're investigating a suspicious death, madam,' said Dave, intervening quickly enough to save Cotton from having to defend himself against this formidable woman.

'My interest at the moment, Mrs Crane,' I began, 'is the dead man, Robert Sharp. When did he arrive?'

'Last Monday,' said Rosemary. 'That would've been the fifteenth of July.' She'd had the foresight to bring her own list from the reception office.

'Did he come alone?'

'No, he was with a black girl.' Rosemary glanced down at her list again. 'A pretty little thing, she was. Name of Madison Bailey.'

'Is she still here?'

'No, she booked out first thing this morning.'

'What time?'

Rosemary glanced back at the list in her hand. 'Two minutes past eight.'

'Are you sure about that?'

'Absolutely. The CCTV camera recorded the time her car left, and I processed her credit card myself. She didn't even stay for breakfast.'

'Was their arrival together a coincidence, d'you think, or did they appear to know each other?'

'I've not the faintest idea,' said Rosemary. 'You'll have to ask her.'

'Did Mr Sharp arrive by car, Mrs Crane?' I asked.

'Yes, he did. I suppose you want the number.' Rosemary displayed her list so that Dave could make a note of the vehicle's registration number. 'And it's still in our car park. Presumably the police will remove it.'

'I'll arrange with Linda for a low-loader to take it for examination, sir,' said Dave. 'It might be worth examining the vehicle under secure conditions.'

'Good idea, Dave. I'll leave it to you to organize it,' I said, and turned back to the general manager. 'One other thing before we get on, Mr Cotton. Apart from the one at the gate, are there any CCTV cameras on the site?'

'At the Pretext Club? Good heavens, no! It's full of naturists. They'd just love being recorded on CCTV.' Cotton's face expressed shock, presumably at my having asked such a scandalous question. If he'd been wearing a monocle, it would have dropped out. 'What's more, we make sure that mobile phones and cameras are handed in on arrival and, for that matter, any other device that's capable of taking photographs. This is a place of relaxation for like-minded people without interference from the stresses of the modern world. People come here to enjoy themselves, not to be made the subject of home movies.' During this high-flown justification for the rule, Rosemary Crane was nodding furiously, like a frontbencher in the House of Commons agreeing with everything the prime minister was saying.

'I appreciate that, Mr Cotton.' For a moment, I thought he was trying to sell me membership. 'I was thinking more of CCTV covering the perimeter. I imagine that your members will occasionally attract voyeurs.'

'All too often,' exclaimed Rosemary vehemently. 'We've even caught the filthy-minded perverts trying to climb up the wall. That's why Mr Cotton had those screens put up on the side of the swimming pool that faces the public road.' She pointed out of Cotton's office window at the unsightly canvas structures.

'They're only temporary, until we can get something more attractive,' explained Cotton.

'Time you got it done, then, Cyril,' said Rosemary.

'How long do you keep the gate CCTV tapes for, Mr Cotton?' asked Dave.

'A fortnight.'

'We'd like to have the ones for yesterday and today.'

'I'll arrange it.'

'As a matter of interest,' I said, 'do you have security of any description? Patrols or an on-site security officer? Anything like that?'

Cotton and Rosemary both shook their heads. 'No, nothing like that,' said Cotton, 'but we do have a team of lifeguards, two of whom are on duty at the pool during swimming hours. It's a health and safety thing. You never know when their inspectors might turn up, unheralded.' He seemed obsessed with health and safety inspectors, or perhaps the fear of them.

'One other question, Mrs Crane,' said Dave. 'Did Madison Bailey have anyone with her in her car when she left this morning?'

'I don't know,' said Rosemary.

I wondered if she did know, but was being awkward, although I had noted that the gate CCTV would only record the registration number of a vehicle. We left it at that. It was too late to start interviewing; that would have to wait until tomorrow.

Despite Linda Mitchell having earlier referred to the fire investigator as a man, it was a woman who arrived at just after eleven o'clock that evening. She introduced herself as Martina Dawson and immediately embarked upon a long and highly technical conversation with Linda and Dr Mortlock.

I later learned that the result of this exchange of views was that the badly charred body would be left where it was until the following day. Martina Dawson would require more

light than was available now in order to conduct her preliminary
survey and crossing the floor of the chalet to get at Robert Sharp's
remains might inadvertently contaminate the scene. We all knew
that if that happened it could seriously jeopardize the outcome
of the entire investigation, particularly when the case got to court.
Although that was some way ahead, care has to be taken right
from the start.

'This is Detective Chief Inspector Harry Brock,' said Linda
as she brought Martina Dawson across to where I was standing.
'He's the senior investigating officer.'

'How d'you do?' Dawson shook hands with a firm grip. I
reckoned she must be at least fifty and her short black hair
gave her a severe, schoolmarmish appearance, but I later learned
that she had a good sense of humour. Her jeans, blue shirt and
no-nonsense black shoes lent her an air of determination,
emphasized by her slightly tinted rimless spectacles.

'What's the plan, Ms Dawson?' I asked.

'It's Martina, but I'm known as Marty. I'll return tomorrow
morning and make a start. I'll explain what I'm doing then.'

'Good. Is there anything you want done to preserve the
scene, Marty?'

'I've had a good look from the outside and the roof of
the chalet seems to be more or less intact, but I wouldn't go
any further than that. According to the weather forecast, it's
unlikely to rain. I'll just have to take a chance on it, because
throwing a tarp over the chalet roof might do more harm than
good. It could bring down debris and, however slight, might
lead us in entirely the wrong direction when it comes to
analysis. I could send for a portable shelter but it would take
time.'

'We're used to preserving crime scenes, Marty,' said Linda.
'My people can erect a marquee arrangement over it. It won't
touch any part of the structure and it'll prevent any contamin-
ation. We've got all the kit with us.'

'That'd be great, thanks, Linda. We'd normally do it ourselves,
but it wasn't until I arrived that I found the police were still
here and treating it as a probable crime scene.' Martina turned
to me. 'There is one other thing the police could do before
tomorrow . . .'

'Name it,' I said. 'We're pleased to do anything at all to help. We're on the same side, after all.'

'I noticed that there is a public road on the other side of the screens next to the swimming pool. I'd be grateful if you could get someone to have a look round there. In fact, all around the perimeter on the outside would be even better. I don't believe spontaneous combustion was the cause of the fire in this case, and arsonists – if that's what we're dealing with – sometimes chuck petrol containers over walls to get rid of them. They'd look a bit stupid leaving the scene of a fire and getting on a bus with an empty jerrycan. Might upset the health and safety people, to say nothing of the bus driver. And you never know, a member of the public might even notice. Mind you,' she added thoughtfully, 'arsonists are pretty stupid anyway.'

'Take it as done, Marty.' I briefed Kate to arrange for some of our uniformed colleagues to search the area around the club's perimeter. 'You must've been doing this job for quite a while, Marty,' I said, turning back to Dawson.

For the first time since we'd met, Martina Dawson smiled, probably because I'd expressed an interest in her and her background rather than confining myself to posing questions about her assessment of the cause of the fire. 'I've been at it for very nearly thirty years altogether,' she said. 'I started as a firefighter in the London Fire Brigade and got really inter-ested in the technical side. I took an external degree – bloody hard work, that was – and started investigating the cause of fires when I found that to be more interesting than putting them out.' She glanced at her wristwatch. 'See you tomorrow morning, about eight o'clock, Mr Brock.'

'The name's Harry,' I said.

Martina Dawson nodded and turned away.

I briefed the team to be back at the Pretext Club at eight the following day, a Sunday, and ignored the groans that always greeted similar inevitable orders. But I often think back to the words of my first detective inspector when I joined the CID as a fresh-faced detective constable. 'If you can't take a joke, you shouldn't have joined, mate,' he would say. Frequently.

I took a chance on Lydia still being up and rang her to say that I'd decided against returning to Esher, as I didn't want to disturb her, and that it would save time and trouble if I went home to Surbiton. After teasingly saying that she rather wanted to be disturbed, Lydia expressed her disappointment but understood. For my part, I'd missed another of her splendid dinners. All I could hope for now was to find a twenty-four-hour McDonald's somewhere.

I finished my chat with Lydia by suggesting that she should expect me when she saw me, a phrase which, regrettably, she was hearing all too often.

I arrived at the Pretext Club on the stroke of eight the next morning, more by luck than skilful route planning, London's traffic being totally unpredictable, even on a Sunday. It came as no surprise that Martina Dawson, the fire investigator, was already at the site and was talking to Linda Mitchell. Henry Mortlock arrived five minutes later, grumbling as usual about having to work on a Sunday. But that wasn't a surprise either.

'Good, the gang's all here,' said Martina. 'Now we can get started. I understand from your Inspector Ebdon, Harry, that nothing of evidential value was found by the police who searched outside the walls. That means that either petrol wasn't the accelerant or some other method was used to bring it in.'

She entered the canvas structure that the crime-scene guys had erected the night before and began her investigation by walking all around the outside of the chalet, absorbing everything she saw. That done, she went inside, through the gap where the door had been until the fire brigade opened it with an axe, and for the next half hour or so examined the entire scene without touching anything. I decided to let her get on with it because I knew from previous suspicious fires that anything she found that needed to be bagged and tagged as an exhibit would be passed to Linda straight away. And it was at that point I would become actively involved.

Martina Dawson must have spent about two hours altogether in the chalet.

'You can move your cadaver now, Doctor,' she said to Henry Mortlock when eventually she emerged.

'Anything to tell me, Marty?' I asked.

'I'd rather keep it until I've analysed what I've found, Harry, but I can say with some certainty that the fire started beneath the bed on which the cadaver was found. There was some sort of accelerant, but I'll have to wait for the laboratory findings to be certain, although I'm pretty sure I know what it was.'

'How long will that take?' I had no alternative but to accept what she said, even though it was essential to get on with the enquiry as soon as possible if, in fact, it turned out to be a murder or manslaughter. The first twenty-four hours are vital in murder investigations.

Martina Dawson pursed her lips. 'I hope we'll get some indication from the lab late tomorrow.' She paused and then grinned. 'If I put a squib up their arse.'

'Good grief! You should never play with fireworks, Marty,' I said with mock severity, 'they're dangerous.'

'You don't have to tell me that, Harry. I spend every Bonfire Night in the pub.'

Plainly there was more to Martina Dawson than was immediately apparent.

'What's next, guv?' asked Kate Ebdon.

'I'd like you to start interviewing those club members who were here yesterday and are still here, Kate. I understand that some more members have started to come in already today. How many of our people d'you need to take statements?'

'I reckon two teams of two will do. Liz Carpenter and Nicola Chance on one team and Charlie Flynn with Sheila Armitage on the other. I suppose all the members will be naked.' Kate looked gloomy about the prospect. 'Well, I'm not joining in just to make them feel relaxed.'

'You never know your luck, Kate. Some of them might be dishy men,' I said. 'In the meantime, Dave and I are off to interview Madison Bailey.'

'Remind me who she is. I think I'm losing the plot already.' But Kate was being disingenuous; she always knew exactly what was going on.

'She's the black girl who arrived with Robert Sharp, but left yesterday morning before the fire was discovered.'

'D'you reckon they were an item, guv?'

'That's something I intend to find out.'

* * *

Madison Bailey lived in a flat at Harlington close to Heathrow, a distance of about nine miles from the naturist club, and we arrived there at two o'clock.

A young brunette answered the door and smiled at Dave. 'Are you Madison's new boyfriend?' she asked before we'd had a chance to introduce ourselves.

'Sorry to disappoint you, but we're police officers,' replied Dave.

'Oh no! There's not been a crash, has there?'

'We wouldn't necessarily know, we're not traffic police,' I said.

'I didn't mean a car accident, I meant an air crash. Madison's a cabin crew member on a long-haul flight. She went on duty at oh-seventeen-hundred Zulu last evening.'

'I assume you mean six o'clock yesterday evening.' Dave was always irritated when people did not speak plain English, particularly when he thought they were showing off.

'I take it you're in the airline business, too?' I said, basing my guess on her use of the term Zulu to indicate Greenwich Mean Time. 'We're from—'

'Yes, I'm cabin crew, too. How did you guess?'

'We're from a murder investigation team . . .' I began, struggling to get our enquiries on the right track before any more confusion arose.

'Oh, God! She's been murdered?' The woman blanched and put a hand to her mouth. 'What happened? Have you caught her killer?'

'If you'd let my chief inspector finish, we'll tell you exactly why we're here,' said Dave, who had already categorized the woman as an airhead, and was getting mildly annoyed by her grasshopper assumptions. He was one of those men who liked a woman to be attractive *and* intelligent. But if only one of those qualities existed then, as far as Dave was concerned, it had to be intelligence.

'I'm Detective Chief Inspector Harry Brock,' I said, 'and this is Detective Sergeant Poole. May we come in?'

'Oh, I'm awfully sorry. Yes, of course.' The woman showed us into a comfortable sitting room and invited us to take a seat.

'Perhaps we could start with your name,' I said.

'Oh, sorry, I should've told you that, shouldn't I?' She smiled sweetly at Dave. 'I'm Jeanette Davis, but everyone calls me Ginny.'

'We're investigating the unexplained death of a man that took place sometime yesterday at the Pretext Club near Harrow, Ginny. It's a naturist club and we've been told that Madison Bailey arrived there on the fifteenth of July. That's last Monday.'

'She had a few days off and she told me that's where she was going.' Ginny did not seem at all fazed at learning her flatmate went to a naturist club and I assumed her generation regarded nudity rather differently from the view taken by older generations. My mother would have been appalled if I'd suggested going to such a club and would have attached the direst motives to the whole concept.

'Did she say if she was going with anyone?'

'No, she didn't, but she was always a bit secretive about boyfriends. Perhaps she thinks I'll steal them from her. It was most likely someone she'd met on a flight, because that sort of thing's always happening to us girls. I've lost count of the number of times I've been chatted up on a flight. I'd put money on her dating a different guy by tomorrow.'

That I could understand. Ginny Davis was a statuesque young woman with curves in the right places but did not seem to be all that bright.

'D'you know her current boyfriend's name?' asked Dave.

'No idea, but, like I said, she always played her cards close to her chest.'

I decided not to prompt Ginny by suggesting that Madison's new boyfriend could have been the Robert Sharp whose death we were investigating. At least, that was the inference I drew from what Rosemary Crane, the receptionist, had told us. I wanted to tell Madison face-to-face of Sharp's death in order to gauge her reaction. If his death was not accidental, Madison Bailey might have had something to do with it.

'When will she be back, Ginny?' I asked.

'Tomorrow midday, I should think. Not that I'll be here. I'm on duty at LHR at oh-nine-hundred tomorrow. Er, that's Heathrow.'

'Zulu?' queried Dave sarcastically.

For a moment, Ginny looked puzzled. 'No,' she said, 'nine o'clock local time. As a matter of interest, why did you want to see Madison? D'you think she had something to with this death you're talking about?'

'Good heavens, no! We're interviewing everyone who was there on the day of the incident,' I said, deciding to refer to it as an incident, rather than a murder. But the more I thought about Marty Dawson's opinion that the fire had started underneath Robert Sharp's bed, the more inclined I was to think that we were dealing with a murder. 'It's just routine,' I added, coining a useful but completely meaningless phrase beloved of fictional detectives.

'Well, Dave, what d'you think of Ginny Davis?' I asked when we returned to the car.

'She's a dimbo, guv, but you couldn't exactly describe her as a flatmate, could you? Not with a figure like she's got.'

THREE

Dave and I returned to the Pretext Club and were greeted by Kate Ebdon. As usual, she was dressed in the man's white shirt and jeans that I said may have irritated Jane Mansfield, the HAT DI, and most certainly displeased our beloved commander. He was, however, ill-disposed to say anything to her because I'd once suggested that any comment about her style of dress might be viewed as sexism – or, given that she was Australian, even racism – by the Scotland Yard diversity police. It did not, however, alter his view that when a woman was promoted to inspector, she immediately became an officer and a lady, and should dress accordingly. It's a pity that he'd not seen her at the Old Bailey, attired in black skirt-suit and black tights, with high heels and gold earrings. She would step into the witness box and smile fetchingly at the judge. Her appearance had been described on more than one occasion by defence counsel as affording the Crown an unfair advantage. But I don't think the commander had ever been to the Old Bailey – assuming, of course, that he knew where it was.

'What's happening, Kate?'

'Linda had a message from Marty Dawson to say that the lab results won't be available until tomorrow morning. Dr Mortlock's removed the remains of the victim and hopes to do a post-mortem on what's left of him, probably at nine o'clock tomorrow morning, but he'll let us know. From what he was saying, it depends on the state of the cadaver once he gets it on the table.'

'How did your interviews go, Kate?'

'It didn't take long for my two teams to talk to all the members who were here yesterday, and I can summarize the statements. The majority seemed not to know Robert Sharp other than by sight, but those who did have contact with him said he was amiable and courteous. Some of them also mentioned that he appeared to be very friendly with Madison Bailey and that the two of them spent a lot of time together. They remembered her in particular because she was black and was described, even by the women, as a beauty.'

'Did any of them strike you as knowing more than they were telling, Kate?'

'Not particularly. Most of the women in Sharp's age group – even some who were a few years older – admitted to being chatted up by him when Madison wasn't there, but said he didn't persist once they told him to get lost, in the nicest possible way, of course. Nearly all of them said that they found Sharp to be personable and sexy. One or two of the younger women described him as good looking and one of them went overboard about his six pack. Another even went so far as to admit that if she hadn't been married, she'd happily have had a fling with him. Incidentally, the first any of them knew of the fire was when they were herded out to the car park and the fire brigade arrived. No one saw anything leading up to it. And that's about it, guv.'

Kate always called me 'guv' in the presence of other officers but would call me Harry when we were alone. This stemmed from a weekend in Paris – on official business – when my friend Capitaine Henri Deshayes of the Police Judiciaire and his wife Gabrielle, a former Folies Bergere dancer, entertained us to dinner at their apartment. Henri, a self-confessed oenophile, was a little too liberal with the wine. At least it was too much for Kate, who needed my help to get her to her hotel room.

'I suppose I'd better visit the address the Pretext Club had for Robert Sharp,' I said, 'in case there's anyone there who should be told about his death. According to Rosemary Crane, the receptionist, he was unmarried, but I think that was only her assumption. All the personal papers he had with him will have been destroyed in the fire, but we might find something at his address that'll put us on the right road to finding a motive if, in fact, he was murdered. From what Marty's discovered so far, it would appear likely.'

It was about six o'clock when Dave and I arrived at Sharp's address, which we had obtained from the club. It was a three-storey house that had been converted into flats, and was in one of the streets that was a turning off The Vale in Acton, West London. Sharp lived in a flat on the ground floor.

I rang the bell at least twice and Dave and I were on the point of trying other flats to see if anyone knew anything about Sharp when the door was opened by a woman. She was probably in her early thirties but her careworn face and lack of make-up made her appear a good ten years older. Her lank hair, already showing signs of greying, was dragged back into a rough ponytail, her sweater had a stain on the front and her jeans were torn, but not 'distressed' in the way youngsters thought was fashionable. This was a woman who had probably been quite attractive once, but her slovenly appearance gave the impression that she no longer cared. A small boy, perhaps five years old, had an arm around the woman's leg while the thumb of the other hand was firmly in his mouth. He gazed up at us with the enquiring eyes of young innocence.

'Good evening,' I said. 'I'm sorry to bother you, but does a Mr Robert Sharp live here?'

'Occasionally,' said the woman. 'I'm his wife. If you've come for money, I'm afraid there isn't any.'

'We're police officers, Mrs Sharp. May we come in?'

'Suit yourselves.' She turned from the door and grabbed the child's hand, pulling him after her. I doubted that her attitude towards us was one of rudeness, but rather one of complete resignation, as though wondering what the fates were about to throw at her now.

We followed her into a room that seemed to be a sitting-cum-dining room and general workshop. There were piles of clothing on a table, and the ironing board had another pile of clothing on one end. Perhaps she took in washing, but on reflection, I don't suppose that anyone did these days, given that washing machines were comparatively cheap to buy, although probably beyond this woman's means.

'Do you occupy the whole of the ground floor?' I asked.

'No. Just this room and the one next door. That's the bedroom. I'd ask you to sit down, but unless you want to move some of that stuff yourselves, you'll have to stand.' Mrs Sharp waved an arm listlessly at the few chairs piled up with all manner of household linen and towels. 'What is it you want? If it's Bob, I haven't a clue where he is. Off with some fancy woman probably. That's what he's usually doing. I suppose his view is that it beats working. He's not had a job in years. I don't know where he gets his money from, but none of it comes my way.'

This was rapidly developing into a delicate situation and I was bent on trying to be as gentle as possible, but there's no easy way to tell a woman that her husband has been burned to death at a nudist camp.

'Mrs Sharp, I'm Detective Chief Inspector Harry Brock and this is my colleague Detective Sergeant David Poole. We're investigating a death that has occurred when a fire broke out. I'm sorry to have to tell you that we believe the dead man to be your husband, Robert Sharp.'

This awful announcement was met with utter silence. There was no startled response. No fainting. No screams of disbelief and no tears. She stayed in this motionless and silent state for some moments.

'Was he with a woman?' she asked eventually.

'No, he was the only casualty.'

'Where was it, this place where it happened?'

There was no alternative but to tell her the truth before she learned it from the media.

'It was a naturist club called the Pretext Club about seven or eight miles from here.'

'He's still up to his old tricks, then.'

'D'you mean he's been there before?'

'I don't know about one called the . . . what did you say it was called?'

'The Pretext Club.'

Mrs Sharp shook her head. 'Doesn't ring a bell, but it was at one of those places we met.' She gave a rueful smile. 'You might not believe it now, but I could look quite presentable without clothes ten years ago.'

'Did you go there with someone else?'

'No. Most of these places accept women on their own, but men usually have to have a partner.'

'How did Robert Sharp get membership, then?'

'He paid for a non-existent wife so they thought he was half of a couple. He was a very personable, charming man and he could talk anybody into anything. He certainly talked me into his bed that same night and then to a register office the following week. Who was he with this time?'

'We're still making enquiries about that.' I decided not to mention Madison Bailey.

'Well, if he didn't go there with a woman, sure as God made little apples he hooked up with one while he *was* there.' Mrs Sharp sounded cynical but then, based on what she'd been telling us, she had every right to be. 'She'll be one of a long line. I almost feel sorry for the poor little bitch, whoever she is.' She paused thoughtfully. 'What's going to happen about the funeral?' she asked, as the practical realities of her situation became apparent to her.

'That depends on when the coroner releases your husband's body,' said Dave, 'but we'll let you know. May I have your first name?'

'It's Holly. Well, I won't be able to pay for a funeral. Bob left us on our beam ends with his crazy money-making schemes and his womanizing. He never seemed to worry about me or the boy and I've got another one on the way. As far as I'm concerned, the council can bury him. I don't owe him anything.'

'What money-making schemes were they?' I asked.

'Oh, one week he was going to make a fortune out of buying and selling antiques. When that didn't work out, he had some stupid scheme about opening an upper-class holiday camp in the Caribbean. None of it came to anything. His schemes never did, but that was Bob all over.'

'We'll be in touch, Mrs Sharp,' I said, and we left Sharp's widow. Not a grieving widow, but one who was very bitter about the way she'd been treated by a philandering pipe-dreaming husband. And, I suspect, her troubles were not over yet. The rent was almost certainly in arrears already and I'd no doubt that she would be evicted before long.

According to Ginny Davis, Madison Bailey wouldn't be home until after midday. That gave me the opportunity to spend

Monday morning in the office attempting to catch up on the
avalanche of paperwork that was routinely inflicted upon us.
The concept of the paperless society that had been promised
to a previous generation of coppers with the arrival of the
ubiquitous computer has actually had the opposite effect.

However, it wasn't long before I received the first phone
call from our press bureau regarding the questions raised by
representatives of the media about the death at the Pretext
Club. These earlier requests came mainly from journalists of
the gutter press to whom the combination of death and nudity
had the makings of an irresistibly prurient series of articles
with double entendres abounding.

I decided to release the name of the victim in the hope that
it might bring fresh information from people we didn't know
existed. Based on what we'd learned so far about Robert Sharp,
I told the press bureau that we would like to speak to anyone
who knew him or had met him. As ever, with requests of this
nature, the only problem would be the resulting avalanche of
information that would descend upon us, taking up our time and
very often proving to be of little or no help to our investigation.
But it had to be done.

Once that phone conversation was finished, I ventured into
the incident room.

Detective Sergeant Colin Wilberforce, the incident room
manager, had already set up a computer file regarding Robert
Sharp's death. It was a file that could easily be expanded if it
turned out that Sharp had been murdered rather than having
died accidentally. If it had been the result of a tragic accident,
then we would pass the matter to the local CID or the Uniform
Branch to handle. But it all hinged on Marty Dawson's opinion
of the cause.

Wilberforce was a great asset and never had to be told what
to do. He was one of those officers with a natural talent for
police administration and organization. Although his name had
never appeared in the media for having arrested a murderer,
his smooth operation was the framework upon which the
investigation depended. Without it there would be no form
to it and we'd be running around like headless chickens.

It would be a sad day if he ever decided to apply for

promotion. I know that's a selfish view, but guys like him are difficult to find. That said, he seems quite happy where he is. He has a settled married life and lives with his wife Sonia and their three teenaged children in Orpington.

He is willing to swap duties with anyone who will give him a Saturday afternoon off so that he can play rugby for the Metropolitan Police when he displays the same ruthless and calculated efficiency on the rugby field as he does in the incident room. Heaven help any individual who interferes with his ordered management. And that includes the commander but, given that that worthy hardly ever emerges from his office save to go home, there is little danger of him even being able to find the incident room.

'You might be interested to know, sir,' said Wilberforce, 'that Robert Sharp was listed on the Police National Computer as wanted on warrant by the Devon and Cornwall Police, the Hampshire Constabulary and the Sussex Police.'

The PNC is a useful tool that is shared by all the UK police forces and enables them to discover, among many other things, if any force in the country, or even Interpol and Europol, has an interest in a particular name or a vehicle or a modus operandi.

'What was he wanted for, Colin?'

'It appears that he specialized in passing off imitation antiques as the real thing. Most times, the potential purchaser suspected that he was a con man and didn't fall for his spiel, but with Houdini-like skill, he always managed to escape the moment the police started to look for him.'

'Still an offence, whether the mark believed him or not. I wonder if a disgruntled punter set fire to him, Colin. What was the value of the cons he did pull off?'

Wilberforce swung back to his computer and scrolled up the relevant page. 'One of them is a Sussex Police job, sir. A couple of years ago, Robert Sharp conned a woman in Brighton into buying a fake Ming vase by claiming it was the real thing. He took her for three hundred pounds. Apparently, she reckoned herself to be an expert as she owns an antique shop and thought that it was worth at least a grand. But when she tried to sell it on for a profit, she found out that it was one of many cheap imitations knocked out in Birmingham and was worth about a fiver at most. A case of the biter bit.'

'Gives an entirely new meaning to the phrase "sharp practice",' I said.

'There's a bit more to it, though, sir. According to the local CID, that particular victim had a brief but torrid affair with Sharp. But by the time she discovered she'd been had over with the vase, Sharp was long gone. Incidentally, the local police said that there was some local scuttlebutt that she'd become pregnant shortly after Sharp's vanishing act and, although never admitting it to police, it was probably Sharp's child. Anyway, she had a termination and she didn't tell the police about that either.'

'Don't tell me all that's on the PNC, Colin.'

'No, sir, but I had a chat with the DC at Brighton who dealt with the job.'

'I think I'll have to talk to this woman, Colin. Do we have a name and address?'

'We do, sir, and I'll give you the name of the Brighton CID officer dealing.' Wilberforce glanced at his computer monitor and then scribbled the details on a slip of paper. 'The victim's name is Sadie Brooks and her shop is in The Lanes, if you know that part of Brighton. As for the other two jobs – Devon and Cornwall, and Hampshire – it was much the same sort of scam, and although they were rarely successful, there were one or two punters who were relieved of money. One particular lady was ripped off for three thousand by him. That was in Hampshire. There may have been others, of course, but the losers were probably too embarrassed to report it to the police.'

'Common enough reaction, Colin. What sort of things did he try to flog?'

'Most times it was a vase of some sort, sir, or candlesticks, pottery figurines, that sort of stuff. Apparently, tea caddies were a source of income for him at one time. I was surprised to find that some can fetch over a thousand pounds. Presumably small items were more easily portable than, for example, a Victorian wardrobe.' Wilberforce chuckled at the thought of Sharp struggling through the streets of Brighton humping a wardrobe or a George II dresser on his back and going from door to door in an attempt to sell it. 'By the way, sir, the commander would like a word.'

I tapped on the commander's office door and waited for his peremptory 'Come!' before entering the great man's presence.

'You wanted to see me, sir?'

'Ah, Mr Brock. Tell me about this suspicious death you're dealing with.' Reluctantly, because the commander loves paper, he closed the docket in front of him and placed it in his out-tray.

One of his many irritating habits was to describe a murder or manslaughter as a suspicious death until the jury's verdict had said it was one or the other, *and* that verdict had been ratified by the Court of Appeal. In this case, however, it turned out to be the truth; it *was* a suspicious death, although I was moving ever closer to believing it was a murder. I outlined what we had learned so far, but rather frustrated him when I said that I couldn't tell him anything else until I got the report from Martina Dawson, the fire investigator.

'Well, I suggest you tell the woman to get a move on, Mr Brock. These laboratory people need to be reminded of the urgency of murder cases.'

'She's not a police officer or a member of the forensic science service, sir. She belongs to the fire brigade.'

'Keep me posted, Mr Brock,' snapped our paper-tiger commander, plucking another of his beloved files from the in tray. He was clearly annoyed that Martina Dawson was not under his command and there was absolutely nothing he could do to hurry her up.

FOUR

Dave and I arrived at the Harlington flat shared by Jeanette Davis and Madison Bailey at about two thirty that afternoon.

'Hello. I'm Madison Bailey and you must be the policemen. Ginny left me a note to say that you'd be coming to see me.' If this confident young woman had been Robert Sharp's latest squeeze, I could quite see why he would have been attracted to her. She had smooth coffee-coloured skin, a perfect figure, shoulder-length jet-black hair and an engaging smile. Her denim shorts and scarlet crop top completed the picture of a young woman who was sexually attractive and knew she was. But I was cynical enough to believe that this and her confident approach were all part of an air stewardess's stock-in-trade.

I introduced us and she invited us into the sitting room where we had interviewed her flatmate, Jeanette Davis. Waiting until the girl had seated herself in an armchair, we sat down on the settee opposite her.

'We are investigating a fire that took place at the Pretext Club, Miss Bailey,' I began. 'I understand that you were there last week.'

'Oh, call me Madison, please. When did this fire happen?'

'As far as we know at about three thirty on Saturday afternoon,' said Dave. 'There was something about it in this morning's papers, at least in the online editions.'

'I've not had a chance to look at anything yet. We don't get much time to read anything when we're working. And I don't usually bother with papers, anyway – I just catch the TV news from time to time or pick it up on my tablet.'

'What time did you leave the Pretext Club?' I asked.

'First thing on the Saturday morning because I was on duty at six that evening, and I only got back at midday today. Was anyone hurt?'

'A man died in the fire,' I said. 'His name was Robert Sharp.'
I sat back and waited for the reaction.

'Really? Good gracious. I'd met Robert.' Madison's response
was unemotional and she remained perfectly composed. 'Funnily
enough we both arrived together on the Monday. That would've
been . . .' She paused as she tried to remember the date.

'The fifteenth of July,' prompted Dave.

'That's right,' she said, and afforded Dave another of her
engaging smiles. 'He seemed a nice guy and we spent quite
a bit of time together. We were both keen swimmers and we
spent most of our time in the pool.'

'D'you have a car?' Dave asked.

'Yes, a Mini convertible. I bought it this year as a matter
of fact. I was lucky enough to get nought per cent finance.'

'And you used that to travel to the Pretext Club, I suppose.'

'Of course.'

'We're checking all the cars that were in the car park,
Madison. I suppose one of them would have been yours.'

'Oh, quite definitely.' Madison laughed. 'It's too much of
a risk leaving a car like that in the street, especially for three
or four days. No, I parked it in the club car park. They don't
charge members to park.' She paused. 'Well, they don't charge
me, anyway.'

'Did Robert Sharp say what he did for a living, Madison?'
I asked.

'Yes, he said that he was in the antiques business. As a
matter of fact, he told me that he had a shop in King's Road,
Chelsea, opposite a pub nearer Sloane Square than World's
End, I think he said. I must admit that he was a bit vague
about it. He said the shop was being looked after by his
manager while he enjoyed a few days of being free of everything, including clothes.' Madison giggled at some secret
thought, doubtless involving a naked Sharp. 'It was a view of
life we both shared. Wonderfully carefree. You should try it
sometime,' she said, glancing at Dave. There was no trace of
embarrassment at having spent a week at a naturist club, but
why should there have been? We seem to live in an age when
many of the old inhibitions have been cast aside. Some for
the better, some for the worst.

'I imagine he must have been very wealthy if he could afford to take a week off and leave a manager in charge,' said Dave. 'And trusting, too.'

'He was certainly wealthy if his conversation was anything to go by. He told me all about the frequent holidays he had in the south of France, and the villa he owned on some Caribbean hideaway. He actually offered to take me on holiday to one of those places. Oh, I'd almost forgotten . . .' Madison leaned over the side of her armchair and picked up a tan suede hobo bag. 'Before I left on Sunday morning, he gave me his card. Would you like it? If the poor man's dead, it won't be of any use to me now, will it?' she said, and handed me a piece of printed pasteboard. 'And no exotic holiday, either,' she added, contriving an expression of regret.

I glanced briefly at the card. It had Sharp's name, the name of a well-known gentlemen's club in central London and a mobile phone number, but no private or business address. What a surprise! I gave it to Dave. 'Did he ever mention opening a form of holiday village for the very rich in the Caribbean, Madison?' I asked.

'Not that I recall.'

'The people at the Pretext Club seemed to think that you were his wife.' Dave stretched the truth quite a long way in his attempt to find out whether Sharp had admitted to having a wife or even if he'd suggested taking his new-found friendship with Madison any further.

'No, he was single,' said Madison adamantly. 'He made a point of telling me that he was divorced. He said that married men at places like the club or on cruises – or even on online dating – would often pretend to be single and spin a tale to girls in the hope of persuading them into bed. But he needn't have worried; in my line of business we learn very quickly how to spot a married man.'

But you didn't spot this one, I thought.

'Did he show you any photographs of the places you mentioned, Madison?' I asked. 'The south of France or the Caribbean?'

'Yes, he had them on his iPhone. They looked wonderful.'

'I imagine they did.' I'd recently learned from Lydia that it was the simplest thing in the world to download such scenes from online brochures. It was, however, difficult to tell whether Madison had believed Sharp and his stories. Perhaps common sense told her that she was being played along but she was so enamoured of the man that she was prepared to cast reason aside.

'Were there any shots of Sharp actually in the photographs he showed you, Madison?' Dave asked.

'No, there weren't, come to think of it,' she said pensively.

I didn't think there would have been. The more I learned of Robert Sharp the more he was proving to be a typical confidence trickster and that broadened the field of those who would want to do him harm.

'Where were you when Robert Sharp showed you these images, Madison?' asked Dave.

'At the Pretext Club.'

'But I thought members had to hand in phones or cameras or anything that took photographs.'

'Oh. I . . . um . . .' Madison faltered. 'He must've smuggled his in.'

'But if he wasn't wearing any clothes, where was he hiding it?' Dave's questioning was pleasantly relentless rather than aggressive, but he was proving that Madison Bailey had either met Sharp elsewhere than the club or she had spent time in his room where he'd secreted his smuggled phone. It didn't matter unless there was an underlying reason for her not telling the truth.

'I can't remember,' said Madison eventually, but she was clearly flustered.

Dave wisely left it with that final question.

'We may need to see you again, Madison.' I handed her one of my cards. 'If you think of anything that might be helpful, perhaps you'd give me a call.'

'Of course.' She smiled again. At Dave.

'What d'you reckon, Dave?' I asked as we drove back to central London.

'She was very confident of herself, guv, but I suppose that goes with the job she does. I'm inclined to believe most of what she said, but she's pretty clever at disguising her feelings and she did lose it a bit when I started asking where she was when she saw Sharp's phone. Mind you, I'm not sure that she was taken in by him to the extent that she led us to believe. Perhaps she's a con artist herself and was going to take him for all she could get and then abandon him. Unfortunately for her, I doubt he'd got any money at all, but having seen her new Mini convertible he thought that she had. I wonder what sort of yarn she spun him.'

'One thing's pretty obvious, though, Dave. Your questions proved that she wasn't telling the whole truth.'

'There's a report from Martina Dawson here for you, sir,' said Wilberforce, the moment I stepped into the incident room.

'Now perhaps we'll be able to get on with it.' I invited Kate and Dave into my office, and spent several minutes scanning the report. 'It looks as though we've got a murder on our hands,' I said eventually. 'Marty's report states that she found evidence of an accelerant, namely petrol, and confirms that the seat of the fire was immediately beneath Robert Sharp's bed. The report also says that the bed was wooden and the mattress was not made of fire-resistant material. That's an offence in a place like the Pretext Club and Marty's referred it to the Commissioner of the London Fire Brigade.'

'I had a team searching all around the outside of the club's premises,' said Kate, 'and they didn't find any sort of container that could have held petrol. Just the usual trash, like coke tins and those polystyrene boxes that fast food comes in.'

'Marty told me that nothing was found. Did you examine the CCTV footage of the outside at the back of the pool, Kate?'

'Yes, but it came up negative. We also conducted a search of the grounds of the club but there was nothing to be found that could've contained petrol. So, how the hell did the murderer get the accelerant into the club and, more to the point, into Sharp's chalet?'

'I think Marty has answered that question, Kate. Among the debris beneath the bed, she found traces of at least two plastic bottles, the sort that are sold by supermarkets containing spring water.'

'There's one other unanswered question, guv,' said Dave. 'Sharp wouldn't have lain there while the killer incinerated him. He must have been rendered unconscious at some stage, although it's more likely, I'd have thought, that he was murdered prior to the fire and the chalet set on fire to cover up the crime.'

'With any luck, Dave, we'll find out tomorrow morning. Henry's conducting the post-mortem at nine o'clock. And while I think of it, would you get Colin Wilberforce to do a search at the General Register Office? Madison Bailey said that Robert Sharp claimed to be divorced, but I don't believe that or Holly Sharp would have told me.'

Whenever Henry Mortlock gives me the time he intends to conduct a post-mortem, I arrive at the appointed hour only to find that he's finished his disembowelling. Perhaps he prefers not to have an audience. And so it was this morning. Dave and I got there just as Mortlock was throwing his gloves into the medical rubbish bin. There was an occasion when I tried to catch him out and arrived an hour before he'd scheduled the post-mortem. He'd looked at me and told me that I'd arrived an hour too early. One of the things I'd learned about Henry Mortlock is that it's almost impossible to wrong-foot him.

'Well, Henry, what news?'

'For a start, Harry, God bless the London Fire Brigade. They arrived on the scene promptly enough to prevent the total destruction of your Mr Sharp. As a result, I was able to find this.' He picked up a stainless-steel kidney-shaped bowl and whipped off the covering cloth with all the deftness of a stage magician. In the centre of the bowl rested a point-two-two round of ammunition. 'Another half an hour and that would have been unrecognizable, but fortunately you can still see the striations.' He handed me the bowl. 'However, Harry, that is your department. I have enough to do without straying into the realm of ballistics.'

'Where did you find it, Doctor?' asked Dave.

Mortlock stared at Dave for a few minutes. 'In his body, Sergeant Poole. Where else would it have been?'

'Yes, I gathered that, Doctor.' Dave grinned. It was all a part of the game that he and Mortlock played. 'But whereabouts in the body?'

'In the heart, Sergeant Poole, where its arrival would have tended to be fatal. Put in layman's terms for your benefit, it buggers up the ticker and that stops the works.'

I returned to Belgravia and, now that I had something substantial to impart, I assembled the team in the incident room. When I'd finished the briefing, I started to allocate actions to be undertaken.

'From Marty Dawson's report, coupled with Dr Mortlock's findings and the time the fire brigade received the call, we can estimate, with reasonable accuracy, that the fire started at about three thirty on Saturday afternoon.'

'That's the time we were told that a member of staff noticed the fire, guv,' said Dave.

'Is there any chance of identifying the weapon that was used to kill Sharp, guv'nor?' asked DI Brad Naylor.

'The round that Dr Mortlock found has gone to ballistics, Brad, and it would be a real stroke of luck if the weapon's on record as having been used before, but we'll just have to hope. Unfortunately, I suspect it'll be a case of waiting until we find the weapon itself. The killer must've got up close to be sure of a kill-shot with a two-two.'

'Yeah, probably.' Brad Naylor emitted an exaggerated sigh. 'But wouldn't it be nice to have an easy murder once in a while,' he said, which brought a laugh from the team.

'Amen to that,' said DS Charlie Flynn.

'The important task now is to interview those members who left the club between ten o'clock Saturday morning and four o'clock that afternoon. Obviously, anyone who left nearer to the time the fire broke out will be of greater interest to us. One of them could be the killer.'

'Isn't there a chance that the killer might still be there, guv?' asked Kate. 'He or she might be cocky enough to brazen it out.'

'Your team spoke to them all, Kate. If there are any you think worth interviewing again then do so. Brad, I'll put you in charge of interviews with those who left on the day. There were six men and five women, including three married couples. Pick your own team. In the meantime, Dave Poole and I will go to Brighton to see one of Sharp's marks.'

'Don't forget to take your bucket and spade, guv'nor,' said Sheila Armitage, which raised another laugh.

Colin Wilberforce gave me the name of the detective constable at Brighton who'd dealt with the fraud perpetrated on Sadie Brooks. I phoned him and told him that Robert Sharp was dead.

'I'm glad to hear that, sir,' replied the DC cheerfully. 'That's one more crime on the computer I can write off as cleared up.' There was a pause before he asked, 'Did you want me to come with you, sir, when you go to see Sadie Brooks?' The formal request sounded reluctant, even over the phone.

'That won't be necessary unless you particularly want to.' I felt that the woman we were going to see might talk more freely without the local law being present. But I'm ever the optimist.

'No, that's fine by me, sir.' The DC sounded relieved at not having to stick around while a Metropolitan DCI made a few enquiries that were really nothing to do with the Brighton police.

'If I learn anything that might help you, I'll let you know.'

'Thank you, sir. It's possible she might know of other scams she hasn't told us about but will tell you.'

We drove to Brighton, Dave having convinced me that to use the car for the seventy-mile journey was both cheaper and quicker than travelling by train. He always manages to put forward a compelling argument for not wasting valuable police time by waiting for trains that might not turn up.

The Lanes in Brighton is a labyrinth of narrow streets and alleyways full of shops large and small where it would appear one could buy almost anything. It was somewhere in this commercial maze that Sadie Brooks had her antiques business.

It was another beautiful day, and the area was thronged with tourists. The majority were traipsers who did little more than stare in shop windows but moved on the moment the proprietor came out in an attempt to entice them inside. There were

Japanese visitors everywhere whose sole pastime seemed to be photographing everything. I often wonder what they do with all those images. Do they ever look at them? Do they bore their friends to death with the video recordings of their holidays? Perhaps they were so busy taking photographs that they didn't have time to look at them.

We came across Sadie Brooks' establishment by accident and I stopped. I'd only spent a few seconds gazing in the window when a woman appeared in the doorway of the shop. She was probably in her late forties or early fifties, had short bottle-blonde hair and was wearing white cropped chinos and a bardot crop top. Curvaceous and brassy, with an assortment of bling adorning her neck, she wore a charm bracelet on her right wrist and a gold chain around her left ankle.

'There's a much better selection inside, love.' The woman spoke with an unmistakeable, coarse London accent and sounded as though she'd be more at home running a stall in the Portobello Road. 'What are you looking for? Anything in particular?' The question was posed in a tired tone of voice that implied we were just wasting her time.

'I'm looking for Sadie Brooks,' I said.

'I'm Sadie Brooks.' Suddenly, with that sixth sense that those living on the fringe of the law have for detecting the Old Bill, Ms Brooks realized who we were. 'Oh Gawd, you're coppers!' It was a statement made in such a tone of voice that I wondered how much bent gear there was in the shop behind her.

'I'd like to talk to you about Robert Sharp, Ms Brooks.'

'That sleazebag. Who's he been seeing off with one of his fiddles this time? You'll never catch him, you know. He's as artful as a wagonload of monkeys.'

'I'm Detective Chief Inspector Harry Brock from the Murder Investigation Team at New Scotland Yard, Ms Brooks, and this is Detective Sergeant Poole.'

'Christ! Don't tell me he's murdered someone now.'

'On the contrary, Ms Brooks, someone's murdered him.'

'Oh, for Gawd's sake call me Sadie unless you're going all formal on me while you think up something you can nick me for.'

'We weren't thinking of nicking you, Sadie,' said Dave.

'Blimey! He talks.' Sadie laughed openly at Dave, probably from relief. 'So, Bob Sharp's dead. Are you sure?'

'Yes,' I said, 'we're sure.'

For a second or two, Sadie savoured the information. 'That's the best news I've heard all day,' she said eventually. 'Here, you'd better come inside.' She glanced at a couple of pensioners who seemed to be taking an inordinate interest in our conversation. 'We're shut,' she told them. 'Come back tomorrow.'

Sadie Brooks was right when she said there was a much better selection of antiques inside her shop. The shelves were laden with small items such as clocks, candlesticks and vases, figurines of nineteenth-century women with unbelievable bodies, and pottery depictions of dirty street urchins with ugly faces. In groups on the walls, there were several paintings of bucolic scenes and a framed print of Terence Cuneo's painting of Waterloo Station and one or two prints of Jack Vettriano's work. The floorspace, what little there was of it, was almost filled by a mid-Victorian mahogany clerk's desk.

'I don't know how I managed to get stuck with that,' said Sadie, as I edged around it. 'Not much good to you when all you've got is a laptop computer, is it? And as for those . . .' She pointed at three mahogany wheel barometers. 'Who uses them these days when you can get an app to find out if it's going to piss down?' She crossed to the door, locked it and pulled down the blind. 'No point in staying open any longer,' she said. 'You're practically the only people I've had in here all day and you ain't going to buy nothing. But at least you've brought good news. How did he die?'

'He was burnt to death at a naturist club just outside London.'

For a moment or two Sadie stared at me, almost in disbelief, but then she burst out laughing. 'D'you mean he was still trying his luck at nudist colonies?'

'Well, yes, but the sort of people who go there aren't too keen on it being called that. From what you say, I take it he made a habit of going to naturist clubs.'

'He certainly did. As a matter of fact, it was at one of those places I met Bob. I've put on a bit of weight since then,' said

Sadie, running her hands down her body. 'What was he doing there this time? The usual con trick, I suppose.'

'What exactly d'you mean by that, Sadie?' asked Dave, deciding not to mention Madison Bailey.

'Oh, do work it out, love. It's his favourite gambit: join a nudist colony and then pick up some unsuspecting gorgeous-looking bird. Ten to one on, he was shafting her within hours, just before he nicked her credit cards and conned her into parting with her PIN.'

'Why d'you say that?' asked Dave.

'Well, that's what he bloody well did to me, innit? Nicked me credit cards just after he'd flogged me a bleedin' vase that he reckoned was Ming but turned out to be pure Brummagem. I thought I could judge men, particularly after the trouble I'd had with my ex, Jim Brooks, the bastard. I thought I could judge Ming vases, an' all,' she said.

'Where's Brooks now?' I asked.

'No idea, love.' Sadie gave an expressive shrug. 'That marriage lasted three months and then I found out he wasn't a professional tennis player on the American circuit after all, and he buggered off with my life's savings, he did. Turned out he'd been a dustman in Liverpool before he got the boot. Then the smarmy Bob Sharp turned up with all the old sweet-talking madam you can imagine, and I really thought he was the genuine article. Oh, we had a rave of a time. Done all the nightclubs in Brighton, but it turned out that it all finished up on my bloody credit card because I always got pissed and didn't remember what I'd been doing. And just before the bastard buggered off, he put me in the family way. I even had to pay for the bloody abortion. I tell you this, Mr Policeman, I'd have topped him meself if I'd had the chance.'

It was a fascinating story, but it was obvious that, try though she might to prove she was streetwise, Sadie Brooks was a sucker when it came to men. I felt sorry for her; so many women have been conned by the silver-tongued fortune hunters of this world and she, it appeared, was an easy mark.

'D'you know of any other women he might've conned, Sadie?' asked Dave.

'Bloody hundreds, I should think, but I don't know any

names. I'll wager it'll have something to do with a nudist colony, though.'

'Where were you last Saturday, Sadie?'

'Is that when he got his comeuppance?

'Yes.'

'I was in bed with my fella. All day. And if you want to check my alibi, you'll have to find the bastard first. He'd had what he came for and pissed off on Sunday morning. I'll bet he's got a wife somewhere an' all.'

'Did Sharp tell you he was married?' I asked.

'No, he never. Well, well, what a bleedin' surprise, I don't think,' said Sadie sarcastically. 'What is it about me and married men?'

'Well, he was and he had at least one child, and there's another on the way.'

'Poor little bitch. And I suppose the silly cow stood by him through thick and thin. I could've told her a thing or two, but it's too late now. For both of us.'

It seemed that Sadie Brooks was the type of woman who never learned from her mistakes and, despite her blasé approach to life, was probably as soft as butter on the inside.

FIVE

'What d'you reckon, Dave?' I asked, during our drive back to London.

'In bed with a bloke who's now done a runner?' scoffed Dave. 'Very useful sort of alibi, that is. Anyway, guv, that would mean she'd shut her shop all day on a Saturday at the height of the tourist season. I don't think so, not if she relies on the business as her only source of income.'

'She might've thought it worth losing money to close for the day in order to get her own back on Sharp by tracking him down and setting fire to him, Dave.'

'What you might call fulfilling a burning ambition,' commented Dave quietly.

'I wonder if she's got a website with her photograph on it.' I ignored Dave's witty remark; to have commented on it would merely have encouraged him. 'If she has, we could download it and show it around the naturist camp to see if anyone saw her there last Saturday.'

'Blimey!' Dave shot me a sideways glance. 'Did I hear that correctly, guv'nor?'

I laughed. 'You did, Dave. I'm fed up with you guys talking computer language all the time and me not understanding it. I bought myself a book called *Computers for Seniors for Dummies* to find out all about it.'

'Very suitable, sir,' said Dave in a voice entirely without intonation.

'And Lydia's very switched on, and she's giving me lessons.'

'I'm sure they're very worthwhile, sir.'

'Watch it, Poole.' I was familiar with Dave's occasional switch to the formal honorific. It usually meant that I'd made a stupid comment or stated the blindingly obvious or, as in this case, he'd read a double meaning into what I'd said.

I decided that we'd go back to our office in Belgravia via Chelsea to check on this story that Robert Sharp had told

Madison Bailey, that he had an antiques business in the
King's Road. I didn't believe for one moment that there was
any truth in it, but thoroughness in a murder investigation is
paramount.

Sharp had gone to the trouble of having cards printed with
the address of a London club and a mobile phone number but
neither a private nor a business address. Experienced fraudsters,
such as he was proving to be, go to great lengths to convince
victims of their credibility but rarely include information that
would enable the police to track them down. I was surprised
that he had so often used his own name. That was pretty naive,
but paradoxically, it might make him more difficult to trace.
He had, after all, managed to get away with numerous crimes
so far.

There is, however, always a risk for confidence tricksters
of Robert Sharp's sort. If the mark decides to check before
parting with his or her money or, worse still, reports the matter
to the police who then make enquiries, the best course of
action for the con man is to disappear as quickly as possible.

It came as no surprise that Robert Sharp's antiques business,
which he had told Madison Bailey was in the King's Road,
Chelsea, was not going to be easy to find. In fact, I'd already
decided that it didn't exist, but I would have to say in any
report I submitted to the Crown Prosecution Service that I'd
looked for it, otherwise they would want to know why I hadn't.
Unfortunately, there are no detectives on the staff of the CPS.

Sharp had told Madison Bailey that his premises were opposite a pub nearer Sloane Square than the World's End. But the
most likely location turned out to be a coffee shop of which
there are many in the King's Road. That is to say, there are
many this week.

Dave found a parking space, not an easy thing to do in this
particular street, principally because it's in London.

The coffee shop was one of those old-fashioned establishments where a waitress took your order and you paid her as
you were leaving. It's amazing that there are still some people
trading in London who are that trusting. Having ordered coffee,
we seated ourselves and when the waitress returned with two
beakers containing an inferior brown liquid, I discreetly

displayed my warrant card and asked if the manager could spare me a moment.

The young man who appeared wore a T-shirt marked 'Barista' and hovered in an agitated fashion by our table. 'I'm the manager,' he announced. 'Is there a problem?' He probably thought we'd discovered the sock in which he kept his stash of cannabis under the bed in the flat where he lived.

'No,' I said. 'Why don't you sit down for a few moments while we have a chat?'

The manager glanced furtively around as though fearing the instant arrival of Her Majesty's Revenue and Customs to do a snap VAT inspection. Eventually, he took the plunge and sat down or, rather, perched on the edge of the chair. His left hand, fingernails bitten right down, played a constant tattoo on the table top.

I told him who Dave and I were, and that we were investigating a murder. 'I've been informed that these premises were until recently an antiques shop.'

'Not as far as I know. This has been a coffee shop for quite some years,' said the relieved manager. 'At least, that's what I was told.'

'Must be a record for the King's Road,' said Dave. 'Have you ever heard of a guy called Robert Sharp who was said to be in business in this area?'

'Sharp? Sharp?' The manager savoured the name for at least three seconds before replying. 'No.'

'Thanks for your help,' said Dave. 'What do we owe you for the coffee?'

'Six pounds twenty,' said the manager.

'Cheap at twice the price,' said Dave sarcastically, and counted out the exact amount.

We'd checked the story that Madison Bailey had told us and the outcome had been exactly as I'd expected. I can only assume that Sharp had created his latest persona with the intention of persuading Madison Bailey into parting with some money. Or persuading her into bed with the promise of marriage to a man of great wealth who owned a Caribbean hideaway and took his holidays on the French Riviera.

As we were not too far from Pall Mall, I decided we'd

check out the gentlemen's club, the address of which Sharp had on his business card.

The fount of information in such places is always the hall porter. I identified myself and told him I was enquiring about a member.

The hall porter, resplendent in a green tailcoat, bridled at this request. 'We don't give out information about our members, sir, unless you have a warrant.'

'We're not asking you to,' said Dave, 'but this finger's been going about pretending he belongs to this prestigious establishment.' He displayed the card that Madison Bailey had given us.

The hall porter took out a pair of glasses and examined the card closely. 'I can tell you, guv'nor, that there's no one called Robert Sharp belonging to this club.'

'Just as I thought,' I said. I had known that before we entered the club's premises, but it had to be done.

My list of suspects for Robert Sharp's murder was looking decidedly short. Madison Bailey had admitted being at the Pretext Club at the same time as Sharp and there was little doubt that was true. She claimed to have left early, a claim that was supported by the CCTV and Rosemary Crane's assertion that Bailey had settled her account when she left at two minutes past eight on Saturday morning. Bailey further stated that she had left the country later that day, although not before the fire was reported. I determined that I would have her alibi checked with the airline she worked for.

Unlikely though it sounded, Sadie Brooks' statement that she had spent the busiest trading day of the week in bed all day with a man who had now vanished would be difficult, although not impossible, to disprove. I thought I might send my Australian rottweiler to see her; Kate Ebdon is very good at persuading people to tell the truth. It did cross my mind that Sadie Brooks' antiques business might be a front for something else, like drug dealing, money laundering or even sex-slave trafficking, given that the ferry port of Newhaven was a mere ten miles away from Brighton. In that case, closing for a day wouldn't have mattered a damn. On the other hand, experience told me that if she was a murderess, she'd have come up with a better alibi than the one she had given us.

As for Holly Sharp, Robert Sharp's wife, I couldn't be sure if she was better off without him or whether she'd nurtured hopes that he might one day return to the marital home and do the decent thing. Like providing for his family. It appeared at first sight that neither option was advantageous to the poor woman. One thing was sure: I didn't see her being responsible for Sharp's murder.

It was half past five by the time we got back to the office. The incident room was buzzing with gossip that ceased the moment Dave and I walked in.

'I'm just going to see the commander, Dave, to bring him up to date.'

'That shouldn't take long, guv,' said Dave gloomily. I think he thought as I did: it was going to be a long haul before we laid hands on Sharp's killer. And I was under no illusions. Sometimes the police never discovered a killer. Such cases would always remain open, but the amount of police time that was expended on them got less and less with the passing years. Naturally, we always hoped for a miracle, like a guy walking into a nick and confessing, or the DNA of someone just arrested for drink-driving would be a match with the DNA found on a victim's clothing twenty years previously. But I doubt Dave was thinking that at all and I was within minutes of discovering what the conversation in the incident room had been about.

I tapped on the commander's door.

'Come!'

'I thought you'd wish to know the progress of the enquiries I'm making into the death of Robert Sharp, sir. It is in fact, a murder.' I began to explain about the accelerant under Sharp's bed when the commander stopped me in mid-flow.

'I'm not really interested in any of this, Mr Brock.'

It was then that I noticed what he was doing. There was a cardboard box on his desk and he was emptying the drawers of their contents. Some items he was putting into the box, others he was throwing into the wastepaper bin. And finally, he placed the photograph of Mrs Commander in the box.

It had been standing on his desk ever since he was appointed to HMCC, and the forbidding appearance of the harridan was clearly meant to serve as an awful warning against matrimony.

'I'll come back, sir.'

'Don't bother, Mr Brock. I'm retiring. Close the door on your way out.'

I returned to the incident room. 'Dave, a word in my office.' I knew that my trusty sergeant would already have got to the nub of the strange and uncharacteristic goings-on in the commander's office.

'The commander's retired, as of today, guv,' said Dave, accepting my invitation to sit down.

'Bit sudden, wasn't it?'

'I had a quick word with my mate across at the Yard who knows about such things,' said Dave. 'Apparently the deputy assistant commissioner sent for him this afternoon and told him in no uncertain terms that it was time he retired or he would arrange a transfer for him. Apparently, some vague offer was made of a job in a north London outpost to do with investigating historic damage to police property. It seems that the commander's laid-back attitude to his hours of work didn't impress the DAC. At least, that's the scuttlebutt.'

'The end of an era,' I said. 'Any suggestions from your source as to who might take his place, Dave?'

'The smart money is on Mr Cleaver, guv.'

That sounded too good to be true. Detective Chief Superintendent Alan Cleaver was a real detective who had been a CID officer for the whole of his service after his first two years beat duty. How Cleaver had put up with the departing commander for the years he was detective chief superintendent of HMCC, I'll never know, but if what Dave said was true, he'd got his reward at last.

'I suppose there'll be a collection to buy a present for the commander to mark his retirement.'

'That's a bit difficult now that there aren't any ha'pennies in circulation, guv.'

'What about a farewell party, then, Dave? That's customary.'

'Somehow, I can't see him pushing the boat out,' said Dave.

'No, perhaps you're right,' I said. *Unless it's a paper boat*, I thought.

On Wednesday morning, I arrived at the office at about half past eight. I was determined to sit down with the two DIs, Kate Ebdon and Brad Naylor, and Dave Poole, to formulate a plan for tackling the increasingly complex case of Robert Sharp's murder.

'The commander would like a word, sir,' said Colin Wilberforce, the moment I stepped into the incident room.

'Who is it, Colin?'

'Mr Cleaver, sir,' said Wilberforce, as though any other officer in the post would be unthinkable. 'He said there's no rush, but when you've got a minute.' This was a revelation indeed. Yesterday's commander, who'd departed so suddenly the previous evening, never appeared before ten o'clock each morning, and disappeared promptly at six, although there had been a few weeks when he'd arrived at nine. But that had been a sop to the DAC and didn't last long before he reverted to his old timetable. The consensus among his subordinates was that he was more frightened of Mrs Commander than he was of the DAC. It had been an imprudent policy that had finally resulted in his peremptory departure.

I knocked on the commander's open office door.

'Come in, Harry, and take a pew.' Commander Cleaver's jacket was on the hat stand in the corner and he'd rolled up his shirtsleeves. His desk was completely clear. Gone were the filing trays and the heaps of paper that his predecessor had so adored. This was the desk of a no-nonsense boss.

'No computer, sir?'

'I've got a secretary, Harry. She deals with that sort of thing.'

Before I sat down, I reached over the desk and shook Cleaver's hand. 'Congratulations, sir. Pleased to see you sitting in that chair.'

'Thanks, Harry.'

'The Robert Sharp murder, sir . . .' I began.

'Felt anyone's collar for it yet?'

'Not yet, sir, but—'

'Let me know when you have, but don't come in here every

day with interim reports. It's wasting your time and mine. The reason I'm here is to make sure you do your job properly and provide any help you might ask for or I think you need.'

'Understood, sir.'

'Another thing, Harry. It's come to my notice that you're not too well clued up on IT. All my chief inspectors should know their way around mobile phones, computers, iPads and all the other stuff that's become the modern face of policing. So, get to grips with it.'

'As a matter of fact, I've started, guv'nor. My partner knows her way around computers and she's teaching me quite a lot.'

'I had a French girlfriend years ago,' reflected Cleaver, 'before I met my missus. That's how I became fluent in French. It's surprising what you can learn in bed, Harry.'

'Oh, we don't discuss computers in bed, guv,' I replied hurriedly. 'It's just that—'

'Get outta here, Harry.' The commander laughed. 'And leave the door open.'

I returned to my office via the incident room, and asked Kate, Brad and Dave to join me. Suddenly the future seemed much brighter.

We discussed the Sharp case for nearly an hour. The conclusion was that Sharp's murderer was either someone who had been ripped off big time by him, probably to the tune of several thousand pounds, or it was a woman to whom he had promised marriage, riches and a jet-setting lifestyle, but who had finally realized that it was all smoke and mirrors, although not before she had parted with a considerable amount of money. There were quite a few wealthy widows or divorcées who were looking for a husband but were wise to fortune-hunters. It would be a motive for murder if one of them had fallen victim to the likes of Robert Sharp.

That thought immediately put several people back in the frame. Sadie Brooks had been seen off by Robert Sharp, although she admitted he wasn't the first to have done so, but he might have been the one who finally tipped her over the edge. Madison Bailey had been told wonderous tales of Sharp's wealth, his Caribbean villa and his exotic holidays and I decided that she would have to be interviewed again. Those members of the Pretext Club who had been present at the time of Sharp's murder would also merit a second interview despite having been cleared by Kate's team originally.

'Did you find a website from which you could download a photograph of Sadie Brooks, Dave?' I asked.

Kate Ebdon raised her eyebrows in surprise at my new-found familiarity with information technology.

Dave handed me a print. 'This is the photograph that was displayed on it, but I think it was probably taken a good ten years ago. She didn't look that glam or that slender when we saw her yesterday.'

'I think we'll have to show it around at the Pretext Club, Dave, although we're probably wasting our time. I'm not sure I'd have recognized her from that.'

'We could get an up-to-date shot,' said Kate.

'I suppose we could, Kate,' I said doubtfully, 'but is it worth the trouble?'

'From what you and Dave have been saying, it looks as though Sadie Brooks is all that we've really got in terms of a viable suspect. If you think it's a good idea, it would only take a couple of hours to get down there, take the pic and come back.'

'Right, do it, Kate. Dave, you can drive Miss Ebdon down there as you know where it is, but don't go anywhere near Sadie's shop or you'll blow her cover.'

'He wouldn't dare,' said Kate, and she wasn't joking.

After Kate had left for Brighton, I decided to go to Heathrow to speak to the security officer of the airline for which Madison Bailey worked. Colin Wilberforce had already discovered her name for me and had told me that she was a retired police officer.

Having worked my way through the maze that is Heathrow, I eventually found the office of the woman I wanted to speak to.

'I'm Clare Hughes,' she said, once I'd introduced myself. 'I don't think we ever ran across each other when I was in the Job. But I was in the Uniform Branch and seemed to spend a lot of my time dealing with admin at whichever nick I was posted to. I suppose I had a knack for it. Frankly, I was glad to have got my time in. You can have too much of the Job, especially these days when we don't get the support we used to get. But it so happened that I was offered this job and it was too good to turn down.'

'How long have you been out, Clare?' She was a brunette of about fifty, perhaps a little older, immaculately dressed in a grey trouser suit with a red silk scarf, and just enough make-up.

'A year now and I'm thoroughly enjoying it. Anyway, enough of me, what can I do for you?'

I gave Clare the short version of the case I was dealing with and Madison Bailey's connection with it.

'Interesting,' said Clare Hughes. 'Unlike my predecessor, I don't believe in sitting in this office all day watching aeroplanes take off and land.' She waved a hand at the window which afforded a view of the runways. 'I get around the terminals and keep my eyes and ears open. It's surprising what you pick up, just by listening. Still, I don't have to tell you that, do I, Harry?' she added apologetically. 'As a result of putting myself about, I've gleaned quite a bit of interesting information from among the women. One of the advantages of being a woman in this job is that you use the ladies' staff loos and believe me, Harry, that's where character assassinations take place and loose-tongued gossip is bandied about.'

'From which, I gather, you've learned something about Madison Bailey?'

'Oh yes. By all accounts, she's quite a forward young lady, and is always on the lookout for a man.' Clare paused and smiled. 'Providing he's got money, of course. It's an open secret that she pushes off to a nudist camp whenever she gets the chance. Well, she's an attractive girl and I can imagine that strolling about the place naked she's going to have the pick of any man she wants. And she has the added advantage,' she said, shooting an arch smile in my direction, 'that she can see what's she's getting. Mind you, she's bound to pick the wrong man in the end. They always do.'

'The staff at the Pretext Club told me that Madison Bailey arrived there with the deceased, Robert Sharp, on Monday the fifteenth of July, but when I interviewed her she claimed it was just a coincidence. Incidentally, does the name Robert Sharp mean anything to you, Clare?'

Clare didn't hesitate. 'I've never heard the name,' she said.

'Madison Bailey also said that she arrived in her own car, a Mini convertible. She certainly left very early on the Saturday morning, at two minutes past eight to be precise. And that was well before the alarm was raised. Which means that there was a considerable time gap between her leaving the club and the discovery of the fire.'

Clare donned a pair of glasses and leaned across to tap a few keys on her computer. 'Yes, that all tallies,' she said after studying the screen for a moment. 'She was certainly on duty that evening, but it wouldn't have taken her long to get ready for her flight. I don't know why she should have left so early. It's not as if she was new to the job. These girls have done it so often that they can get ready for a flight in next to no time. Of course, she might have had another appointment somewhere.'

'I think I'll need to interview her again, Clare,' I said. 'Can you tell me when she's next off duty?'

'Yes, she's scheduled to land at ten hundred hours tomorrow morning, after which she's off duty for five days. You'll probably find her on the prowl back at that nudist club during her five days' leave.'

'Ten hundred hours tomorrow, you say. Is that Zulu or BST?'

'BST.' Clare laughed. 'I can see you're familiar with the jargon, Harry. You could get a job here when you retire.'

'There's absolutely no chance of that,' I said. 'I'm going to find a nice quiet place in the sun and relax with my rich widowed girlfriend.'

'You should be so lucky,' scoffed Clare. She obviously didn't believe me.

'Maybe. Before I go, let me ask you a question, Clare. D'you think Madison Bailey is the sort of woman who is capable of murder?'

Clare Hughes shrugged. 'I honestly don't know, Harry. Maybe if you pushed her too far, she might, but you could say that of a lot of women. Depends entirely on the circumstances and the woman, I suppose. At least, that's my partner's view.'

SIX

Dave parked the car in Duke Street and spent the next few minutes giving Kate instructions on how to reach Sadie Brooks' antiques shop. He then described Sadie Brooks herself, including the jewellery and the clothes she had been wearing when he last saw her, and mentioned that she spoke with a London accent.

Kate grabbed her shoulder bag and set off to saunter through The Lanes, stopping from time to time to peer in shop windows. She deliberately walked past Sadie Brooks' shop just to check it was the right place. Going on a few yards, she stopped, turned and made her way back and looked in the window.

Sadie Brooks appeared from inside the premises, dressed almost identically to the description Dave had given. 'There's lots more stuff inside, love. Were you looking for something in particular?'

'G'day,' said Kate, immediately hamming up her Australian accent. 'I'll bet you've got a whole load of stuff I'd just love to have, but I'm flying back to Oz tomorrow and there's no way I can take anything else.'

'Oh, lucky you,' said Sadie. 'I've always wanted to visit Australia. They tell me it's a lovely country.'

'It's beaut, mate, especially Port Douglas in Queensland where I come from.' Kate moved closer to Sadie and lowered her voice. 'Me and my mates used to go skinny dipping in the Coral Sea. But every once in a while, some wowser would tip off the cops, then we'd have to grab our clobber and run like hell for it.'

For a second or two, Sadie Brooks appeared baffled by Kate's quickfire Australian slang. 'Sounds wonderful,' she said eventually, 'but with a figure like mine, I'd probably get arrested for being the wrong shape if I did it.'

'Could I ask you a favour, Miss . . .?'

'It's Sadie Brooks, but call me Sadie. What can I do for you, love?'

'I'm Kate, Sadie. When the folks back home knew I was coming to the Old Country they said to be sure and take lots of photos. D'you think I could have one of you standing outside your shop?'

'Sure.' Sadie struck a pose and smiled as Kate used her phone to capture a few images of the antiques dealer.

'That's great, Sadie,' said Kate when she'd finished and put her phone back into her bag. 'The folks will love that. A real bit of old England. If you ever get Down Under, be sure to look me up. I'll give you my address in Port Douglas. We could have a special barbie and a few tinnies. Might even go skinny dipping. What d'you say?'

'Sounds good. If I do get to Australia, I'll make sure I look you up.'

Kate took out a notebook, jotted down a fictitious address and handed it to Sadie. 'If you don't feel like skinny dipping, I can lend you a cossie.'

DI Kate Ebdon returned at three thirty.

'There you are, Harry. What d'you think of that?' Kate displayed the series of photographs she had taken with her mobile phone. Each one was an extremely good likeness of Sadie Brooks and confirmed that Kate was a competent photographer. Or a lucky one.

'Excellent,' I said. 'Well done, Kate. Did she suspect anything?'

'Nah! She was as sweet as apples. She wished me a happy holiday and said she'd like to visit Australia one day so I gave her a bogus address and told her it was where I lived with my brother in Port Douglas. I doubt she'll ever get Down Under though. I reckon she's a dreamer. She's certainly dreaming if she thinks she'll make a fortune out of that junk shop she's running. A bit of a loser, if you ask me.'

'D'you reckon she's the sort who could resort to murder?'

'Any woman could if you pushed her far enough and hard enough,' said Kate. 'I certainly could if some bastard had me over the way that poor cow was stitched up. Mind you, I'd probably settle for breaking both his legs.'

And that, more or less, was what Clare Hughes at the airport had said about the propensity for women to commit murder.

'By the way, Harry,' Kate continued, 'I had another look at the CCTV footage from the club. The last time I checked, it was to see if anything had been thrown over the boundaries or whether there was anyone loitering with intent, so to speak. But then I thought about vehicles. The CCTV camera at the entrance showed Robert Sharp's car entering at five past nine on the morning of Monday the fifteenth of July. The camera was deliberately aimed at front number plates and it isn't possible to see who was in any of the vehicles.'

'Yes, I discovered that the first day we were there.'

'It's done for security so that the receptionist can record the number and check it against the booking. When it tallies, she opens the electronically controlled barrier and lets the vehicle in. And as Madison Bailey claimed, her car is recorded leaving at two minutes past eight on the Saturday morning.'

'I didn't doubt what she said about leaving at that time, and no one but a fool would leave a car like that in the street for several days. Nevertheless, I'll speak to Madison Bailey again and this time I'll take you with me.'

'D'you have a moment, sir?' Colin Wilberforce asked as he appeared in the doorway of my office.

'Come in, Colin. Sit down and tell me what's on your mind.'

'Sadie Brooks, sir.'

'What now?' Whenever Wilberforce appeared asking if I had a moment, I always had a dread feeling that he'd discovered something that would upset the direction of my enquiry. Although, having said that, it more often saved me from taking the enquiry in a direction that ultimately would lead nowhere.

'Sadie Brooks was married to a James Brooks five years ago.'

'Yes, she told me that, but she didn't say when the wedding took place.'

'Well, the truth is, sir, they weren't married. Not legally anyway, because James Brooks was already married. It turns out that he's a serial bridegroom. When the Devon and Cornwall Police arrested him last year for bigamously marrying a woman in Exeter, they found that he had entered into a form of marriage on three previous occasions, including his wedding to Sadie Brooks. The motive was, of course, to relieve each of his "wives" of the contents of her bank account by sweet talking them into some get-rich-quick scam.'

'Was there any suggestion that he used the alias of Robert Sharp, Colin?' I was beginning to wonder if Sadie Brooks had been entirely honest with us and it wouldn't have surprised me if she had lied. I'd come to the conclusion that after her experiences, she'd probably lie automatically to any man. Even if he was a police officer.

'Well, it's possible, I suppose, sir,' said Wilberforce dubiously, 'but I can't see any profit in a con man pretending to be another con man. However, Brooks is currently serving five years in Ford open prison.'

'That's a bit strong for bigamy these days, Colin.'

'The bigamies were only taken into consideration, sir. The police were originally investigating a series of frauds, but during that investigation they discovered the bigamies. He was sentenced for defrauding various persons by false representation.'

'D'you know if Sadie Brooks gave evidence at his trial?'

'No, sir, she didn't.'

'I'd already decided to see her again, but now I'll have her bigamous marriage to talk about. Thanks for all that, Colin.'

'All part of the service, sir.'

Because most police officers either work shifts or have done so in the past, they are particularly careful not to disturb others who have occupations that follow a similar pattern. There is nothing worse than being woken by a nine-to-five-Monday-to-Friday type when you've been working all night. However, in view of what Clare Hughes at the airport had said about Madison Bailey almost certainly going to the Pretext Club, I decided not to wait until the afternoon of Thursday to interview her a second time. We arrived at her Harlington flat at about ten fifteen.

In the event, it wouldn't have mattered what time we'd arrived.

'I always catch up on sleep at night,' said Madison. 'I don't like sleeping during the day, it's such a waste of off-duty time. In fact, I was just throwing a few things into a bag before I push off to the Pretext Club.' She giggled. 'Not that I'll need much.'

'This is Detective Inspector Kate Ebdon, Madison,' I said.

'G'day,' said Kate.

'Oh, hello.' Madison held out a hand, but despite her customary confident response, Kate's brash greeting appeared to bring a brief frisson of concern across the younger woman's face. Maybe it was Kate's Australian accent, or it might have been that I'd brought a woman with me this time instead of my black sergeant. Women officers are not as easily taken in by female suspects as male officers are, and have an intuitive ability to detect when they are lying. And right now, Madison, in common with everyone else involved in this murder, was a suspect. That said, I didn't think she was a viable one, but rather a silly girl who frequently disappeared into a fantasy world of her own.

Madison invited us to sit down and offered tea or coffee.

'No, thanks, Madison,' I said. 'You must get fed up with doing that when you're at work.'

I'd briefed Kate on how to play the interview, knowing that she'd give no quarter, and she immediately tackled the young woman in a typically uncompromising Ebdon manner.

'Why did you lie about arriving at the Pretext Club in your own car? You didn't, did you? You arrived in Robert Sharp's car.'

The directness of Kate's allegation took Madison Bailey completely by surprise. In fact, I think it would be fair to say that she had probably never been spoken to like that before. She stared at Kate with a shocked face, as if trying to convince herself that it hadn't happened, and it was some moments before she was able to formulate a reply.

'No, that's not true. I used my own car.' Madison looked at me. 'I told you, when you were here before, that I wouldn't have left my new Mini out in the street for four or five days, because it wouldn't have been there when I got back. You can check with the club. They keep a note of everyone's car when they come in and when they leave.'

'When did you hear about the fire, Madison?' Kate changed her line of questioning, having satisfied herself that the Bailey woman was telling the truth about her movements that day.

'When I got to the airport, someone mentioned that there had been this fire at the Pretext Club and that someone had been killed.'

'When I told you about the fire and the death, you gave me the impression that it was news to you,' I said.

'Oh, did I?' asked Madison innocently, and paused. 'Are you sure about tea or coffee?'

'Quite sure, thank you.' I concluded that her repeated offer was to give herself time while she sorted out a suitable answer.

'Why didn't you mention to my chief inspector that you knew about the fire when he and Sergeant Poole came to see you on Monday?' asked Kate, once again taking back the questioning. 'Are you hiding something?'

'Well, I—'

'You were having an affair with Sharp, weren't you?' continued Kate relentlessly. 'And you wanted to keep it a secret. Why didn't you admit it instead of wasting our time?' she added, giving Madison no chance to deny the allegation.

'I didn't want the airline to find out.' The lame responses continued to tumble out, one after another. Madison was now much less confident than when we'd arrived just under half an hour ago.

'Why not?' persisted Kate. 'Was he married? Was that the problem?'

'No, he was single.'

Kate glanced at me. I knew that look; it said that we're not going to get any more out of Madison Bailey until we've found out a hell of a lot more about her.

'I think that'll do for the time being, Madison,' I said, 'but we may have to see you again.'

Kate and I left Madison Bailey to her own thoughts, but she must have been worrying about how much we knew about her – not that it was much. But it was apparent that she thought we knew more than we did. I was now determined to find out why. Kate summed it up as we drove back to Belgravia.

'That woman is up to something, Harry.'

I had a feeling that things were beginning to move at last. After leaving Madison Bailey's flat, I returned to the office.

'Colin, find out as much as you can about Madison Bailey, but without showing out,' I said to Wilberforce.

'Of course, sir.' The slight tone in Wilberforce's voice indicated that he didn't need me to tell him to be discreet.

'I've spoken to Clare Hughes at the airport and she passed on the scuttlebutt that has been doing the rounds about the Bailey girl. But when Miss Ebdon and I spoke to Madison this morning, we both got the impression that she was hiding something.'

'Leave it with me, sir.'

After grabbing a quick lunch at my favourite Italian, Dave and I set off for Brighton once again.

The Lanes were no less crowded than they had been two days ago. On the contrary, there were probably even more tourists about. Not that it made any difference to Sadie Brooks: her shop was devoid of customers.

'Oh, it's you again.'

'Yes, it's us again, Sadie.'

'What is it this time?' Sadie didn't bother to lock the door or pull down the blind on this occasion. Either she thought we would not be staying long or she sensed that her line of business was not attractive to the traipsers who continued to peer in shop windows and take photographs but didn't buy anything.

'James Brooks.'

'What about that loser? You haven't brought more good news, have you? Is he dead an' all?'

'No, Sadie, he's doing time in Ford open prison.'

'Ha! The law's caught up with him at last. What did he get done for?'

'Bigamy, among other things.' I didn't mention that the bigamy cases had been taken into consideration when the sentence was imposed for the more serious offence of fraud.

'Don't tell me some other poor cow fell for his charms.'

'Four altogether, Sadie, including you. The form of marriage you and he went through was a sham. You weren't legally married to him at all.'

Quite suddenly, Sadie sat down on a rather ornate armchair upholstered in green leather. For some moments she remained silent, gazing unseeing at a brass bedwarmer hanging on the opposite wall. 'Where's this Ford prison you were talking about, Mr Brock?' she asked eventually, as she looked at me again.

'It's not far from Arundel, about twenty-five miles from here, I suppose. Why? Are you thinking of visiting Jim?'

'Yes, I am.'

'Have you forgiven him, then, Sadie?' asked Dave.

'No, I just want to kick him in the nuts.'

'I don't think the prison authorities would like you to do that, Sadie. They really don't like having their inmates damaged.'

'I don't give a toss what the prison authorities like or dislike,' responded Sadie emphatically. 'Anyway, why's he not in a proper nick, like Dartmoor for instance? That's where the bastard deserves to be.'

'Incidentally, you were number two on his hit list of brides, Sadie,' I said. 'I presume he didn't mention his first marriage.'

'Yes, he did, and the shyster told me he was divorced.'

'Did he ever show you any divorce papers?'

'No, stupid naive bitch that I am. I trusted him and what thanks did I get? He emptied my bank account, nicked my credit cards and took off. Not that the credit cards did him much good – they were topped up to the limit and I put a stop on them as soon as I found out they'd gone.'

'Now, about last Saturday, Sadie. You said that you were in bed all day with a man, but that he disappeared straight afterwards and you didn't know where he'd gone. Is that the truth?'

'Not really, no. It was the first thing that came into my head because I didn't want to admit that I'd been stupid again. I met this fella in the local boozer on Friday night and got bloody pie-eyed. He came back here, had his way with me and then buggered off. Well, I s'pose that's what happened because he'd gone when I woke up in the morning. But I felt so bad after putting away all that booze that I didn't feel like getting up, so I stayed in bed.'

'All day, Sadie?'

'Yeah, all bloody day. God knows what it cost me because, being a Saturday, I might have got rid of some of this junk.' Sadie waved a hand around the shop; the stock seemed exactly the same as it had been the last time we called on her. She started to laugh but then, quite suddenly and uncharacteristically for the tough, brassy woman she was, she burst into tears, great sobs shaking her body.

I wasn't quite sure what had brought that on, although I imagine she had plenty of reasons, but decided that it was best to leave her until the moment had passed.

Finally, Sadie looked up, not bothering to wipe her eyes. 'That bastard Jim Brooks,' she said. 'He was only with me for a year, but it was the best time of my life. We'd go out a lot, do all the nightclubs and really enjoy ourselves. Then we'd come back here to the flat, go to bed and he'd screw the arse off me. D'you know, he was the only man I ever knew who could hit the spot every time.' The tears started again, mascara running down her cheeks unnoticed. 'Men just don't fancy me any more, Mr Brock. All they want is money. They think I'm rich because I own this millstone.' Again, she encompassed the interior of her shop with a sweep of her hand. 'And sex, of course, but they'll soon start to think that I'm getting too old for that. I ask you, what's left for me?'

'What was this man's name, Sadie? The one who spent the night with you last Friday.'

'Man?' Sadie scoffed. 'I should think he was young enough to be my son. I think he said he was called Lance or some poncey name like that. What's more, when I eventually got up and had a shower, I discovered that I'd paid for the night out on my credit card, but I don't remember doing it. I was blotto.' She paused to blow her nose. 'You must think I'm a bloody fool, Mr Brock. I let men walk all over me. Always have done and I don't suppose I'll ever change.'

'Did he say where he lived?'

'No. Could be anywhere. He might live in Brighton, but, on the other hand, he might be down here on holiday and getting his end away as often as he can. Anyway, I've decided to sell this place for what I can get and move to Australia.'

'What brought on that sudden decision, Sadie?' I asked.

'There was a nice Australian girl here yesterday called Kate and she told me all about where she lived in Oz, as she called it. It sounded great. I thought to myself, *Sadie, what the hell are you doing in a bloody Brighton junk shop? Start a new life.*'

We walked back to the car and drove off with the intention of returning to London.

'What d'you think, Dave?' I asked.

'Call me cynical if you like, guv'nor, but I think Sadie Brooks is a bloody good actress. I still think it's worth showing the staff at the Pretext Club the picture of Sadie that Miss Ebdon took. And I shouldn't mention to Miss Ebdon that Sadie's thinking of going to Australia.'

'You're right, Dave. I'm not sure whether to believe Sadie Brooks or not. I still can't accept that she would shut her shop for a whole Saturday just because she'd got a hangover.'

As we left Brighton, I telephoned Colin Wilberforce to see if there had been any developments in my absence and found him in a bad mood.

'What's wrong, Colin?'

'You asked me to find some background on Madison Bailey, sir. So, I decided to check on whether she and Robert Sharp had been at the Pretext Club at the same time on any previous occasions.'

'And had they?'

'The woman at the club wouldn't tell me, sir.'

'Who did you speak to, Colin?'

'Someone called Rosemary Crane, sir, who kept banging on about data protection.'

'Leave it with me, Colin. It's time these people were put right about obstructing a murder investigation. Where's Miss Ebdon?'

'In her office, sir.'

'Transfer me, Colin.'

'Before I do, sir, I've discovered some interesting information about the Pretext Club. I've passed it to Miss Ebdon. I'll put you through now, sir.'

When Kate answered, I explained the problems that Wilberforce had been having with Rosemary Crane.

'D'you want me to go up there and rattle their bars a bit, Harry?'

'I think we'll get a brief first, Kate. Go to the nearest Crown Court, smile sweetly at the judge and obtain a search warrant to seize their membership database and details of when members stayed there. Then, meet me at the Pretext Club and we'll give their tree a shaking just to see what falls out.'

'Sounds like fun, Harry. By the way, Wilberforce gave me some info about the two who run the club. I'll fill you in when I get there. But I'll get the warrant first.'

SEVEN

D ave and I left it long enough to afford Kate sufficient
time to persuade a circuit judge that her application
for a warrant was valid. Then we drove out to the
Pretext Club.

After a short and rather terse conversation with Rosemary
Crane via the gate intercom, we drove into the club's grounds.
As we got out of the car, the first person we saw was a naked
Madison Bailey. She waved, dropped the large beach bag
she'd been carrying and dived gracefully into the pool.

'Any chance of mixing business with pleasure, guv?' asked
Dave.

'What would Madeleine say, Dave?' Dave's wife, Madeleine,
was a principal dancer at the Royal Ballet. 'Don't forget that
ballet dancers are extremely strong, even the female ones.'

'You don't have to tell me that, guv,' said Dave, nodding
sagely. 'It's not worth the risk of two broken legs.' There had
always been rumours that Madeleine assaulted Dave from time
to time, but it was all a big joke. Dave was devoted to his
wife, and there was no chance of him ever taking a fancy to
another woman or she to another man.

Kate Ebdon was seated on a bench close to the general
manager's office. She took a document out of her shoulder
bag and handed it to me.

'The warrant, guv.'

'Any trouble, Kate?'

'No way. The moment I mentioned a nudist colony and a
murder, the judge had his pen out ready to sign.'

I took the warrant and briefly scanned it. 'That should stop
them complaining.'

'Probably start them off again,' said Kate. 'Before I left the
office, Colin Wilberforce told me that his bit of digging turned
up an interesting snippet of information. Cyril Cotton is actually the joint owner of the Pretext Club. The other joint owner

is Rosemary Crane who is divorced and by all accounts enjoys a close relationship with Cotton that's much more than a business relationship. Cotton has never married.'

'Well, there's a surprise. I reckon they're made for each other simply because I can't imagine anyone else fancying either of them. I wonder why they're so reluctant to give us any assistance.'

'Could be money laundering,' said Dave. 'There's a lot of it about.'

'Possibly,' I said. 'I had thought of that. However, let's have a chat with the aforementioned lovebirds.' I pushed open the door of the general manager's office to find both Cyril Cotton and Rosemary Crane there. This time neither of them was wearing clothing but didn't seem in the slightest embarrassed by it. Perhaps this bravado was an attempt to embarrass us so that we'd run away red-faced. Which just went to show they didn't know much about coppers.

'I've already told one of your people who had the audacity to telephone me that I don't intend to part with any more information about our members,' announced Rosemary Crane at her haughty best. Her reaction made me wonder if she and Cyril Cotton had had something to do with Sharp's murder after all. They certainly hadn't gone out of their way to be helpful to us.

'I'm afraid you don't have an option, Mrs Crane.' I showed her the search warrant. 'Failure to comply with a Crown Court judge's warrant is a serious offence and could result in imprisonment for contempt.'

'Well, I don't know what you hope to achieve by harassing our members. All they want to do is come here to relax and enjoy themselves in this beautiful sunshine.'

'And get murdered,' said Dave.

'Pah!' Rosemary tossed her head. 'What d'you want to know, then? I see I have no alternative.'

'Robert Sharp and Madison Bailey were here last Saturday,' Dave stated. 'When were they last here together before that?'

'How d'you know they were here before? Madison certainly was, but I'm not sure about—'

'You're wasting my time, Mrs Crane.' Dave was beginning to get a little annoyed. 'I might even go so far as to suggest that you're deliberately obstructing us in the execution of a warrant. Just look it up.'

With a toss of her head, a gesture of irritation that she repeated frequently, Rosemary Crane crossed to the computer on Cotton's desk, her ample derrière wobbling as she did so, and began scrolling through the entries.

'They were here from Monday the third of June to Saturday the eighth of June. There, does that satisfy you?'

'Not yet,' said Dave. 'Did they arrive together?'

'I don't think so.' Rosemary studied the monitor again. 'No, they didn't. Robert Sharp arrived at eight thirty and Madison arrived at eleven minutes past ten.'

'I thought naturist clubs restricted their membership to couples,' suggested Kate archly, 'and yet these two appear to be unrelated singles.'

'Who *are* you?' demanded Rosemary. So far, Kate hadn't spoken a word, and her Australian accent may have caused the Crane woman to wonder if we'd brought a journalist with us.

'Detective Inspector Ebdon, Murder Investigation Team. And your answer?'

'We have to make money, Inspector.' For the first time since our arrival, Cyril Cotton joined in. 'This place is very expensive to run and if a suitable applicant turns up, then we take him or her, whether or not they have a partner.'

'And that's how Sharp and Bailey became members, is it?'

'Yes.'

'It's not something I agree with,' said Rosemary Crane. 'Cyril happily accepts anyone who turns up. It'll get us into trouble one day, and I . . .' She suddenly realized that she was talking to three police officers, but it was too late to retract her admission.

'Yes, go on,' I said.

'Well, no, I mean . . . there are always issues with health and safety and hygiene and that sort of stuff.' Rosemary's flustered protestation was weakened by the scarlet glow that rose rapidly to her cheeks.

'I think you mean that the behaviour of some members might cause the police to take an interest in the running of this establishment,' I suggested.

'Why would you take an interest?' asked Rosemary innocently, attempting unsuccessfully to backtrack.

'Running a brothel, perhaps?' said Dave uncompromisingly.

But instead of responding to Dave, Rosemary turned on Cotton. 'Didn't I always tell you, Cyril, that if you were too lax about the sort of people you admitted you would eventually run foul of the law? But you wouldn't take any notice, would you? No, you were the one who wasn't interested in anything but money, and that was your all-important god, wasn't it?' It appeared now that, far from being involved in the murder, Rosemary Crane was far more worried about a visit from the burgeoning army of jobsworths who were likely to descend unheralded to enforce one of their pettifogging rules.

'But I'm always very careful about who we admit,' said Cotton lamely.

'That's absolute rubbish and you know it.' Rosemary was not giving up yet. 'This scheme of yours to admit sexy young women at a lower rate than middle-aged men is just one example. Take that Madison Bailey. She pays next to nothing to be a member here, and if I didn't respect that young lady's judgement, I'd think there was something going on between you two. Fat chance!' She laughed scornfully at the prospect of Madison even giving the overweight, unattractive Cotton a second glance, let alone anything else. But ironically, according to the information that Wilberforce had turned up, Rosemary Crane was more than willing to hop into Cyril Cotton's bed. 'There are laws now about sexism and ageism and gender equality, Cyril, but you just sail along as though nothing but the bank balance matters to you. Have you ever wondered what goes on in the chalets during the night? Have you ever noticed how often members creep from one chalet to another? Have you ever walked around the place after dark? No, you're too busy poring over your precious bank statements.'

'If I may just interrupt your discussion for a moment,' said

Dave sarcastically, 'perhaps you could tell me if Robert Sharp was a single member?'

'Yes, he was,' said Cotton. 'And so is Madison.'

'Have a look at this photo, Mrs Crane.' Kate handed a six-by-ten blow-up of one of the photographs she had taken of Sadie Brooks. 'Is it anyone you recognize?'

Rosemary Crane studied the photograph for some seconds before shaking her head. 'I don't know that woman at all.'

Kate took the photograph back and handed it to Cyril Cotton. 'And you, Mr Cotton, have you ever seen this woman here at any time in the past?'

Cotton studied the photograph for longer than Rosemary Crane had done before replying. 'Yes, I'm sure she was here some weeks ago. Don't you remember, Rosemary? She spoke with an American accent and said she lived in New York. Mind you,' he said, 'it might be easier to recognize her if she wasn't wearing any clothes.'

'Well, I don't recognize her at all,' said Rosemary.

'Perhaps you'd show it to members of your staff,' said Kate, 'and ask them if they know her.'

'What's her name?' asked Cotton.

'That's what we're trying to find out.' Kate saw no advantage in revealing the name of the woman. In fact, if someone were to recognize Sadie Brooks *and* name her, that would be extremely useful.

'That seems to be all for the time being,' I said. 'I don't think we need to take up any more of your time now, but we'll undoubtedly have to return with more questions as our enquiries progress.'

'I don't doubt that for one moment,' said Rosemary Crane acerbically.

I was in the office next morning at just after eight o'clock. At eight thirty, Linda Mitchell arrived.

'We've completed the examination of Sharp's car, Harry, but there seems very little in the way of evidence that's likely to help you. Of course, you may think differently. Anyway, it's all in my report. But we did find this.' Mitchell handed me a document enclosed in a plastic sleeve. 'It's a credit card account that we found under the front passenger seat of Sharp's car. I doubt that Sharp knew it was there. In fact, he probably thought he'd lost it.'

'He seems to be up to the limit on this one, Linda,' I said, quickly scanning the document. 'His credit limit is shown as eight thousand pounds and he's got seven thousand, nine hundred and sixty-five pounds outstanding, including interest. I think we'll have a chat with this company, see what they can tell us about Robert Sharp.'

'Anything on there that might help, guv?' asked Dave.

'Quite possibly, Dave. Several of the entries are for hotels in various parts of the country. If they can tell us who he stayed with and, in turn, find out if one of them ever went to the Pretext Club, we might get lucky and find out who topped him.'

'You could well be right, sir,' said Dave.

'Shut up, Poole.' No doubt, he thought it was a long shot. And so did I, in truth.

I walked through to the incident room. 'Colin, find out where this credit card company has its offices,' I said, handing him the account. 'And please don't say Edinburgh.'

Wilberforce turned to his computer and tapped a few keys. 'That makes a change,' he said. 'It's in London. And, as usual, the director of security is ex-Job.' He turned the screen so that Dave could note the details.

The director of security at the credit card company was named Ron Clark and had retired a year previously from the fraud squad of one of the county constabularies.

'It's a different world after thirty years in the Job, Harry,' said Clark, once introductions had been effected. 'It takes a bit of time adapting, and I'm still learning. Anyway, what can I do for you?'

I summarized the investigation into the murder of Robert Sharp and explained about the discovery of the credit card account in his car.

Clark glanced at the account number and keyed it into his computer. 'This is one curious punter, Harry. He's running what's known in the trade as a yo-yo account. He's got no credit left at the moment, but last year the same thing happened. Then he paid in a lump sum – six and a half grand to be exact – and cleared his debt in one go. Then the debt started mounting again, but now he's back to square one. Let me try the credit reference agency we use. They might help you even more.' He keyed another address into the computer and waited. 'I thought so. Sharp's rating is rock bottom. It seems that he owes money all over the place.'

'How did he get the sort of credit you gave him, then, Ron?'

'He's been a cardholder with us for quite a few years, so we obviously gave him a card before his balance started its see-saw behaviour. But how he managed to get the others is a mystery. And I don't know why we didn't withdraw his credit facility altogether. According to this credit agency,' said Clark, tapping the computer screen with his pen, 'he's got six credit cards, all topped up to the limit, and there's a bank very keen to talk to him about mortgage arrears.' Clark keyed in another address. 'Yeah, that reckons. There are County Court Judgements out against him all over the place – from Cornwall to Yorkshire.' He swung round to face me again. 'There's going to be a hell of a lot of unhappy creditors when they learn he's snuffed it, Harry. Unless he's left any assets that none of us know about.'

Dave laughed. 'I very much doubt it, Ron. His wife's on her beam ends and the poor cow hasn't got two pennies to bless herself with. It's rented property so she'll probably be served with an eviction order very soon, if she hasn't been turned out already, but I wonder why he's got a mortgage?'

'You'll have to ask the bank,' said Clark, and handed me a slip of paper on which he had written details of Sharp's mortgage.

'I'll see if I can persuade them to give me some information,' I said. 'Are any hotels mentioned in his account history, Ron?'

Clark swung back to his computer. 'There are four over the past year. There's one interesting one, though. On the twelfth of May this year, he tendered his card at a hotel and it was refused. We make a note of such incidents because ultimately it affects his creditworthiness. Would you like a printout of those transactions?'

'Please, Ron. It might be that one of the women he wined and dined was responsible for cremating him, particularly if he stole all her money before doing a runner. That's his usual MO, at least, as far as we know.'

'Nor hell a fury like a woman scorned,' quoted Dave, taking the printout from Clark and handing it to me. The hotels where Sharp had stayed, I was pleased to see, were in London or the home counties.

'One other thing, Ron,' I said. 'How the hell does this guy manage to use other people's credit cards without knowing their PIN?'

'Easy if you know how, Harry.' Clark paused. 'Give me your credit card for a minute or two.'

I handed it over and watched Clark insert it in a reader that he then plugged into his computer. After tapping a few keys, he turned the monitor so that I could see it. Displayed in large numerals was my four-digit PIN.

'Like I said, Harry, it's easy when you know how.'

The five-star hotel where Sharp's card had been refused on the twelfth of May was only a couple of streets away from the office we'd just left, and I decided to call there on the way back to Belgravia.

It was one of those hotels that thrived on the tourist trade. As we approached the entrance, I saw unlicensed minicabs circling like vultures, waiting for the opportunity to rip off unsuspecting foreign visitors.

Inside the hotel there was a rack full of pamphlets depicting Buckingham Palace, the Tower of London, the Royal Festival Hall, Windsor Castle and other attractions in and beyond the capital. The foyer was crowded and voices in a variety of foreign languages could be heard attempting to converse with each other and with the hotel staff. A world-weary hall porter was standing behind the place of safety provided by his counter, fielding questions as fast as he could.

Waiting until the latest coachload of international sightseeing travellers had checked in, Dave and I approached the reception desk.

'We're police officers, miss. I'm Detective Chief Inspector

Harry Brock, Murder Investigation Team, and this is Detective Sergeant Poole,' I announced quietly to the receptionist, discreetly displaying my warrant card at the same time. 'I'm told that a Mr Robert Sharp stayed here a couple of weeks ago. I wonder if any member of the staff remembers who was with him.'

The young lady receptionist's badge said her name was Estelle. 'If you'll excuse me, I have to get the manager's permission before I'm allowed to give out any information about guests.' She tapped out a number on her phone and explained the situation to whoever had taken the call. 'The manager will be along shortly,' she said, replacing the receiver.

The middle-aged woman who appeared was smartly dressed in a tan-coloured trouser suit. Her name badge said she was called Greta and showed her to be the manager.

'I'm Greta, gentlemen. Estelle tells me you're enquiring about Robert Sharp.' Her accent sounded Germanic and reminded me of my ex-wife Helga, originally from Cologne, whom I'd divorced some time ago after sixteen years of tempestuous marriage. The catalyst was the loss of my four-year-old son, Robert, who had drowned in the pond of a neighbour with whom Helga had left him while she went to work. 'Perhaps you'd like to come into my office.'

We followed Greta into a small but comfortable room close to the reception area. I imagined it was where uncomfortable interviews were conducted with long-stay guests who'd 'omitted' to settle their accounts on a regular basis.

I told Greta who we were and explained that we were investigating Sharp's murder. I said that we'd learned that he'd stayed at this hotel and left on Sunday the twelfth of May this year.

'Huh! It sounds as though he got his just deserts at last,' exclaimed Greta vehemently, and then apologized. 'I'm sorry, that wasn't very Christian of me, but I'm afraid people like Sharp really annoy me.'

'Why d'you say that?' I asked.

'They take unfair advantage of women and, unfortunately, all too often, the women let them.'

'D'you have a reason for saying that, Greta?' I couldn't imagine any man being foolish enough to try taking advantage of Greta.

'Sharp produced a credit card when he arrived and, as usual, it was swiped into our system, but when he came to settle his account the next morning, the card was rejected. At that point, the receptionist called me to the desk, and I asked Sharp what he proposed to do about it. After a short discussion with the young lady who was with Sharp, she produced her own credit card and paid the bill. I have to say that she didn't appear to be very happy about it. It was for almost four and a half thousand pounds.' She glanced at her computer screen where she had already turned up the details. 'Four thousand, four hundred and ten pounds and fifty-five pence, to be exact.'

'Who was this young lady, Greta?'

'She was a rather gorgeous young black girl, mid to late twenties, I should think. Actually, her skin was quite light.'

'But d'you remember her name?' Dave asked.

Greta turned back to her computer. 'It was Sabrina Holt. She really was lovely. God knows what she was doing with that Sharp person, apart from paying for their weekend.'

Dave took out his mobile phone, scrolled through it and turned it towards the manager. 'Is that her, Greta?' It was a shot of Madison Bailey waving.

Greta needed only a glance. 'Yes, that's Sabrina Holt, but she's not wearing any clothes.'

'It was taken at a naturist club just outside London. It was where Sharp died.'

'Ah, that would explain it. We have many such clubs in the south of Germany, but I didn't know there were any in this country. Usually the weather here is too cold for that sort of thing. Either that or it's raining.'

Having been to Cologne with my ex-wife on several occasions, I didn't think that Germany's climate was too good for wandering about naked either.

'Can you give me details of that credit card, Greta?' said Dave. 'I think it may be false.'

'You do? But the account was settled by the card company.'

'Yes, it would have been, if what I think happened, did happen,' said Dave, and wrote down the details.

'Two questions, Dave,' I said as we drove away. 'How did you manage to get a photograph of a naked Madison Bailey?'

'It was when we went to the club yesterday to interview Cotton and Crane, guv.' Dave offered no further explanation than that. 'And the second question?'

'How in hell's name did Madison Bailey get a credit card in the name of Sabrina Holt? I doubt that a company would willingly have issued one in a false name.'

'There are two answers to that,' said Dave. 'Either Sabrina Holt is her real name or she was using a cloned credit card. It's easily done. People are too trusting. They go into a restaurant or a bar and allow the waiter or barman to take their card away in order to prepare the bill or whatever. At least, that's what they pretend to do, but you and I know that it's not necessary.'

'Yes, I know. They usually deal with the bill at the table or wherever, with a handheld machine.'

'With the right kit, you can clone a credit card in seconds,' continued Dave. 'And very often it'll take a month or even longer before the card holder realizes there are transactions on the card that they didn't incur.'

'You suggested that Sabrina Holt might be her real name, Dave. Supposing she comes from Jamaica, for example, and she got the card there.' I looked sideways, but Dave was already shaking his head even though he was keeping his eye firmly on the road ahead.

'If that was a genuine card, it would mean that she actually intended to pay the bill. No, I'm not wearing it, guv, not when you consider her salary is probably twenty grand a year. Maybe twenty-five grand at a stretch.'

'I can check that with Clare Hughes, the airline security officer. I should've asked her when I saw her.'

'I reckon Madison was part of Sharp's scams,' Dave continued, 'and that Greta misinterpreted her being unhappy about footing the bill. Madison's display of reluctance might have been part of the pretence or she was nervous about using a cloned card. D'you intend to 'front her with it and see what she says?'

'No, not yet, Dave. I'll put Charlie Flynn on to it. He knows his way around the financial markets.'

EIGHT

Back at our Belgravia headquarters, Kate Ebdon joined me in my office.

'I've been out to the Pretext Club again today, Harry. And I took Tom Challis with me, although I don't suppose the new Mrs Challis will be too chuffed about him mixing with all those naked ladies.' Tom Challis had recently married Heather Douglas, who had very nearly become a victim in a series of murders we had investigated. Her knowledge of science enabled her to set a trap that ultimately led us to arrest a serial killer.

'Was it profitable, Kate?'

'Possibly. Tom and I spent some time chatting to the staff. Frankly, I don't rate the Cotton and Crane duo to be much help, but the girls who clean the accommodation and change the beds, that sort of thing, were much more forthcoming. One of the things that was apparent is that the people who work for them hate the two bosses. As a result, there's a regular turnover of staff.'

'I'm not sure that's too much help to the investigation, Kate.'

Kate laughed. 'You're right, Harry. I was straying from the point. The interesting fact that emerged concerned Madison Bailey. It seems that during the week leading up to the murder, she became very friendly with a guy called Geoffrey Sykes who was staying there. This came from three of the cleaning staff and one of the lifeguards at the pool, each of whom was interviewed independently. They were all women, and they tend to take more notice of such things. The really interesting fact is that one of the cleaners barged into Sykes' room in the accommodation, thinking it was empty, only to find Madison in bed with him.'

'It looks as though Madison Bailey was prepared to put herself about a bit. Still, there's no law against it whether they're single or they're both married, even if they're not married to each other. What's known about this Geoffrey Sykes, Kate?'

'It was his one and only visit to the Pretext Club, Harry. Apparently, they take casuals, as they call them, from time to time. I made a few more enquiries from the reluctant pair who own the place, and they told me that Geoffrey Sykes checked out on the Saturday morning, ten minutes after Madison Bailey.'

'I suppose Rosemary Crane didn't have an address for this Sykes finger, did she?'

'You suppose right, Harry, but I got the details of his credit card. We can trace him through that.'

'We'll have a word with him when we've time, but it looks as though he took advantage of a willing Madison. Can't really blame him for that, I suppose. And the fact that Sykes and Madison booked out within ten minutes of each other is probably a coincidence.'

'They were certainly booked to stay for that week and were scheduled to leave on the Saturday morning. Oh, and one more thing. Rosemary Crane showed the staff the photograph of Sadie Brooks, but no one recognized her. It looks as though that's a blowout.' Kate stood up to leave. 'Charlie Flynn's waiting to have a word, Harry. He said you wanted to see him.'

'Yes, I do. Leave the details of Sykes' credit card with me, Kate, and I'll get Charlie to look into that as well.'

Detective Sergeant Charles Flynn is a suave ladies' man. He had been divorced twice by the time he was twenty-eight and was now touching thirty and in an on-off relationship with a woman police officer stationed at Bishopsgate in the City of London. Frankly, I don't think he's really cut out for marriage.

Flynn's years as a member of the Fraud Squad had fine-tuned an astute brain that was capable of analysing facts in a comparatively short space of time. But he's not only a desk jockey. He's also very good at prising facts out of those who are reluctant to part with information. All in all, he was the ideal officer to find out about the credit card that Madison Bailey, alias Sabrina Holt, had used to pay a hotel bill. And to track down this Geoffrey Sykes who had become a person of interest.

'There's a lot of it about, guv,' said Flynn, once I'd explained about the Sabrina Holt credit card. 'Not to put too fine a point on it, the general public are easily taken for a ride. Believe it or not, it can often take weeks, months even, before someone twigs that they're being cheated. Some people pay the minimum amount on their card by direct debit without even checking their account. And there are those who clear the whole amount every month, again by direct debit, to avoid paying any interest.'

'See what you can find out, Charlie.'

'Right, guv.' Flynn stood up. 'D'you want me to have a chat with this Madison bird?'

'Not yet. Get the story behind the credit card first, and then I'll work out what to do next.' I decided that allowing Flynn to interview Madison Bailey was really putting too much temptation in his way. An amalgam of the sexy Madison and the roving-eyed Flynn was a dangerous mix. I've seen cases fall apart before, simply because a police officer has become personally involved with a witness, let alone a suspect. And I was beginning to wonder if Madison was now a suspect in the murder of Robert Sharp.

It was proving to be a busy afternoon. The next to appear in my office was Colin Wilberforce.

'I've been doing a bit more research on Madison Bailey, sir.'

'Sit down and tell me about it, Colin.'

'She studied physics at Leeds University, sir.'

'Did she indeed!' This opened up an entirely new side to the woman. 'Did she graduate?'

'No, sir. She dropped out after a year and decided to become an airline attendant instead.'

'Physics, eh? So, she'd probably be qualified to know how to start a fire by remote control, say a mobile phone, even after a year's study. Presumably she had suitable A-levels.'

'I imagine so, sir. I haven't found out which school she went to, yet.'

'Don't bother, Colin. It's not important. At least, not at this stage. What you can do is leave a message for Martina Dawson and ask her to ring me.' I was hoping that the fire investigator would be able to answer some of the questions formulating in my mind.

Rather than telephone me, Martina Dawson appeared in my office an hour later.

'I much prefer talking about things face-to-face, Harry, rather than using the phone. What's your problem?' She sat down in the one armchair that my office boasted and crossed her legs.

'It's about the fire at the Pretext Club you investigated, Marty.' I repeated the information that Wilberforce had discovered about Madison Bailey's time at university. 'I was wondering whether a year of a physics degree course at Leeds might have given her sufficient knowledge to have started that fire by remote control.' I was guessing and I knew that she would destroy my theory very quickly if I was on the wrong tack. But she didn't.

'It's possible, I suppose.' Martina Dawson remained silent for some time, deep in thought. I waited, having previously formed the opinion that she was not a woman to be rushed. 'I daresay that she could have acquired enough knowledge to set a device that could be triggered with a signal from a mobile phone,' she said eventually. 'If that were the case, such a device would likely have been destroyed beyond recognition in the resulting conflagration.'

'Would that call show up on her mobile phone or on her phone account?'

'Only if she's naive enough to have used her own phone, Harry.' Marty laughed. 'But I doubt she'd be that stupid. She'd have picked up a phone from a supermarket for cash, one that couldn't be traced – ironically it's what the Americans call a burner – and throw it in the river once the job's done.' After a lengthy pause, she added, 'Does that get you any further forward?'

'Not in terms of the investigation itself, no, but it does move her up the list of suspects. My main problem at the moment is to find a motive for her to have murdered Sharp. If, in fact, she did.'

'It's not my field of expertise, Harry, but from a female perspective, I can tell you that if a man swindles a woman out of a large amount of cash there's no telling what she might do. Do you think that your dead man could've swindled her?'

'It's something I'm in the process of finding out, Marty. Thanks for your help, and I'm not only talking about the fire.'

'Mind you, there is one thing that can tip a woman over the edge, and that's if the man in her life abandons her in favour of a newer model.'

It was a comment that made me wonder if Marty Dawson was speaking from experience.

After one or two false starts at the credit card company, Flynn was eventually shown into the office of a woman who, he had been assured, would be able to answer all his questions. She was a brunette with a pageboy hairstyle, whom he estimated to be in her mid-thirties.

'I'm Detective Sergeant Charles Flynn, Murder Investigation Team, New Scotland Yard, Mrs . . .'

'My name's Patricia, Sergeant Flynn, although everyone calls me Trish, and I'm one of the security staff,' said the woman, skilfully dodging the implied question about her marital status, having got Flynn's measure immediately. 'Please take a seat and tell me how I can help you.' She seemed unaffected by her visitor's suavity and her response was impassive, but then he wasn't the first police officer with whom she'd had dealings in her job.

Flynn explained about the credit card, in the name of Sabrina Holt, that was used to pay the hotel bill on behalf of Robert Sharp on the twelfth of May. He didn't immediately mention that it was almost certainly Madison Bailey who had used the card.

'What seems to be the problem, then?' asked Trish, still maintaining a dispassionate attitude as if to convey that she was not in the least impressed by Charlie Flynn or the job that he did.

'We think it may have been cloned,' said Flynn.

'Oh, Christ!' exclaimed Trish, abandoning the false reserve that she had deployed until then. 'D'you have the details?'

'Certainly do.' Flynn chuckled at the sudden collapse of Trish's original iciness. He handed her the piece of paper with the account number and the dates of the stay at the hotel.

Donning a pair of managerial-type spectacles, Trish turned to her computer and entered all the details. 'There is an item here for four thousand, four hundred and ten pounds, fifty-five pence on the twelfth of May this year.'

'That's the one,' said Flynn. 'Was the hotel paid?'

'Yes, of course.'

'What about the cardholder? Did she settle her account?'

'She pays the total sum by direct debit each month. I don't suppose she even bothers to check her account.'

And that is exactly what Flynn had suggested might have happened when he'd spoken to DCI Brock.

'Unfortunately,' Trish continued, 'there are all too many people who don't bother to check their accounts or even download them. They just pay. It may be that she has a job where most of the transactions are settled by her employers anyway. She just puts in receipts and gets reimbursed, puts the money into her bank account and forgets all about it.'

'Why d'you say unfortunately?'

'When they eventually discover what's happened, they come bleating to us, but there's nothing we can do except attempt to investigate it and issue them with a new card. And sometimes we decide to close the account as being too much trouble. Even so, they expect us to reimburse them. Well, I'm afraid they end up being disappointed.'

'Have you ever met this Sabrina Holt, Trish?'

'No, but then we rarely meet our customers. They're just names on a computer.'

'Then you wouldn't know whether she was a light-skinned black woman.'

Trish giggled girlishly. 'No, I wouldn't. What makes you ask that?'

'Because that's how I'd describe the woman who incurred that debt with the hotel. She is an air hostess. If you would let me have the address of this Sabrina Holt, I may have to interview her.'

Turning once again to her computer, Trish furnished Sabrina Holt's details.

'Thanks very much. You've been very helpful, Trish. But there is one more thing you could help me with . . .'

'Yes?'

'I passed an Italian restaurant just down the street from here. What's it like?' Although on the face of it, it was an innocent enquiry, this was in fact one of Charlie Flynn's more subtle chat-up lines and usually led to an invitation.

'Very nice. I usually have lunch there myself. I don't believe in eating sandwiches in front of a computer.'

'Why don't you join me, then?'

Trish smiled. 'What would your wife think about you taking me out to lunch, Charles? May I call you Charles?'

'No, you can call me Charlie, and I don't have a wife. But what would your partner think?' Flynn had noticed that Trish was not wearing a wedding ring, but that didn't mean a thing these days.

'I don't have a partner, Charlie.' Trish stood up and grabbed her handbag. 'Let's go.'

Flynn appeared in my office just after three o'clock. First of all, he told me what he had learned about Sabrina Holt's credit card account.

'Where does this Holt woman live, Charlie?'

'Yuppy territory, guv. She's got a flat in the Isle of Dogs, down the East End near—'

'I do know where the Isle of Dogs is, Charlie.'

'Sorry, guv. But she must be filthy rich because the price of flats there are calculated in millions rather than thousands. I did an electoral roll check and she is the only one shown as living at the address I got from the credit card company.'

'Or she's got an illegal immigrant living with her who can't vote. Get down there and find out what this is all about, Charlie. Now, what about this Geoffrey Sykes who was found sharing a bed with Madison Bailey at the Pretext Club?'

'He lives in Motspur Park, guv. His credit card is paid off on the thirtieth of each month by direct debit, which means the charge on the naturist club won't have gone through yet.'

'I'd better have a talk with him, to see if he's got anything useful to say about his fling with Madison Bailey. And then, I suppose I'll have to speak to Madison Bailey again and find out what she was doing in Sykes' bed. Apart from the obvious.'

Geoffrey Sykes lived in one of the quiet roads close to Motspur Park railway station. These days, it seems that many people are in jobs where Friday is treated as if it were a half-day. Nevertheless, I telephoned Sykes before setting out on what might be a wasted journey if by some chance he was out or on holiday. But he answered my call and was naturally curious to learn why two officers from a murder investigation team at Scotland Yard should wish to talk to him. I told him it was not something I wanted to discuss over the phone.

I decided to take Kate Ebdon with me rather than Dave, because she lives in a part of New Malden which is very close to Motspur Park. My idea was that after we'd spoken to Sykes, Kate could drop me at my place in Surbiton and then go home, keeping the car with her until the following morning.

The overall impression of the Sykes residence was one of neatness. The garden was neat, the front of the house was neat and appeared to have been recently repainted. The green front door had a polished brass lion's-head knocker that was probably for decoration as there was also a bell-push on the door frame.

The man who answered the door was also neat. Wearing a collar and tie – unusual these days, except for detectives – he had neatly trimmed hair, a pencil moustache and wore rimless spectacles.

'Mr Sykes?'

'Yes.' There was no move to admit us. Yet.

'I phoned earlier, Mr Sykes. Detective Chief Inspector Harry Brock and this is Detective Inspector Kate Ebdon.'

Sykes raised his eyebrows a fraction, presumably having difficulty in accepting the idea that a detective inspector was wearing jeans and a white shirt *and* was a woman. But women are now an essential part of the police in general and the CID in particular. All those I'd met were as good at the job as the men and some were a damned sight better, Kate Ebdon being a good example.

'Please come in, Inspector.'

'It's *chief* inspector, sir.' I blame the television scriptwriters who seem to think that it's acceptable to demote an officer when speaking to him. But a chief inspector is of a higher rank than an inspector and the difference can be as much as ten thousand pounds a year.

'Oh, I'm sorry.' Sykes led the way into the sitting room at the front of the house. 'This is the wife,' he said, indicating a grey-haired, dumpy little woman who was sitting in an armchair. 'This is the lady and gentleman from Scotland Yard, dear,' he added, by way of introduction.

'Charmed, I'm sure.' Mrs Sykes afforded us a syrupy smile, closed the book she'd been reading and paid attention.

'Do sit down,' said Sykes, indicating a couple of armchairs, 'and tell me why you would want to talk to me about a murder.' I thought I detected a slight north-country accent that had not been eradicated by the years I imagine he'd spent in the south.

This interview could develop into a delicate situation. I could hardly ask to speak to Sykes alone, but if he was engaging in nudism without the knowledge of his wife, it would probably cause a row, depending, of course, on her view of such matters. Not that it would be our fault. However, the question about intimate relations with a sexy young black girl called Madison Bailey was undoubtedly guaranteed to blow their comfortable little existence sky high. The last thing I needed was to become involved in divorce proceedings between Mr and Mrs Sykes. The Commissioner of the Metropolitan Police takes a very poor view of officers who are careless enough to be subpoenaed to give evidence in the divorce court.

'It concerns the Pretext Club near Harrow, Mr Sykes.' I tried to picture Sykes cavorting in the pool and making love to Madison; it was not an edifying vision. Less believable even than that was Madison wanting to share a bed with a man who had the appearance of a middle-aged pedantic clerk with adenoidal problems.

'I've never heard of it.' Sykes looked genuinely baffled.

'What is it, a nightclub of some sort? The wife and I never go to nightclubs. Anyway, Harrow's miles away.'

'It's a naturist club, a nudist colony,' said Kate, who tended not to pussyfoot around.

'Good grief!' exclaimed Sykes. 'What would I be doing in a nudist colony?'

His wife laughed, as if to confirm the stupidity of it.

'But why should you ask?' continued Sykes. 'I mean, what led you to my front door?'

'Because a man claiming to be Geoffrey Sykes and using a credit card in that name stayed there between the fifteenth and twentieth of this month. And on the twentieth, a man was murdered there,' I said.

Sykes' face expressed utter bewilderment at this revelation. 'There must be other men named Geoffrey Sykes, surely,' he said. 'It's not exactly unique.'

'The credit card company gave us this address as being that of the cardholder, Mr Sykes,' said Kate.

'This is all most extraordinary,' said Sykes, shaking his head. 'I'm retired, you see, Chief Inspector, and we were here for the whole of that week including the weekend,' he protested, genuinely appearing to have difficulty in following this turn of events. 'We were supposed to be going to Greylake nature sanctuary in Somerset, being keen ornithologists, but our car was stolen.'

'Where was it stolen from, Mr Sykes?' asked Kate.

'Arundel. From one of the town-centre car parks.'

'If you were going to a nature reserve in Somerset, what were you doing in Arundel in West Sussex?' asked Kate, who seemed to be having as much difficulty as Sykes in making sense of this whole narrative.

'Ah, no, you see that was . . .'

'What my husband is trying to say,' said Mrs Sykes, finally joining in, 'is that we were in Arundel on the Saturday before the weekend when we intended going to Somerset. That was . . .' She reached for her handbag, took out a small diary and thumbed through its pages. 'Yes, here we are. We went to Arundel on Saturday the thirteenth of July. We stopped there for lunch before going to the wildlife and wetlands reserve in

Mill Road. Well, that was our intention, but when we returned to the car park our car had gone. Which meant that we couldn't go to the wildlife sanctuary. And it meant we couldn't go to Somerset the following weekend either.' She consulted her diary again. 'Saturday the twentieth of July was when we should have been going to Somerset.'

'I see,' I said, having finally grasped what had happened. 'So, you were here all that weekend?'

'Yes, but fortunately there was one of David Attenborough's wonderful programmes on television, so it wasn't a totally wasted weekend.' The Sykeses were obviously keen nature lovers, but not, it was becoming clear, the sort to be found in naturist clubs.

'The police in Arundel were very good about it,' said Geoffrey Sykes. 'They took all the particulars and said they were sure it would be found.'

'Didn't your insurance company cover the cost of hiring a car, Mr Sykes?' I asked.

'Oh, would they do that?'

'How d'you explain your credit card being used on the twentieth of July, Mr Sykes?' asked Kate, saving me from getting into a discussion about car insurance.

'I can't,' said Sykes. 'I've got three cards altogether, but I usually use the one that gives me cashback every so often.' He walked across to a small table and took his wallet from one of its drawers. 'Oh, Lord!' he exclaimed. 'One of the cards is missing.'

'Would it be this one?' asked Kate, opening her pocket-book to display where she had written the number of Sykes' account.

'Just a minute.' Sykes returned to the open drawer and took out a bundle of accounts held together by a bulldog clip. 'Yes, it is. But how on earth did this person get hold of it?'

'Did you by any chance leave it in the car, Mr Sykes, or perhaps it fell out of your wallet when you were looking for something else?' persisted Kate, trying to establish precisely the circumstances under which this nature lover's card had finished up in the hands of whoever had used it at the Pretext Club.

'I suppose I must've done,' said Sykes. 'How very silly of me.'

'The credit card company have probably suspended it as a result of our visit, but you should report its loss as well, Mr Sykes,' I suggested. 'Unfortunately, I think you'll have to pay for any transactions that were incurred by this individual at the Pretext Club.'

'Oh dear,' said Mrs Sykes. 'It's all a mystery.'

It was a mystery to me, too.

NINE

I was concerned that someone like Sadie Brooks might talk to the media and that it would result in inaccurate reporting or, worse still, reveal the extent of the enquiries we were making. In an attempt to prevent this, and perhaps secure some useful information, I decided on Thursday to release the information that Sharp had been murdered.

This morning, Saturday, one week after the murder, two calls were received on the dedicated telephone line that had been installed for that very purpose. Each was from a woman and each claimed to have known Robert Sharp. One of the women, a Janice Greene, lived on the outskirts of Guildford, and the other, Gina Page, resided at Dorking. Interestingly, no crimes that bore Sharp's style had been reported in the Surrey Police area. I decided that I would speak to the two women, sooner rather than later, in the hope that they might have some vital information that would solve the case for me. But I have been disappointed before. Many times.

I took Kate Ebdon with me as it was possible that the women might be more forthcoming if it got to the point that they would rather speak to her than me.

We found Janice Greene in a flat close to the University of Surrey.

'Ms Janice Greene?'

'That's me.' The woman who opened the door was tall, probably in her mid-twenties, and had long blonde hair and an engaging smile.

'We're police officers, Ms Greene, from the investigation team dealing with the murder of Robert Sharp. You telephoned our hotline this morning.'

'Gosh, that was quick. I didn't expect anyone so soon.'

'How did you meet Robert Sharp, Ms Greene?' I asked,

once we'd introduced ourselves and were settled in the flat's comfortable sitting room.

'Oh, please call me Janice,' she began. 'I met Bob at a naturist club on the south coast about nine months ago. I'd gone there with a number of friends, just for a bit of a lark really.' She spoke as though going to a naturist club was an everyday occurrence. Perhaps it was for her and her group of friends and really no different from going to a nightclub. 'Anyway, as I said, I met Bob Sharp and we got talking. He asked me out and . . .' She faltered and glanced at Kate.

'You had an affair?' suggested Kate.

'Yes, but that wasn't the real reason I got in touch with you.'

'What was the reason, then?' Kate asked, but we both knew what she was going to say.

'I really wanted to know if there was any chance that I'll get my money back now he's dead?' Janice blurted out the question as though glad that she'd finally admitted that Sharp had swindled her.

'I think you'd better tell us about it.' I sensed that was the start of what was now becoming a familiar pattern.

'We were together for about three months and we got on really well. So well, in fact, that when he proposed to me, I accepted.'

'Were you in a relationship with someone else when you met Sharp, Janice?'

'Yes. I was going out with one of the guys who worked at the uni.'

'What was his name, Janice?' asked Kate.

'Stephen. Stephen Hall.'

'What did he think about you breaking off your relationship with him? I presume that's what happened.'

'He was furious. We had a blazing row and he said he couldn't understand what I saw in Bob Sharp. Anyway, he packed in his job at the uni and moved away to Swindon. I think it was Swindon. I never saw him or heard from him again apart from him telling me where he'd gone. Not that I know why he did that.'

'It'd be helpful to us if you wrote down his present address,

Janice.' Kate handed the woman her pocketbook. 'And where he's working now. If you know, that is.'

'I'm sorry I ever split up with my boyfriend. All things considered, it was a stupid thing to do,' said Janice, as she returned Kate's pocketbook, 'but I was really in love with Bob – or thought I was. He was absolutely charming and thoughtful, unlike any man I'd met in the past. On reflection, I suppose I was besotted with him – infatuated is the word my ex used. He was suave and courteous to a fault.' She stared momentarily into the middle distance, a dreamy expression on her face. 'Anyway, we sat down in this very room to plan the wedding. He told me he was in a good way of business and showed me a photograph on his smartphone of a place he owned in the Caribbean. He said that we'd spend our honeymoon there. Either there or in the south of France where he had many contacts.'

'You mentioned money just now, Janice,' said Kate. 'How did that come about? You did lend him some, I suppose.'

'Yes, I did. He said that he'd spotted a house not far from here that he thought would be ideal once we were married. I was pleased about that because it meant I could carry on working at the university.'

'What d'you do there, Janice?' I asked.

'I'm an assistant librarian. Anyway, Bob took me to see this house and it was ideal, really lovely. He told me that it was necessary to put down a deposit straight away otherwise someone else would snap it up.'

'Didn't he have sufficient cash, then?' But Kate knew exactly what was coming next.

'He did, yes, but he told me it was all tied up in stocks and shares and other investments and it would take a little while to release it. He was afraid we'd lose the house if we didn't act quickly.'

'Did he tell you what he did for a living, Janice?' I asked.

'Yes, he said he worked on the stock exchange trading in the futures market, whatever that meant. Anyway, I loaned him three thousand pounds. It was what my grandmother left me when she died. But after I'd lent him the money, he disappeared. I eventually rang the estate agent and asked what was happening, and he told me that they'd heard from Bob. He said that after we'd viewed the property, Bob had telephoned the agency and told him that we were no longer interested. I asked about the deposit that had been paid, but the estate agent said Bob hadn't paid anything.'

'Where was he living at this time, Janice?' Kate was busily taking notes as she posed the questions.

'He told me he lived in Chelsea.'

'Did you ever go to his place?'

'No. When I suggested it, he said it would be a couple of weeks before I could see it because he'd got the decorators in and they were giving the whole place a makeover. I suppose that was a lie, too.'

'Didn't you think it odd that he had a place in Chelsea, but was talking about buying a house here in Guildford?'

'I think that was my fault because I said that I'd like to carry on working at the uni, but it wasn't that important. I'd loved to have lived in Chelsea and I'm sure I could have got another job up there, probably at London University. But now that he's dead, I don't suppose I'll ever see my money again. Do you know who murdered him? I read something about it being at another naturist club miles from here. I think that was the one genuine thing about him – he seemed to be dedicated to the naturism business.'

'Yes, it was called the Pretext Club,' I said, although I didn't think Sharp was dedicated to naturism. As far as he was concerned, it was a means to an end. 'We're still looking for his killer and it'll take time, but we'll find him or her. Incidentally, did he ever suggest that you should join him at that naturist club?'

'No, he didn't, but I'd have been delighted because I'm keen on it, too. It's so relaxing and carefree.' Then, quite suddenly Janice Greene dissolved into tears. I was surprised at Kate Ebdon's reaction. I say surprised because I'd always thought of her as a hard-nosed copper, but she moved swiftly across to the settee and sat down next to Janice. Putting her arm around the girl's shoulders, she asked, in an almost motherly fashion, 'When's the baby due?'

'Next month,' mumbled Janice in between sobs.

*   *   *

Sabrina Holt lived on the fifth floor of an apartment block on the Isle of Dogs. Fortunately for Charlie Flynn, the lift was working and he reflected on the fact that if it had been a council-owned block, he would undoubtedly have had to climb the stairs. And he'd done that a few times.

'Sabrina Holt? I'm Detective Sergeant Charlie Flynn from the murder investigation team. I phoned earlier.' The woman who answered the door looked to be about forty-five. Probably old enough to have amassed a fortune and to be thinking about retiring.

'Come in.' She showed Flynn into a large open space that was furnished minimally but comfortably. There was a huge television set against the wall adjacent to windows that comprised the whole of one side of the room and gave a panoramic view of the River Thames. A kitchen-diner occupied a space at the far end. 'Do sit down. I must admit I'm a little puzzled as to why someone from the murder squad at Scotland Yard should want to see me.'

'It's about your credit card, Miss Holt.'

'It's Sabrina, Sergeant Flynn. You make me sound like someone's maiden aunt.'

'It's Charlie, Sabrina. Have you ever lost your credit card?'

'No. I've got three altogether and I have them here. D'you want to see them?'

'If it's no trouble.'

The woman picked up a canvas tote bag from the floor by her chair, ferreted about in it and eventually handed her holder to Flynn.

'Have you ever parted company with this particular credit card, Sabrina?' Flynn held up the card he'd identified from the account number.

'No. I told you that I've never lost any of my credit cards.'

'That wasn't quite what I meant. Can you recall if this card was ever out of your sight when you were paying for something with it?'

'Of course not. In a restaurant for example they always bring a hand-held device to the table and complete the transaction there. And the same sort of system operates at checkouts in shops and supermarkets.' Sabrina took a moment to consider the question further. 'But now you mention it, Charlie,' she said slowly, 'there was one occasion. It was on a flight to Bogotá.'

'What were you doing in Bogotá, Sabrina? Business trip, was it?' Flynn was trying to discover if it was a business credit card that was settled by her employers without too much questioning, as one of the credit-card company's security staff had suggested might be the case.

'No, I went there for a holiday. It's a beautiful city and very interesting. If you're ever there, make sure you visit the Gold Museum.'

'I'll bear it in mind, Sabrina,' said Flynn, although he doubted he would ever visit Bogotá and certainly had no taste for museums.

'Anyway, I bought a bottle of duty-free vodka on the plane and paid for it with my credit card. That card.' Sabrina gestured at the card that Flynn was still holding. 'The stewardess said that she would have to take it and process it in the galley as they weren't allowed to bring hand-held devices into the cabin area. She said it was something to do with aircraft safety.'

'A likely story,' muttered Flynn. 'D'you happen to remember the stewardess's name or what she looked like?'

'Good heavens no. I don't suppose I even looked at her name badge at the time and I certainly can't remember anything about her appearance. They all look the same in uniform. But why are you asking all these questions, Charlie, and what does it have to do with a murder? I assume there's some connection as you're from the murder squad.'

'This card was used by an air stewardess to pay a hotel bill in central London, Sabrina. It was for four thousand, four hundred and ten pounds and fifty-five pence.'

'But how could that possibly be?'

'Before I answer that, d'you mind telling me your profession?'

'I'm a commodities trader.'

'I'm certain that your credit card was cloned, Sabrina.' Flynn pondered the incongruity of a commodities trader who didn't understand the simple basics of a common fraud.

'What on earth does that mean?'

Flynn explained the simple way in which the fraud was perpetrated.

'But how could it have been?' Sabrina sounded genuinely puzzled, even after Flynn's explanation.

'The most likely scenario was that it happened when the stewardess took your card having spun you some specious story about aircraft safety. However, don't you ever check your credit card account when you receive it?'

'Not really. It's cleared every month by direct debit.'

Flynn thought how pleasant it must be to have so much money that you didn't notice when over four grand that you hadn't incurred appeared on your account and wasn't even questioned.

'But you still haven't said what this has to do with a murder,' continued Sabrina.

As succinctly as possible, Flynn told the commodities trader about the murder of Robert Sharp and how an air stewardess was connected.

'Well, it's certainly opened my eyes,' said Sabrina as she conducted Flynn to the door of her apartment. 'I certainly won't let my credit card out of my sight in the future.'

And that, thought Flynn, *is too bloody late.*

Kate Ebdon and I drove straight on to Dorking where our interview with Gina Page produced a set of circumstances almost the same as those that Janice Greene had experienced.

She was also a tall girl, much the same age as Janice Greene. She, too, had long hair, although in her case it was jet black.

Sharp had told Gina a story similar to the one he had told Janice Greene. Early last year she had met Sharp at a naturist club and they had started an affair. He'd proposed marriage a couple of weeks after the meeting, and she admitted to having fallen 'head-over-heels' in love with him. The same story unfolded. The Caribbean hideaway that he talked about to Janice Greene and, incidentally, to Sadie Brooks, was backed up with photographs, none of which included him. The purchase of a house was mooted and visited, and then out came the same old story of funds being tied up in stocks and shares, and poor naive Gina was persuaded to make a short-term loan until he could lay his hands on his own money.

'How much, Gina?' asked Kate.

'Four and a half thousand,' said Gina, 'but he promised he'd pay it back the following week.'

'But you never saw him again and when you spoke to the estate agent, he told you that Sharp had telephoned to say that he was no longer interested in the house the two of you had viewed. Furthermore, the estate agent denied receiving any money by way of a deposit.'

'How did you know that?' Gina was wide-eyed at Kate's apparent omniscience.

'I'm sorry to have to tell you this, Gina,' I said, 'but we've heard it all before.'

'So, that's that, I suppose. No chance of getting my money back now that he's dead.'

'I'm afraid you're in a rather long queue, but I think it's safe to say that Sharp probably didn't leave any money when he died. Or if he did, it'll be in some offshore account and impossible to get at. But that's extremely unlikely.'

'Were you in a relationship with someone else when you met Sharp, Gina?' asked Kate.

'Yes, I was living with Kevin.'

'Who is Kevin?'

'I'd met him at the same naturist club where I met Bob. But before, of course. Before I met Bob, I mean.'

'Was Kevin with you at this naturist club when you met Sharp?'

'Yes.' For a moment or two, Gina had the grace to appear shamefaced.

'I imagine Kevin was upset when you walked out on him?'

'That's putting it mildly,' said Gina. 'He was hopping bloody mad. I still get messages on social media calling me a slag and a tart and a whore.'

'I think you'd better give me his details, Gina,' said Kate. 'It would appear that this Kevin has already committed several offences.'

In the event, prosecuting Kevin for his internet bullying

proved to be too difficult for us and it was left to the police in Australia.

We got back to Belgravia by eight o'clock that evening, only to find that there had been another call from a member of the public complaining that she'd been swindled.

'It's a Mrs Nina Harrison who lives in Bromley, sir,' said Gavin Creasey, the night-duty incident room manager.

'D'you want to do that this evening, guv?' asked Kate.

'No, it can wait until Monday, Kate,' I said. 'It's bound to be the same as the stories we've just heard from Janice Greene and Gina Page.'

And that's how it turned out, more or less, but this time there was a twist that made it much more interesting and possibly pointed us in the right direction. But as I've said many times, I've often been disappointed.

Before settling down to an hour's work reading some of the statements that had been taken over the past few days, I telephoned Lydia and suggested dinner that evening at a restaurant that had only recently opened in Kingston.

'I know it's no good asking you to come out to Esher, not while you've got an investigation running, Harry, but I've got a better idea. Why don't I come to your place and get dinner for you? Then you can relax.'

'Sounds like a plan,' I agreed. I don't know what it is about Saturday evening traffic during high summer, but it took me very nearly two hours to get from Belgravia to my flat in Surbiton. It must be the popularity of that day of the week for going on holiday or coming back from one. My journey wasn't helped by an accident on the A3 that caused our traffic unit colleagues, known affectionately to the CID as the Black Rats, to close the southbound road between Tolworth and, with the cooperation of Surrey Police, Pain's Hill.

I had given Lydia a key to my flat some time ago and she greeted me with a kiss and a large whisky.

'I met your cleaning lady, Mrs Gurney, today, Harry, darling. How on earth d'you get her to clean for you on a Saturday afternoon?'

'I didn't know she did,' I said. 'She turns up whenever she can manage to fit it in, I suppose.'

'She's an absolute gem. I wonder if she'd be prepared to come out to Esher from time to time?'

'I hope you're not trying to kidnap her, my love,' I said. 'I can only manage my life if there are two women in it.'

'She insisted on calling me Mrs Brock,' said Lydia, having given me a playful punch in the ribs for that last remark. 'Do you have some plan you've omitted to tell me about, Harry?'

I laughed. 'That's probably wishful thinking on her part. I think that deep down she thoroughly disapproves of me sleeping with a woman I'm not married to and tries to pretend it's not happening.'

'Well, I don't disapprove. In fact, I quite like the idea,' said Lydia, and promptly changed the subject. 'How are you getting on with your nudist colony murder?'

'It seems that the victim made a point of swindling women out of money. He'd met quite a few of them at the Pretext Club and had affairs with them. He also visited some other naturist clubs where he picked up unsuspecting women he eventually finished up swindling. But it seems they all fell under his spell.'

'What you might call naked flames, I suppose,' said Lydia drily. 'Dinner's ready whenever you are.'

It was a magnificent meal, as usual, and Lydia invariably manages to select the perfect wine to complement whatever she'd cooked.

'Are you staying the night?' I asked, once we were relaxing in the living room.

'Of course.' She gave me a wicked smile over the rim of her brandy balloon. 'Unless Mrs Gurney would rather I didn't. D'you want to call her and get permission?'

TEN

In her telephone call on Saturday, Mrs Nina Harrison had complained that she'd been swindled by Robert Sharp. I returned her call on Monday morning, learned that she would be at home all day, and made an appointment to visit her.

Nina Harrison's home proved to be a large, detached house in a quiet road in Bromley, Kent. Parked on the drive was a middle-of-the-range Volvo and behind it a BMW. Each had number plates showing that they had been registered this year.

'You must be the policeman who telephoned this morning,' said the woman who opened the door. She could have been a year or two either side of forty; it was difficult to tell. Her hair may have been naturally blonde – I'm not too good at telling the difference – but from what little I knew of ladies' hairdressing salons, the way in which it had been styled would probably have cost a small fortune. Her white trousers were well cut and her sweater was cashmere. Overall, it would be fair to describe her as a mature, confident and elegant woman.

'It's Mrs Harrison, is it?'

'Yes, please do come in,' she gushed, forcing a smile.

We were conducted into a large, airy sitting room that looked out on to a perfect garden. The room's few pieces of light oak furniture were low enough to enhance the air of spaciousness, and the chairs and settees looked, and proved to be, comfortable. If the Harrisons owned a television set, it was presumably in another part of the house that was dedicated to viewing. I noticed that there were one or two *objets d'art* in various parts of the sitting room, but they were not displayed ostentatiously.

'I'm Detective Chief Inspector Harry Brock, Mrs Harrison, and this is Detective Inspector Kate Ebdon.' I'd decided to take Kate with me for continuity; each interview was beginning to shape up in much the same way as the others.

'I'm pleased to meet you,' said Nina Harrison, and insisted on shaking hands with each of us. 'Please sit down.'

But before we were able to take a seat, a tall, well-built man entered the room. Probably a few years older than Nina, his chinos and check shirt had the unmistakeable stamp of Jermyn Street and he was wearing Gucci loafers. His guardee moustache was neatly trimmed, as was his wavy, greying hair. He struck me as the sort of man who'd be thoroughly at home on a golf course, and was the type who probably wore red trousers when he was playing or dominating the conversation at the nineteenth hole. But he had a deceptive smile that reminded me of the limerick about the smile on the face of the tiger. Instinct, and long experience of dealing with people of all classes, made me wonder if he possessed a sadistic streak. I'm not usually wrong.

'I'm Paul Harrison, Nina's husband.' He, too, shook hands, holding Kate's hand for a little longer than was necessary while he engaged her eyes with his and smiled. If only he knew that this was a very dangerous gambit. I've seen bigger men than Harrison hit the floor after Kate had deployed her karate know-how to subdue a fractious suspect she was intent upon arresting. And God help any man who touched her inappropriately. 'Please, take a seat.' He must have noticed the questioning look I aimed at his wife. 'It's all right, I know all about Nina's little spot of silliness,' he said condescendingly. 'I'm sure you won't mind if I sit in on the interview.'

'Not at all,' I said, 'if your wife doesn't mind.'

'Oh, she won't mind, old boy.' It was not phrased as if he was seeking his wife's approbation, but more as if he took her consent for granted and that she wouldn't dare argue.

'Perhaps you'd tell me how you came to know Robert Sharp, Mrs Harrison,' I said, determined to get on with the interview in the hope it might reveal something useful. So far, I wasn't holding out much hope.

'It was at an auction, as a matter of fact, in London. I dabble in antiques . . . well, we both do. Paul and I.' Nina shot a coy smile at her husband who was now seated in an armchair next to her. 'And I got talking to this man.'

'This was Robert Sharp, presumably?' Kate had a record-of-interview book on her knee and was beginning to take notes.

'Er, yes, although I didn't know his name at the time because we'd never met before. Anyway, as I was saying, we got talking and he seemed to know an awful lot about antiques and the antiques market, more than just a casual buyer. He eventually told me that he was a dealer, although he was mainly concerned with buying specific items on demand for wealthy Americans or Arabs and then arranging for their shipment back to their own country. There's apparently an awful lot of paperwork involved and Robert's become something of an expert, so he claimed. The sort of man you simply must go to if you want something badly enough to pay the earth for it and then have it shipped home for you.'

'Did he tell you all this straight away, Mrs Harrison?' I was already a little sceptical about the story she was relating.

'Not really, no. It sort of came out in dribs and drabs over the two hours we were together. After the sale had finished, you see, he invited me for a drink, and then I caught the train home.'

'But you met him again, presumably?'

'Yes.' This time Nina Harrison looked a little embarrassed, although I wasn't sure if it was genuine. 'Robert mentioned that he'd be attending a sale at another West End auction house the following Tuesday and asked if I was likely to be there. I said maybe, but I knew I'd go. There was something compellingly attractive about him. There was no pressure, he wasn't overbearing and he appeared genuinely interested in everything I had to say.' She stopped and put her head in her hands. 'Oh, God! I'm beginning to sound like the woman in that film *Brief Encounter.*'

'Did he mention a property he owned in the Caribbean, Mrs Harrison?' asked Kate.

'Yes, he did.'

'And did he show you photographs of this West Indies hideaway?' Kate was having a problem containing her sarcasm, but she was rapidly tiring of stupid women who fell for the most hackneyed of chat-up lines.

'Yes, as a matter of fact. On his mobile phone.'

'And did he ever appear in these photographs?'

'No, he didn't, now you come to mention it.' Nina raised her eyebrows. 'That doesn't seem to surprise you, Inspector.'

'Probably because, so far, I've heard it three or four times.'

'I suppose you think I've been very silly.'

'It's not for me to judge, Mrs Harrison.' Kate's response was one of commendable reserve. 'But perhaps you'd continue.'

'Well, to cut a long story short, we met three or four times, always at auctions. And then he invited me to have lunch. Just lunch.'

'By which I take you to mean there was no auction?' I suggested.

'No, no auction. We had a wonderful lunch at a hotel in the West End. Then, out of the blue, he said he'd booked a room. He didn't ask me if I was interested, but he placed his wine glass on the table and then gazed at me, almost compelling me to agree.'

'And you did,' said Kate.

'Yes, I'm afraid I just said, "All right." That was all. Neither of us said another word. I remember dabbing my mouth with a napkin and standing up. Then we went up to a room on the third floor and made love for the rest of the afternoon.'

I glanced at Paul Harrison.

'I know all about it, Chief Inspector. Nina confessed to everything and I forgave her.' Harrison sounded like a head of state pompously bestowing a presidential pardon. As if to confirm his acquiescence, he leaned across and took hold of his wife's hand, but I suspected it might have been a gesture of control rather than one of sympathy.

'Can we now turn to the matter of the money, Mrs Harrison?' I said, ignoring her husband's comment and his outward display of absolution.

'At one of the sales we were at, Robert asked me what sort of antiques interested me. I told him that I loved art deco jewellery and that I'd got one or two pieces but would like a few more.'

'What did he say to that?'

'Nothing. At least not then. It was later, on another of the occasions when we were in bed at the hotel, that he told me

about an art deco platinum, diamond and sapphire bracelet
that he'd spotted in a catalogue. He said it was valued at about
eight thousand pounds, but he thought it was overpriced. He
reckoned he could get it for me for about four thousand by
directly approaching the seller, whom he claimed to know. He
asked if I was interested and I said I was. It was only later
that I remembered the old adage that if it sounded too good
to be true, it probably was.'

'What happened next?' Kate knew what the answer would
be, but was as interested as I was to find out exactly how
Sharp had pulled it off.

'Well, a woman is probably at her most vulnerable when
she's making love. She doesn't really think of other things,
which is probably why I fell for it.' Nina Harrison made a
pretence of looking coy. 'Frankly, I'd no idea of the real
value of that style of bracelet, but when I checked later, I
found that eight thousand was marginally on the low side.
Robert would never have got it for as little as four thousand.
Anyway, the upshot was that I gave him a cheque for four
thousand and told him that I wasn't prepared to pay a penny
more.'

'And that was the last you saw of Robert Sharp or your
money, I presume, Mrs Harrison,' I said.

'Sadly, yes. You must be thinking I've been a bloody fool,
Mr Brock. I suppose being a policeman this sort of thing isn't
exactly novel in your experience.'

'It happens,' I said. 'Unfortunately, much too often.' I
glanced at Paul Harrison, whose face bore the trace of a smirk.
'Did you ever meet Sharp, Mr Harrison?'

'No, Chief Inspector. I might've been tempted to do him
an injury if I had.'

I got the impression that it was the loss of the money rather
than having been made a cuckold that annoyed him.
Nevertheless, it set me wondering. Was it a double bluff and
he did have something to do with the con man's death, or was
it the naive comment of an innocent man?

'As a matter of interest,' said Kate, forestalling the question
I was about to ask, 'have you ever been to a naturist club?'

Harrison laughed. 'No, although I've no objection to such

places. Trouble is, I wouldn't go without Nina, and she's not too keen, are you, old girl?'

'You've never asked me,' said Nina, somewhat churlishly, 'so you wouldn't know.'

'Just one other thing, Mrs Harrison. D'you remember the name of the hotel Sharp took you to?'

'I'm afraid not. I'm awfully bad at remembering the names of shops, pubs and hotels.'

'I think that's all we need to bother you about, Mrs Harrison.' I stood up. 'But if I need to see you again, are you likely to be at home?'

But it was Paul Harrison who replied. 'We're both here most of the time, Chief Inspector. I work from home.'

'Lucky you,' said Kate. 'What d'you do?'

'I own several online businesses,' said Harrison. 'It's the coming thing these days. Shops are old hat. And we don't have any children to get in the way when we feel like taking a holiday. Occasionally, I have to fly to New York because I have business interests there.'

'And you, Mrs Harrison?' I asked.

'Oh, my wife doesn't do anything,' said Harrison, 'except occasionally go to bed with strange men. Don't you, Nina?'

'That's not funny, Paul.' Nina Harrison was furious and I wondered if her husband's claim that he'd forgiven her was really true. 'You may have been too occupied with other things to notice that my antiques business has made quite a profit this year.'

I learned later that rather than 'dabble in antiques', as Nina Harrison had claimed, she and another woman ran a very successful antiques business in central London. Such dealers often think they've spotted a bargain – as she had done with the platinum bracelet – only to find that for once they've been outsmarted.

'One last question,' I said, as Kate and I stood up to leave. 'Where were you both on Saturday the twentieth of July? It's a routine question that we're asking everyone we interview. It was the day that Robert Sharp was murdered.'

'We were both here all day,' said Paul Harrison.

'Yes, we were,' agreed Nina Harrison, a little too hurriedly.

*   *   *

'Any thoughts, Kate?' I asked, as we drove back to central London.

'I wouldn't be surprised if he'd topped Sharp, Harry. He's a control freak and I doubt that Nina's allowed to do anything without his say-so. And I very much doubt that he has forgiven her. But I wondered how many women *he's* got on the side. That man has womanizer written all over him and seems to have enough money to indulge himself.'

'I'm not much impressed with either of them, Kate. Did you notice that her initial show of confidence when we arrived wasn't repeated when her husband was there? And neither of them used endearments to each other. I got the impression that they remain together because they're too idle to split up. Either that or it would be too expensive to divorce. I don't think that overall it's a happy marriage. They're typical self-satisfied dinkys.'

'What the hell's a dinky?' Kate appeared genuinely puzzled.

'It's an acronym: "double income, no kids . . . yet".' I was delighted at being able to come up with a colloquialism that Kate didn't know. More often, it was other way around when the rest of us were struggling to understand the Australian argot into which she occasionally lapsed in moments of great annoyance.

'But do *you* think Harrison could've topped Sharp, Harry?'

'It's possible, but there again we have to find out about the reaction of the two boyfriends of Janice Greene and Gina Page.'

'And we probably haven't heard the last of Sharp's conquests,' said Kate. 'How these silly bitches fall for it, I'm damned if I know.'

'Another thing,' I said. 'I think Nina Harrison is lying about arranging trysts at a hotel with Sharp. I'd put money on her being another naturist club conquest. Did you notice how quick she was to complain she'd never been asked to go au naturel when her husband said it sounded like fun?'

'You could be right, Harry. I don't think there was a hotel at all, simply because Sharp couldn't have afforded it. I reckon it was nonsense about dining at some swish hotel and going upstairs to have it off. Sounds like something out of a chick lit novel.'

* * *

After grabbing a quick bite to eat, Kate and I were back in the office by two o'clock. While we'd been interviewing the Harrisons at Bromley, seven more calls had come in on the hotline from women claiming to have met Sharp. Five were in London, one was in Edinburgh and the other in Birmingham.

'Would you organize a team to get in touch with these women, Kate? Probably a DS and a DC. The information will probably turn out to be useless, like *I met him on a bus, but I never saw him again.* You know the sort of thing, but if they come up with something that might be useful, I'll interview them later.'

'I think that DS Liz Carpenter and DC Nicola Chance will be right for that job. D'you want them to do the Edinburgh and Birmingham calls?'

'Not immediately. We'll ask the local police to deal with that at the outset.' I glanced back at Wilberforce. 'Perhaps you'd organize that, Colin.'

'Very good, sir. Incidentally, one of the calls was from a Mrs Michelle Taylor. She declined to give her address, but she did give her mobile phone number.' Wilberforce wrote the number on a slip of paper and handed it to me.

'Did she say why she'd phoned? Any clue as to what she wanted to tell us?'

'All she'd say was that she'd met Sharp and it ended in a row. She said that she'd only talk to the officer in charge of the investigation.'

'She's either got an inflated sense of her own importance,' said Dave, 'or she's got something worthwhile to tell us.'

'Come into my office, Dave, and I'll ring her.'

It was a short conversation. Michelle Taylor still refused to give me her address but was willing to meet us in Starbucks in Chelsea. She ended the conversation by giving me a detailed description of herself.

ELEVEN

The particular Starbucks nominated by Michelle Taylor was on a corner and Dave parked the car where we could see it from inside the shop. In the near anarchy that now exists in London, thieves take a delight in stealing police cars and ours, being unmarked, was even more vulnerable. We needed to keep an eye open for traffic wardens, too. The only real problem in becoming a victim of either was the amount of paperwork involved. But particularly the former. The Commissioner takes a dim view of officers who lose valuable police property like motor cars, although these days does little to prevent it happening.

She was seated alone at a table at the far end. An attractive woman who appeared to be in her late twenties, she had titian hair that brushed her shoulders, and was clad in a white sweater. She'd also mentioned that she was wearing white jeans and white loafers, but they were not immediately visible. It was a very good description she'd given us. But there was something about her that gave an impression of vulnerability.

Dave bought two lattes and we moved towards the woman's table.

'Mrs Taylor?' I asked quietly.

'Yes. Are you Mr Brock?'

'I am, and this is DS Dave Poole. Would you like another cup of coffee?'

'Please. A cappuccino, and could I ask you to get me a Danish pastry? I'll pay for it, of course.' She smiled at Dave.

'From your phone call, I gather that you have something to tell me,' I said, once we were settled.

'I'm sorry about the cloak-and-dagger business, Mr Brock, but I'm very worried about my husband.' There was a brief pause while Michelle Taylor summoned the courage to add, 'Actually, I'm frightened of him.'

'Please go on.'

'Frank and I are members of the Pretext Club and we decided to take a week's break there in June.' Michelle Taylor didn't look up when she made that admission but concentrated on stirring her coffee. I noticed that she had added two small sachets of brown sugar and I found that unusual, given her age and slender build.

'I presume that Frank is your husband.'

'Yes, he is.'

'D'you remember the exact dates you were at the Pretext Club, Mrs Taylor?' Dave asked.

'It was Monday the third of June to Saturday the eighth.'

'Yes, please go on,' I said. Dave and I knew that Sharp and Madison Bailey had been there during that week.

'The Pretext Club is a very friendly sort of place. There are no inhibitions and people just wander around, swimming or playing volleyball or chatting with each other, having coffee or just doing nothing. It's very relaxing. The first afternoon, Bob Sharp started a conversation with me by the swimming pool but there was nothing strange about that. As I said, it's all very friendly and I thought nothing of it. It was just a casual conversation with no sexual overtones, but then there rarely are, even though there are some ill-informed people who think that these clubs are actually a place for swingers to commit adultery. The next morning, I went for a swim and Bob was by the pool again, and we got talking. The weather was wonderful and I said as much but he said it was much better in the Caribbean where he had a villa.'

'Did he show you any photographs of this villa, Mrs Taylor?'

'No. He said they were all on his smartphone and he'd had to hand it in when he arrived. As it's a club rule, we all hand in our phones the minute we get there. Jolly good thing, too. You can't relax if you're playing with a mobile phone all the time.'

'Forgive me for asking, Mrs Taylor,' I said, 'but where does your husband come into this?'

'I was just getting to that, Mr Brock. The second morning, I went for a swim as usual. When I got out of the pool, Bob was there and he invited me for a cup of coffee. It was at that point that my husband Frank arrived on the scene. I think he must've been spying on me.'

'And he took objection to you talking to Sharp, I suppose.'

'Very much so. I've never known him to be that jealous before. All right, he's always been a bit jealous of other men taking an interest in me, however innocent, but this time he really went mad. He told me to go back to our room and pack because we were leaving. But before I went, Frank turned on Bob and really went for him. He accused him of trying to get me into his bed and he was shouting that he knew what Bob was up to and he'd met men like him before. It developed into a full-scale row. Frank was red in the face by this time and I was afraid of what he might do, but then a couple of the other members arrived and separated them.' Michelle paused. 'Actually, they might have been staff. I'm not sure. But it was just as well, because I thought Frank was going to hit Bob.'

'And did you pack, as your husband had asked, or did you stay?'

'We stayed. We had a row in the room and I told him that if he wanted to go, then he should go, but I was staying. I think that set him off again because he thought I was going to start something with Bob. But then he hit me, Mr Brock. He slapped my face really hard. He's never struck me before and we've been married for three years.' Michelle Taylor suddenly emitted a convulsive sob and a few tears rolled down her cheeks. 'I have to admit, however, that our marriage hasn't always been plain sailing.'

'What does your husband do for a living, Mrs Taylor?' I asked.

'I'm sorry. I didn't mean to break down,' said Michelle, dabbing at her cheeks with a tissue. 'He's a rep for a company that sells stationery.'

'And is he successful at it?'

'He always has been, but he's worried now that he might lose his job. It's not that he's no good at it – in fact, he was the company's top salesman last year – but the online busi- nesses are cornering the market and the trouble is that he's not really qualified to do anything else. He's well up on IT, but then so are a lot of other people. I'm not sure that he'd get a job with an online company, even though he knows the paper business thoroughly.'

'I'm sorry, Mrs Taylor, but I don't see that this has any connection with the death of Robert Sharp.'

'We were there when it happened.'

'When was this?' I was beginning to wonder whether this woman had got the dates mixed up.

Michelle Taylor opened her handbag and took out a give-away diary from a bank. 'I just want to make sure I've got the dates right,' she said as she thumbed through it. 'Yes, here we are. We went back there for our second week's holiday from the fifteenth to the twentieth of July. To my surprise and, I have to admit, with a certain amount of apprehension, Bob Sharp was there again. I wasn't interested in starting anything with him – frankly, he wasn't my type – but Frank thought differently.'

'When you were there in June, Mrs Taylor, did you tell Sharp that you'd be returning the following month?' asked Dave.

'No, I didn't know we would be, not then. As a matter of fact, I didn't think we would ever go there again, not after the showdown between Frank and Bob, but Frank had sort of calmed down and said he didn't see why we should be deprived of going there simply because a man had tried making a play for me. Which I denied, of course.'

'What happened when you got there?'

'Bob stayed well away from me, which was just as well. But when Frank spotted him in the cafeteria, he dragged me back to our chalet and accused me of setting up a meeting with him. He made these wild allegations, accusing me of somehow getting Sharp's phone number and telling him when we'd be there. There was another row and Frank started slapping me again. I was beginning to get frightened of what he might do, to me as well as to Bob.'

'In view of what you've told me, Mrs Taylor, I have to ask you for your address, and I also have to ask you if you're afraid your husband might attack you again?'

'Yes, I think he might. He really scares me. I've started to wonder if he's heading for a mental breakdown of some sort.

Anyway, I'll give you the address of the house my husband and I shared. It's in Pinner, but I've moved out.' Michelle gave me the details.

'Perhaps you'd also tell me your husband's date of birth, Mrs Taylor.' Once Dave had noted Frank Taylor's personal details, I asked, 'Where are you living now that you've moved out of the marital home?'

'With a girlfriend in Hendon. She's an old university chum.'

'What are you doing in Chelsea, then, if you live in Hendon?' Dave asked.

'I've got a part-time job with an estate agent not far from here. But today, I've been to see a divorce lawyer,' said Michelle. 'I honestly can't see any future with Frank, not after the way he's behaved.'

'Does your husband know where you're living at present?' asked Dave.

'No. And I'd prefer he didn't find out,' said Michelle, as a frisson of fear crossed her face.

'You said just now that you were there when Sharp died, Mrs Taylor. Where exactly were you and your husband?'

'I was swimming, but I've no idea where Frank was. The first I knew that something had happened was when I heard people shouting "Fire". And then, within minutes, there was a message over the tannoy telling us to assemble in the car park. The next thing that happened was the arrival of the fire brigade.'

'You've no idea what happened, then.'

'No more than the next person, no.'

'Did your husband arrive in the car park at any time?'

'Yes, a minute of two after me. I asked him where he'd been and he said he'd been swimming. Well, I knew that was a lie because I was in the pool and he wasn't.'

'Have you any idea where he might've been, Mrs Taylor?'

Michelle Taylor didn't answer immediately, but then she said, 'I think he was taking an interest in a rather gorgeous black girl who was staying there. I'd seen her once or twice with Bob Sharp and I think Frank rather fancied her. Ironic, isn't it? He objected to me talking innocently to Bob, but was quite prepared to leap into the bed of any woman who asked him.' She paused reflectively. 'Or even if they didn't ask.'

'Was this black girl the only black girl staying there, Mrs Taylor?'

'Yes,' said Michelle quite firmly.

'The black girl left that morning, so while your husband was missing, it wasn't because he was talking to her.'

'Well, in that case, it was probably some other woman. What do I owe you for the coffee and the pastry, Mr Poole?'

Dave laughed. 'That comes courtesy of the Metropolitan Police, Mrs Taylor.' He wasn't joking either. I knew he'd claim the cost as an expense involved in talking to an informant.

We returned to Belgravia at just after five o'clock that afternoon, and Dave immediately searched Metropolitan Police records to see what was known about Michelle Taylor's estranged husband. The result did not surprise either of us.

'Frank Taylor received a sentence of four years imprisonment when he was nineteen, guv,' said Dave, 'for an act of grievous bodily harm on the girl he was living with. According to his record, he beat her up quite badly and she spent several days in hospital. He was living with her at the time.'

'Any children, Dave?'

'Nothing in his antecedents mentions children. He was released fifteen years ago after serving half his sentence.'

'I wonder if Michelle Taylor knew about his record of violence. I think it's time we had words with Frank Taylor, Dave.'

'As he's a rep, guv, he might be difficult to track down. Could be anywhere in the country.'

'You're such a pessimist, Dave. For all we know, he might have got the sack and has been fooling his wife. We'll go there this evening. I'll put money on him being at home.'

'Or out with a bird or taking his clothes off at the Pretext Club,' suggested Dave pessimistically.

It was a semi-detached house in Pinner. The front garden was overgrown, but it wasn't excessively out of control yet. Nevertheless, I suspected that the neighbours, all of whom seemed to have pristine front gardens with manicured lawns, were unimpressed, and doubtless in fear of the weeds spreading from Taylor's garden to their own. I assumed that Frank Taylor couldn't be bothered to get the lawn mower out or, maybe, it was one of the jobs that Michelle had always done. There was a ten-year-old Honda on the drive and washing it clearly didn't rank high among Taylor's priorities. The brass door knocker was in need of some metal polish, as was the letter plate.

'Frank Taylor?' I asked.

'Yeah, and who the hell are you?' Taylor's gaze went from me to Dave and back again. 'Are you some sort of Bible-bashing evangelists?'

'We're police officers, and we'd like a word with you.'

'Well, I'm busy right now. I'll come down to the nick when I can spare the time. But if it's about a parking ticket, I've paid it.' Taylor showed all the signs of being an aggressive individual ready to pick a fight with anyone. He had the smooth, fleshy features that are attractive to some women but which very often disguise both a lack of intelligence and a weakness of character. I imagined that he was the sort of bully who would cave in at the first sign of strong opposition.

'I'm Detective Chief Inspector Brock of the Murder Investigation Team at New Scotland Yard and this is Detective Sergeant Poole.' There were windows open in the houses on either side of Taylor's and I'd deliberately raised my voice so that any neighbours who happened to be listening would have heard me. It had the desired effect.

'Oh, er, you'd better come in.' As I'd predicted, Michelle's husband surrendered.

Dave and I followed Taylor into an untidy front room and he indicated, with an unspoken gesture, that we should take a seat.

'What's this about, then?'

'I understand that you and your wife were at the Pretext Club on two separate occasions recently, Mr Taylor. The first occasion was from Monday the third of June to Saturday the eighth, and the second was from Monday the fifteenth of July to Saturday the twentieth.'

'So what? It's not a crime, is it?' sneered Taylor.

'No, but murder is a crime, Mr Taylor,' said Dave, his educated delivery appearing to disconcert Taylor.

'What are you talking about?'

'On the second occasion you were there, a man named Robert Sharp was murdered.'

'Are you suggesting that I had something to do with that?'

'You had an argument with Sharp and were separated by other people before the pair of you were able to come to blows.'

'Who told you that? My slut of a wife, was it?'

'We have made extensive enquiries at the club, Mr Taylor,' continued Dave, 'as we are obliged to do in cases of murder. Are you saying that your wife was a witness to this argument?' He knew very well that she was but had no intention of letting Taylor know that we had already interviewed her. 'If that is the case, perhaps you'd tell me when she is likely to be here so that we can speak to her.'

'My wife's not here any more.' Taylor made the admission tersely. 'I threw her out. She's been telling people that I hit her. Well, she's a lying bitch. I've never hit a woman in my life.'

'Don't take us for fools, Mr Taylor. When you were nineteen you were sent to prison for four years for inflicting grievous bodily harm on the woman you were living with.'

'I only served two years, so that conviction is spent.' Taylor, his voice trembling, sounded outraged that we should have raised the question of his prison sentence. 'You've no right to mention it.'

'You were sentenced to four years and that's what decides whether it is spent or not,' said Dave mildly. 'And it's not, but perhaps you would now tell my chief inspector what this argument with Sharp was all about.'

'He was making a play for Michelle.'

'Who is Michelle?' asked Dave, with feigned innocence.

'My bloody wife.'

'Is that why you threw her out?'

'One of the reasons, yes. She was making up to him; believe me, I know the signs. She's an attractive woman, especially when she's strolling around naked giving men a come-on look.'

'If that was a risk, Mr Taylor,' I said, 'why on earth did you take her to a naturist club? That, surely, was asking for trouble.'

'Why shouldn't I? It's supposed to be a free country.'

'Where were you when the fire broke out on the Saturday? That was the twentieth of July.'

'What time was that?'

'About half past three.'

'I can't remember. In the pool, I think. What's this all about? D'you think that I set fire to Sharp? At least, the TV news said that he'd died in a fire.'

'Did you set fire to him?'

'Of course not.'

'But at your first visit you had an argument with him about your wife and if other people hadn't stepped in, there's no telling what might have happened. The next time you were there, I suggest that you went to Sharp's room and deliberately murdered him.'

'For Chrissakes, man! I might have knocked my girlfriend around a bit when I was a youngster, but that's all in the past. I don't go around killing people.'

'What's your occupation, Mr Taylor?' Dave asked.

'I haven't got one. I'm currently unemployed.'

'What happened, then?'

'I chucked the job in. Got fed up with it.'

'We'll very likely need to see you again, Mr Taylor,' I said. 'Are you thinking of moving?'

'Can't afford to,' said Taylor churlishly. 'Mind you, it's out of my hands because the building society is getting all arsey.'

As we reached the sitting-room door, Dave paused. 'You'd better keep your nose clean from now on, sunshine,' he began, his voice barely above a whisper, 'because if you don't, it'll give me great pleasure to drag you out of the house in hand-cuffs and put you into a marked police car.' Dave had a deep loathing of men who attacked women.

'Are you threatening me?' demanded Taylor.

'On the contrary,' said Dave, 'I'm making you a promise.'

TWELVE

'I think he's well in the frame, guv'nor.' Dave accelerated away from the house in Pinner as though trying to put as much space as possible between himself and the unsavoury Frank Taylor. 'He'd lie through his teeth, that one. He obviously got the sack, as his wife forecast, and I wouldn't be at all surprised to find that he's up to some sort of villainy. If only to make ends meet.'

'I think you're right, Dave. However, as we're not far away, let's call in at the Pretext Club and see if we can find a member of staff who can give us an unbiased account of this spat between Taylor and Sharp.'

Rather than tackle either of the joint owners of the club, Dave and I made our way directly to the swimming pool where two lifeguards, a man and a woman, were on duty.

We introduced ourselves and I asked the man if he knew which of the lifeguards had been witness to an altercation with a couple of members on the fifth of June.

'That was me, Don Rogers. And Mel Cameron.' He pointed to a young woman who was keeping a watchful eye on the swimmers. Rogers was a muscular young man of about twenty-three and, I imagined, spent much of his time working out. There was not an ounce of fat on him and he appeared to be made entirely of muscle. I got the impression that spending all day without clothes gave him the welcome opportunity to show off his physique and I wondered, idly, how many ladies he had 'charmed' during their stay at the Pretext Club.

'And you say you saw this argument between Robert Sharp and Frank Taylor.'

'Yeah, well, we both did. Mel, come over here a minute and have a word with these detectives. Mel was a junior county swimming champion,' Rogers explained. 'She does a great butterfly stroke and she's into the martial arts in a big way.'

Mel Cameron was a slender young woman and obviously at the peak of physical fitness.

'Tell me about this argument, Don. You don't mind me calling you Don, do you?'

'No, everyone does. Well, it took place right here by the pool. Taylor was quite a big guy and he was squaring up to Sharp and calling him names and accusing him of screwing his wife.'

'Was his wife there at the time, Don?'

'Oh, yeah. She'd been talking to Sharp. Mind you, I don't blame him – she's a good-looking bird is Taylor's missus. She and Sharp had both been in the pool and got out at the same time. That might've been a coincidence because they got out at opposite ends but, there again, Sharp might have been waiting for the chance to chat her up. Anyway, they were making their way across there,' said Rogers, pointing at the four open showers, 'but then Sharp said something to Michelle – that's Taylor's wife's name – and they both stopped and started talking.'

'Did you hear what was being said, Don?' asked Dave.

'No. I think Sharp was making a joke or something because Michelle laughed.'

'They were just having a quiet conversation,' said Mel. 'Nothing sexy about it at all. Just finding out where each of them lived and how often they came to the club. All that sort of thing. It sounded quite innocent to me.'

'Did you see Sharp touch Michelle at any time?'

Mel only needed to think about that for a moment. 'No, they were actually standing a couple of feet apart.'

'Yes, go on.'

'Well, there was nothing unusual about two people having a chat. This has always been a very friendly place, Mr Brock,' continued Mel, 'and people chat to strangers all the time but, as far as I can tell, there's never anything in it, although you never know, do you?'

'But Taylor seemed to think there was,' Dave suggested. 'Was that it?'

'It looked very much like it,' said Rogers, taking up the story. 'Taylor had been lying on one of the sunbeds watching 'em, when he suddenly leaped up and stormed across to Michelle and Sharp. Straight away, he starts having a go at Sharp, accusing him of having taken Michelle to his chalet and then . . .' The lifeguard paused. 'I won't repeat what he actually said, but I reckon you can guess, being coppers, like. Well, I thought to myself, "Don, old son, you'd better step in before there's bloodshed." So, I got in between 'em and told 'em to grow up and behave themselves because they were upsetting the other members. Taylor looked like he still wanted to have a go, so I grabbed him and moved him away from Sharp. He muttered something about having me for assault and I . . .' Rogers stopped. 'Well, I won't tell you what I said.'

'It was me who grabbed Sharp and pulled him back, out of harm's way,' said Mel. 'Don likes taking all the glory,' she added, and they both laughed.

'And they then stopped arguing, presumably?' I couldn't imagine anyone in his right mind picking a fight with Rogers or, for that matter, with Mel Cameron.

'Oh, yeah, they stopped.'

'We had one report, Don, that it was other members who stopped the argument from becoming a fight.'

Rogers laughed. 'They couldn't get out of the way fast enough. They were quite happy to stand on the touchline and watch, but they weren't going to get involved in the game. If there wasn't a ban on bringing smartphones into the club, they'd all have been making a video of the action.'

We thanked Don Rogers and Mel Cameron and took our leave. But we were no further forward. As I'd predicted when I'd first met Frank Taylor, he was the sort of individual who, faced by someone of the stature of Rogers, would cave in at once.

It was half past seven by the time we got back to Belgravia after what had been a tiring and frustrating day. But it wasn't over yet.

Gavin Creasey, the night-duty incident room manager, who had relieved Colin Wilberforce at six o'clock, followed me into my office.

'Colin left a message for you, sir, about James Brooks.'

'Sadie Brooks' husband?'

'Yes, sir, that James Brooks. Colin decided it might be a good idea to enter Sadie Brooks' name on the Police National Computer. When he did so, James Brooks' name came up in connection with her. He's escaped from Ford open prison.'

'When was this?'

'Saturday the thirteenth of July, sir.'

'That was the date that Geoffrey Sykes had his car stolen from a car park in Arundel, guv,' said Dave, 'and if I remember correctly Ford is less than four miles from Arundel. I went there once to interview a prisoner.'

'But how did he get to Arundel? He wouldn't have walked because the screws would have been out looking for him straight away.'

'Not necessarily, sir,' said Creasey. 'I've been doing a bit of checking and there's quite a bit of freedom of movement there. He might just have walked out and caught a bus. I'm told there is one that goes from Ford to Arundel.'

'How very handy,' I said. 'Is there any indication that Geoffrey Sykes' car has been found, Gavin?'

'I'll have to check that, sir.'

'I'd be very surprised if he'd hung on to it,' said Dave, but my query was answered with the return of Creasey.

'Sykes' car was found burned out in a lay-by between Brighton and Peacehaven on Tuesday the twenty-third of July, sir.'

'That's the day we interviewed Sadie Brooks at Brighton, guv,' said Dave.

'Why do I get the feeling that Sadie Brooks has not been entirely honest with us, Dave?' I glanced at my watch; it was now eight o'clock. 'Well, I'm not going down there now – she's more than likely out on the town.'

'Or in bed with her latest toy boy,' replied Dave. 'So, what's the plan?'

'We'll not miss anything by waiting until tomorrow morning,' I said. 'If he was there, he'll be long gone by now. On the other hand, he might've made for that area because he knows it but didn't pay Sadie a visit. In the meantime, Gavin, get on to the Sussex Police and ask them if they managed to lift any fingerprints from that burned-out vehicle.'

Creasey was back within ten minutes. 'Nothing, sir. Brooks obviously did a good job of torching it.'

We arrived in Brighton at about ten o'clock on the Tuesday morning. The weather was still holding, the sun was out and all in all it promised to be another blisteringly hot day. Crowds thronged the streets, many of whom were making for the beach intent upon spending the day getting sunburned. Some had already donned swimsuits and there were children optimistically carrying buckets and spades, unaware that Brighton's beach was all pebbles, not sand.

The area known as The Lanes was crowded, too, mainly with tourists, as had been the case the last time we visited. As before, the majority of the overseas visitors seemed intent upon photographing everything in sight.

Dave and I entered Sadie Brooks' shop and the ringing of the bell above the door brought the woman herself from the office at the back of the premises. She was wearing an off-the-shoulder blouse and short denim shorts. Despite having good legs, her outfit would have been more suited to a teenager than to a woman fast approaching fifty, if not beyond that landmark age.

'Oh, no, not again! What is it this time?'

Dave pulled down the blind over the shop door. 'When did Jim Brooks come to see you, Sadie?' he asked, as he turned to face her.

'Jim Brooks? He hasn't been near here since the day he ran off with my life savings.' Sadie sounded genuinely surprised by the question and a little annoyed. 'But the last time you were here you told me he was in the nick.'

'He was, Sadie, but he did a runner from Ford open prison just over a fortnight ago. On Saturday the thirteenth of July to be precise.'

'I'd be bloody surprised if that two-timing bastard had the brass neck to come anywhere near me, after what he did,' said Sadie. 'But even if he did chance it, there's only two things he'd want. Well, he's not getting any more money and he can whistle for the other. Like I said before, the only thing he'll get from me is a kick in the nuts.'

'Has the local law been to see you?' I asked.

'No, why should they?'

'Because he was in prison for bigamously marrying you, Sadie, among other things, and that's on his record. I thought they might've asked you if you'd seen him or heard from him.'

'Believe me, Mr Brock, he's one bloke I would quite happily grass on and he probably knows it. I reckon he'd steer well clear of me. Anyway, why are you so interested in him that you've come all the way down here? People are always breaking out of prison. It ain't exactly the crime of the bleedin' century, is it?'

'Because I suspect him of having murdered Robert Sharp on Saturday the twentieth of July at the Pretext Club. I mentioned the murder the last time we were here.' I hadn't a great deal of evidence to support this allegation, but the more I looked into Sharp's murder the faster Brooks was rising to the top of the midden of suspects.

For several seconds Sadie Brooks stared at me before bursting into almost uncontrollable laughter. 'Gawd bless your little cotton socks, Mr Brock. You've made my day,' she said, making a partial recovery and wiping away the tears of mirth and the mascara from her face with the back of her hand. 'It'd be a double, that's what it'd be, if Brooks got life for topping Sharp. I think I'll buy a lottery ticket today. I reckon I might scoop the bleedin' jackpot. In fact, I might even go for an accumulator at Brighton races on Saturday.'

'If you do hear from him, Sadie, let me know, eh?' I handed her one of my cards.

'You can put money on it, Mr Brock,' she said, and tucked the card into the pocket of her shorts.

Dave raised the blind as we turned to leave the shop but paused with the door half open. 'Purely out of curiosity, Sadie, whereabouts d'you come from?'

'Hoxton, born and bred,' said Sadie, and laughed. 'And I wouldn't say no to you, love.'

'What's the name of the officer dealing with Brooks' escape from Ford prison, Colin?' I asked when we'd returned to Belgravia.

'It's a detective sergeant at the headquarters at Lewes, sir.' Wilberforce wrote down the details on a slip of paper and handed it to me.

I called the number, but the officer I wanted was out on an enquiry. After a lot of toing and froing, I eventually reached the sergeant's line manager, a DCI.

I told him who I was and why I was interested in Brooks, and filled him in about our visit to Sadie Brooks before going on to tell him about the murder of Robert Sharp.

'The car that was stolen from Arundel was used by Brooks when he stayed at the Pretext Club,' I said, 'but he left on the day of the murder. I've interviewed Geoffrey Sykes, whose credit card Brooks used to pay for his stay at the naturist club, and Sykes assumes he must have left the card in the car on the day it was stolen.'

'Thanks for all that, Harry,' said the Sussex DCI. 'If I hear anything of use to you, I'll give you a bell. And I'll let you know if he's knocked off on our patch. I presume you don't want us to question him about the Sharp murder.'

'No, just detain him and I'll come down there to interview him, preferably before you give him back to the Prison Service.'

'As a matter of interest, why should Brooks want to murder this guy Sharp, Harry? Is there an obvious motive that I don't know about?'

'Your guess is as good as mine. Perhaps Sharp put the arm on him for money, knowing he was on the run, or he'd shop him to the law.'

The Sussex DCI laughed. 'Honour among thieves, eh, Harry?'

Last Friday, Ron Clark, the director of security at the credit card company that held one of Sharp's accounts, had given me the name of the bank that had granted Sharp a mortgage. As the bank was in central London, I decided to try my luck with the manager to save going to the trouble of getting a warrant from a Crown Court judge.

The moment I mentioned to one of the staff that my enquiry concerned a murdered mortgage holder, Dave and I were ushered into the manager's office with an almost indecent haste.

'How can I help you, Chief Inspector?' The manager, a woman who clearly didn't believe in power-dressing and was wearing a floral summer dress, invited us to take a seat.

I explained about Robert Sharp's murder and told her that we had learned through a credit agency that he was in arrears with his mortgage at this bank.

'Damned right he is,' said the manager with refreshing candour. 'In fact, we're about to foreclose on the property. But you know that client confidentiality prevents me from giving you any information.'

'Yes, I know.'

'So, what d'you want to know?' The manager smiled at Dave.

'The address of the property would be very helpful.'

The manager consulted a docket. 'I'm not allowed to tell you that it's flat five, Hoedown Court, Hoedown Lane, Carshalton.'

'Was it just Sharp living there, as far as you know?'

'Sorry, once again, I'm not allowed to tell you that he shared the property with his wife, Mrs Emily Sharp.'

'Thank you very much,' I said. 'You've been very helpful.'

'There's no need to be sarcastic, Chief Inspector,' said the manager, and laughed. 'I haven't told you a single thing. I'm not allowed to.' She shook hands and winked. I wish she was my bank manager.

There is always a tendency to put off until tomorrow what you don't want to do today. However, I managed to overcome the onset of this inertia and Dave drove me straight from the bank to Carshalton.

There was nothing special about Hoedown Court. It was unmistakeably a property built in the twenties to the art deco design popular at the time.

The entrance to the flat was along a solid concrete balcony on the first floor. It was some time before our knock was answered, but eventually the door was opened by a woman who I reckoned to be no more than nineteen. She had auburn hair and wore a full-length green negligée, the sort of garment that women often wear about the house during very hot weather.

'Mrs Emily Sharp?'

'Yes, what is it?' She glanced suspiciously at Dave.

'We're police officers, Mrs Sharp.' Seeing the look of doubt on her face, I produced my warrant card and Dave produced his. 'May we come in?'

Emily Sharp showed us into a sitting room and invited us to sit down.

'What's this about?'

'It's about Robert Sharp,' I said, hoping against hope that she read newspapers and already knew what I was about to tell her.

'I'm not sure where he is at present,' she said. 'He's got a very important job and travels all over the country. But what is this really about? Has something happened to him?'

Here we go again, I thought.

'I'm sorry to have to tell you that he's dead, Mrs Sharp.'

'Oh!' Emily Sharp did not seem at all upset by this news. The impression I got was that the demise of Robert Sharp, at best, was a bit of a nuisance. After all the death messages I'd delivered, and there had been many over the years, it seemed that I was still capable of being surprised by the reaction of an aggrieved party. And Emily Sharp's reaction did surprise me.

'Did you know? I mean, did you read about it in the newspaper or see it mentioned on television?'

'I don't read newspapers,' said Emily. 'I've got a smartphone that lets me know when there's anything important. Anyway, why should it have been on the telly?'

'You don't seem shocked by the news.' I was struggling to get through to this woman and concluded that the death of a pop star would be more her idea of a devastating tragedy.

'Actually, I'm not really bothered. I didn't think it would last, but it was good fun while it did. We weren't in love, if that's what you're thinking.'

'Were you actually married to Robert Sharp?'

'Good heavens, no! But he told the bank that we were because he said it would give us a better chance of a mortgage. I don't know why because he always seemed to have plenty of money and I hadn't got any. Anyway, you don't have to be married to get a mortgage these days. That's what my mum said, anyway.'

'What's your name, then, if it's not Sharp?'

'Emily Cutler.'

'What was this important job you said Robert Sharp had, Emily?' asked Dave.

'I don't know exactly. He was always a bit vague about it, but it did involve a lot of travelling and he'd be away sometimes for two or three weeks.'

'Did he ever take you to a naturist club?'

'What's that?'

'It's a club where people take off all their clothes and swim and sunbathe.'

'Oh, a nudist camp. Yeah, we first met at one. Why?'

'Because that's where he died, Emily,' I said. 'He was murdered.'

'I suppose I'll have to move out of here, then. I can't afford to pay the mortgage.' Emily didn't seem at all put out that Sharp had been at a naturist club when he was, supposedly, away on business.

Too right you'll have to move, I thought. Sharp was behind with payments and the bank was about to foreclose on the flat.

'What will you do now, Emily?' Dave asked.

'Go home to my parents, I suppose.' Emily Sharp née Cutler didn't sound too pleased at the prospect.

'Where do they live?'

'It's a village in Cornwall a few miles from Redruth. There's never anything to do there and when I met Robert, he told me that he owned a place in the Caribbean and often went to the south of France for a holiday. It sounded like a different world.'

'Did he ever show you photographs of this place in the Caribbean, Emily?'

'Yes, he had them on his phone.'

'Were there any that included him in the photo?'

Emily Cutler gave that a bit of thought. 'No, there wasn't.'

'Did he tell you what he was doing in Cornwall when you met him?' I asked.

'He just said he was down there on business and, like I

said, we met at a nudist camp near there. He said I deserved better and he set me up in this flat. It was only about sex,' Emily admitted candidly, 'but he treated me very well.'

'Did he ever ask to borrow money from you, Emily?' I asked.

'Good heavens, no! It wouldn't have done any good if he had. As I said just now, I haven't got any money and Bob was against me getting a job anyway. It got pretty lonely and boring, though, being here on my own for weeks on end. But he always said that he wanted me to be here when he got back from wherever he'd been.'

'Perhaps you'd give Sergeant Poole the address of your parents, Emily,' I said. 'We may need to speak to you again.' Actually, that was unlikely. She'd confirmed what I'd thought, that Sharp had set her up in this cosy flat and took her out to the bright lights of London from time to time. It was the price he paid for having a pretty girl in his bed and she was, after all, an attractive young lady. One could hardly blame him, except for the fact that he was ratting on his cash-strapped wife in Acton and defrauding people so that he could pay for it.

THIRTEEN

Dave and I eventually returned to Belgravia at half past six. As most of the team were there, I thought it was a good time to bring them up to date. But before I started, Gavin Creasey said, 'I had a call from a Mrs Nina Harrison an hour ago, sir. She'd like to speak to you if you'd telephone her on this number. She'll be in all evening.' He handed me a slip of paper with a mobile phone number on it.

'Thanks, Gavin.' I turned back to the assembled team. 'Robert Sharp was a womanizer and as a result he's racked up debts all over the place, not least with the credit card companies that were daft enough to give him credit. He also swindled several women out of sums of money and, for all we know, there may be more who are too embarrassed to come forward.'

'Can I just mention, guv'nor,' said DI Brad Naylor, 'that the enquiries we pushed out to Cornwall and Hampshire didn't really help us at all. The women concerned, all single or widowed, had been done out of substantial sums. Each of them claimed that Sharp promised marriage and they finished up in bed with him, believing they were on the brink of a romantic future.'

'That's what my ex-wives thought,' said Charlie Flynn, and got a laugh.

'It's fairly obvious,' I continued, when the laughter had died down, 'that he upset somebody on the way and they topped him and then set fire to him to destroy any evidence that might've been useful to us. It's my opinion that whoever murdered Sharp had been at the Pretext Club for some days and, I would suggest, that it was a premeditated killing because the murderer must've brought in a firearm and sufficient petrol to ignite a blaze that destroyed almost all of Sharp's body.'

'It's beginning to look as though somebody didn't like him,' said Sheila Armitage, sounding innocent, and received another laugh. 'But seriously, guv, doesn't that open up the list? It means that everyone who was at the Pretext Club at the time of the murder is a suspect.'

'That's true, Sheila, but at the moment, James Brooks is at the top of my list. Unfortunately, he'll be keeping a very low profile because he's on the run from Ford open prison. It may be, however, that Brooks and Sharp have got history, given that they were both associated with Sadie Brooks at one time. Dave and I have interviewed her, but there's nothing she can tell us. Or if she does know something, she won't tell us. There again, it may be that Sadie wasn't a party to whatever took place between Brooks and Sharp, if anything did.' I glanced at my watch. 'I think that'll do for tonight. Go home and get some sleep and we'll start afresh tomorrow.'

I went into my office and rang Nina Harrison. She responded almost immediately, as though she had been holding her phone in anticipation of my call.

'Mrs Harrison, it's Chief Inspector Brock. I understand you wished to speak to me.'

'Thank you for calling back, Mr Brock.' She sounded breathless. 'I had to wait until my husband was in New York so that I could speak freely. I just wanted to tell you that I wasn't quite honest when you were here the other day.'

'In what way?'

'I told you that I'd met Robert at an auction but that's not true. My husband and I often have weekends away separately. I know it didn't sound as though we did, but the truth of the matter is that we enjoy what is called an open marriage. He has a woman that he visits in New York – at least that's what he told me – and I have a young man who's available whenever the fancy takes me. Paul puts up this pretence that we enjoy a terribly respectable marriage, but I'd put money on him being in bed with his New York tart right now.'

'Is this what you wanted to tell me, Mrs Harrison?'

'Not really. I'm sorry but I have this tendency to ramble on. Anyway, to cut a long story short, I spent a weekend alone at the Pretext Club and that's where I met Robert. The rest of the story, unfortunately, was true. After that, we did meet at auctions and there were days when we spent hours in a hotel bed. I know Paul said he'd forgiven me, but he can be a bit virtuous occasionally and, as I said just now, tries to pretend that we have an exemplary relationship.' She giggled. 'Not that I think that applies to the rest of Bromley, mind you. In reality, Paul couldn't have given a damn about Robert and me, but when he learned that I lost four thousand pounds, it really annoyed him. Although it was my money, he seemed to think it somehow reflected on him. He was probably worried that if people somehow found out about it, they might snigger when he walked into the clubhouse of his precious golf club.'

'Were you and your husband going your separate ways on Saturday the twentieth of July?'

There was a pause and I imagined that Nina Harrison was consulting her diary. Eventually, she said, 'Yes, we were, Mr Brock. I was with my toy boy.' She giggled. 'All that day and all that night.'

'Have you any idea where your husband was that weekend?'

'Not a clue, I'm afraid, but there's bound to have been a woman involved.'

'And when will he be back from New York?'

'Tomorrow.'

'Thank you for putting the record straight, Mrs Harrison,' I said, and terminated the call. Unfortunately, this admission by Nina Harrison meant that Paul Harrison's movements on the day of Sharp's murder were unaccounted for. We would, therefore, have to interview him again given that when Sharp was mentioned at the first interview, Harrison happily declared that he 'might've been tempted to do him an injury'.

Dependent on any further enquiries, it might even be necessary to interview Nina Harrison's toy boy. Not that I could visualize her murdering Sharp, but you never know.

At nine o'clock the following morning, I got a phone call from Ron Clark, the director of security at the credit card company that held Robert Sharp's account.

'Harry, something interesting has cropped up. I didn't know

about it when it happened, but it was before you came to see me. One of the managers has just drawn my attention to it.'

'I think it'd be best if Dave and I came over, Ron.'

Clark agreed and we grabbed a cab for the ten-minute journey. Clark greeted us with cups of coffee.

'Sharp's credit card has been used, Harry. It occurred on the twenty-fourth of this month, two days before you came to see me. It wasn't until I authorized a stop on the card that the transaction came to light.'

'What was it for, Ron?'

'I don't know. All we have are details of the transaction and where it took place. I can tell you that the charge was just under two hundred pounds.'

'If you can give me the date and the name of the outlet, Ron, I'll follow it up. It might just be that it was used by Sharp's killer. In fact, the more I think about it, I can't see that anyone else would have used it. And now that you've explained how it's done, it would make sense.'

Fortunately, the purchase had been made at a central London department store that, even more fortunately, hadn't gone into liquidation. If it had been an online transaction, we probably wouldn't have got anywhere as the vendor never meets the purchaser, so any thought of physical identification would have been stillborn.

The accounts manager at the store was extremely helpful once I'd explained who we were and why we were interested in this purchase. After a deft bit of computer work, she was able to tell us that the transaction had taken place in the luggage department and she escorted us down there.

The senior customer adviser, as they call shop assistants now, was an elegant redhead with green twinkling eyes and was introduced to us as Karen. She remembered serving the customer because it was a man. 'In my experience, it's a woman who purchases a make-up case, Chief Inspector,' she said, 'but this man told me it was a surprise birthday present for his wife.'

'It seems a lot of money to pay for a make-up case,' I said.

'We have plenty of similar cases much cheaper than the one we sold, which retailed at a pound under two hundred, but the man was adamant that he wanted the best.' She paused. 'It was originally priced higher at two hundred and fifty pounds, but this item was in the sale.'

Now I asked the all-important question. 'Can you describe the man who bought this case, Karen?'

'Oh, yes.' Karen's green eyes twinkled again. 'As I said, it was the week of the sales and we had hundreds of customers looking for a bargain, but this man was memorable. He was well-spoken and I think probably in his thirties or possibly forties. He had fleshy good looks and fancied himself as a ladies' man. It certainly didn't take him long before he started chatting me up. He went from presenting his credit card to inviting me out to dinner in about ten seconds flat.'

'Did you take up his offer?' asked Dave.

'I think my husband would have had a few words to say about that,' said Karen, and laughed.

'You've been very helpful,' I said, 'and thank you.' Karen's information had edged us forward a little more.

'Strange business,' said Dave, as we left the store.

'The buyer has to be Sharp's killer, Dave, but what the hell did he want a make-up case for?'

'Perhaps he found the credit card,' suggested Dave, ignoring his question.

'What, complete with the PIN that he would have to use to complete the purchase?' I didn't often trump Dave.

'True, guv'nor. But that doesn't explain why he bought a make-up case.' And it wasn't often Dave admitted to a mistake. 'The only way the killer could've got Sharp's PIN is for him to have given it up when he was looking at the wrong end of the handgun that killed him.'

I doubted that he had the necessary ability to discover it in the way that the chief security officer of the credit card company had shown me.

Kate and Dave joined me in my office to discuss the latest developments. I brought Kate up to speed about the make-up case and my theory that Sharp's killer could well have been the purchaser. Kate agreed that there seemed no other logical explanation and, despite what our previous commander thought, she knew about make-up cases and knew how to dress when occasion demanded.

'But I thought Sharp's card was topped up to the limit,' said Kate.

'Yes, it was, and although the credit card company was unhappy about the way the transactions and the settlements were dealt with, they hesitated to withdraw credit as the outstanding amount and interest were always settled, albeit at the last minute. That said, according to this credit-card company, there was sufficient credit at the time to allow for the purchase of this make-up case.'

'Assuming that the killer was the guy who drove out of the Pretext Club using Sykes' credit card, I suppose he must've taken Sharp's card after the murder so that he could use it at a later date, guv'nor,' suggested Dave.

'Possibly, Dave, and he probably burnt Sykes' card when he set fire to Sykes' car, which was on . . .'

'The twenty-third of July between Brighton and Peacehaven,' said Dave, as usual having the facts at his fingertips. 'And the make-up case was purchased the day after he'd torched the car, following which he must've hopped on a train back to the Smoke. But where was he staying?'

'Supposing for a moment that the murderer is Brooks,' said Kate, 'we haven't yet established a motive.'

'The only possibility, as I said at the briefing yesterday, is that there was history between Brooks and Sharp, the common factor being Sadie Brooks, and that Brooks decided to settle an old score. Unfortunately, there's no evidence to support that theory. Yet.'

'This business of the make-up case puzzles me,' said Dave. 'But I have had a thought.'

'Be careful, Dave,' said Kate. 'You might damage your brain.'

'Noted, guv,' responded Dave and carried on. 'Supposing that Madison Bailey and James Brooks met at the Pretext Club and hatched a plot to murder Sharp.'

'Why would they do that, Dave?' asked Kate.

'I'm coming to that, ma'am.' Dave grinned at Kate, as he always did when he addressed her formally. 'At some time when all three of them were there, Sharp took exception to Brooks taking Madison off him and an argument ensued. On the other hand, Brooks and Madison might've hatched some get-rich-quick plot and invited Sharp to join in. But he disagreed and threatened to blow the whistle because he suspected that they might implicate him anyway. After all, Sharp was a small-time swindler, had never been prosecuted and had no desire to go to prison. But he realized that if he got involved, either actually or by implication, in what he knew was a dangerous scheme, he could end up doing time. Particularly if all his previous frauds caught up with him.'

'Nice theory, Dave,' I said, 'but without evidence it's all pie in the sky.'

'Drugs could be the answer to why he bought a make-up case,' said Kate suddenly. 'And that carries a hell of a lot of jail time.'

'Would you care to expand on that, Kate?' I said.

'Supposing he bought the make-up case for Madison,' continued Kate, warming to her theory. 'She's a stewardess on the Colombia run. That country's unofficial principal export is cocaine. The Colombian government is doing its best to put the kibosh on it but without much success.'

For a moment or two, I pondered Kate's proposition and the more I did so, the more I thought she might've hit on a motive.

'I think we need to talk to the customs and excise section of the National Crime Agency,' I said eventually.

That afternoon, after numerous phone calls to colleagues who knew about such things, I was directed to a senior customs official of the National Crime Agency who was stationed at Heathrow. Dave drove me there, my view being that face-to-face conversations are more satisfactory than phone calls or an exchange of emails.

'Peter Sullivan, gents,' said the NCA officer, once I'd introduced Dave and myself.

I gave Sullivan a thumbnail sketch of the murder of Robert Sharp and described as briefly as possible how we had arrived at the point where we thought drug smuggling might be involved.

'What's the name of this stewardess, Harry?'

'Madison Bailey.' I gave Sullivan details of where she lived and which airline she worked for.

'And you say she's on the Heathrow to Bogotá run. Sounds very interesting. The make-up case interests me, too. One of the advantages of using a make-up case to carry drugs is that they tend to be undetectable to our drug-detector dogs. There are so many smells in a woman's make-up case and that causes the dog to become confused. In short, we've little chance of finding any illegal substances by that method unless it's what we call intelligence-led, and your information puts it into that category.'

'There's one other thing, Peter,' I said. 'We think this may have something to do with the murder I was telling you about. I believe that if this is a drug-smuggling operation, Madison Bailey and Sharp's killer are in it together. I'd be the first to admit that there are a lot of "ifs" in this whole scenario, but it's all we've got at the moment.'

For a few moments, Sullivan sat in silence as he thought through the best way of dealing with this problem so that the National Crime Agency and my murder investigation team both achieved what we wanted. Eventually, he formulated a plan that seemed to fit the requirements of the law enforcement agencies Sullivan and I represented.

'How about this, Harry?' said Sullivan eventually, and outlined what he had in mind.

'I agree,' I said. 'Of course, it might all come to nought, Peter.'

'Even if it does, we'll not have wasted much time,' said Sullivan.

'Sounds like a plan,' said Dave.

After leaving Peter Sullivan, we went to see Clare Hughes, the security officer for the airline that employed Madison Bailey. Heathrow airport is huge and getting from one place to another sometimes involves walking miles. Fortunately, however, Clare's office was not far away.

'What's she been up to now, Harry?' asked Clare, assuming we were there to make further enquiries about the young naturist.

'Nothing that I know of, Clare,' I said, 'but it would be helpful if you could tell me when she's next likely to take some leave.'

Clare Hughes turned to her computer and, after a flurry of keywork, said, 'She's due to take two weeks off starting next Monday, the fifth of August.' She swung back to face me, and her old copper's instinct kicked in. 'Anything I should know about, Harry?'

'Not particularly. I'm still trying to discover who murdered Robert Sharp and we know she was friendly with him at the Pretext Club. I'm clutching at straws really.' I had no intention of telling Clare about the plan Dave and I had just agreed with Sullivan. I wouldn't even discuss it with a serving police officer who was not involved, let alone one who'd retired and now had other loyalties. 'Has she left her holiday address with you?' I asked.

Clare laughed. 'This is the outside world, Harry. Haven't you heard about trade unions? For the sake of industrial tranquillity, we don't ask, but the airline has a note of her mobile phone number and if it's necessary to recall her that's how we'd do it. Mind you, if she turns the bloody thing off, that would be that. And most of them do. If they're ever challenged about it, they'll say they were somewhere where they couldn't get a signal or were swimming or in the sauna and forgot to look for missed calls. I tell you, Harry, this is nothing like the Job.'

'She'll probably be going to the Pretext Club again,' said Dave.

Back at the office, I rang Peter Sullivan and gave him the dates of Madison Bailey's holiday.

'I didn't ask the date of her last flight before she starts leave, though, Peter. I didn't intend to give too much away, even to the airline security officer.'

'Don't worry about that, Harry,' said Sullivan, 'we can find it out easily enough. I'll keep you posted. Incidentally, d'you want to be here when we start the ball rolling?'

'Not a good idea, Peter. She knows Dave and me, and if she spotted us in your neck of the woods, I think she might smell a rat.'

Dave looked at me when I finished the call. 'You really ought to get some new clichés, sir.'

We had exhausted nearly all of our lines of enquiry into the murder of Robert Sharp and although there were a number of suspects, there was no hard evidence to support our suspicions. Frank Taylor, who had a previous conviction for severely beating his girlfriend and was witnessed by several people having an argument with Sharp, was the nearest we'd got to a viable suspect. But there was no way in which we could prove he'd killed Sharp. The evidence simply wasn't there.

I decided to have a quiet day in the office and deal with my mountain of paperwork. Although, being an old-fashioned copper, I call it paperwork, most of it consists of emails that arrive on the ubiquitous computer. One of the things I've learned since being forced on to a steep learning curve about IT is that it's all too easy to press a key and send out a host of emails to people who 'might' be interested in the contents. Half the trouble arises from when certain senior members of the hierarchy demand a hard copy, as a consequence of which printed copies are made and commented upon. And filed! All of which defeats the concept of the paperless society we were promised when all this cyber gismo started.

However, my good intentions amounted to nothing when Colin Wilberforce came into my office.

'A woman has just walked into Charing Cross nick, sir, and told the DI, when eventually she got to see him, that she had important information about Robert Sharp.'

'Did the DI say what this important information was, Colin?'

'No, sir. Apparently, she refused to tell anyone but you.' Wilberforce grinned. 'That's what comes of letting the press bureau put your name out, I suppose, sir.'

'Where's Dave, Colin?'

'In the incident room, standing by, sir.'

'I wonder what rubbish this bloody woman will serve up. Oh well, better go and speak to her. Just as well she didn't walk into Glasgow Central police station, I suppose.'

FOURTEEN

The woman seated in the interview room had an imperious look about her that, at first sight, appeared to characterize a contempt for those about her. But to offset that perception there were lines on her face that seemed to indicate some recent tragedy. Perhaps the one begot the other. And so it proved to be. I guessed her age to be about forty-eight, maybe younger, and she had blonde hair flecked with grey. The white linen dress she was wearing had undoubtedly cost a lot of money, but she was that sort of woman.

'Mrs Rebecca Chapman? I'm Detective Chief Inspector Harry Brock of the team investigating the murder of Robert Sharp.'

'How d'you do.' Mrs Chapman shook my proffered hand.

'And this is Detective Sergeant David Poole, Mrs Chapman.'

'How d'you do, Mr Poole.' Rebecca Chapman paused for a moment or two, as if searching her memory, before shaking hands with him. 'I thought your name was familiar. I understand your wife Madeleine is a principal dancer in the Royal Ballet Company.'

'How on earth . . .?' But that was the most that Dave was able to say. For once, he was lost for words.

Mrs Chapman smiled and the air of aloofness vanished in an instant. 'My sister-in-law is one of the Friends of Covent Garden and she was telling me about your wife. Mrs Poole is regarded as an extremely talented ballerina and I've had the pleasure of watching her perform on several occasions. You must be very proud of her, Mr Poole.'

'I am, ma'am.' Dave was completely overawed, a most unusual state for him.

'I was told that you have something important to tell me, Mrs Chapman,' I said, as Dave and I sat down opposite her.

'I'm afraid I do.' Mrs Chapman became serious again. 'My daughter Fiona committed suicide two years ago.'

'I'm sorry to hear that,' I said.

'Thanks entirely to that bloody man Sharp.' Rebecca Chapman remained perfectly calm, which made her use of the expletive seem even more effective, spoken as it was in her modulated, educated tones.

'Would you like to tell me the circumstances?'

Before replying, Mrs Chapman took a framed portrait photograph from her handbag and passed it me. 'That's him. He promised to marry Fiona. They fixed a date and everything, and Charles and I – Charles is my husband – arranged a wedding breakfast for about twenty of Fiona's friends and our family.'

'Were Sharp's family not represented, then, Mrs Chapman?' asked Dave.

'He told us that he had no family but he did have a friend who would act as best man. Robert was very good looking and personable, too. I hate to admit it, Mr Poole, but my husband and I were completely taken in by him. He was suave to a fault and he never once put a foot wrong when it came to the social graces.'

'So, what happened? Did he fail to turn up for the wedding?'

'Yes, but that wasn't all. Not only did he leave Fiona pregnant, he stole from us. We kept quite a lot of cash in the house that Charles left in his study. I suppose it was about five thousand pounds in all and it was for Charles to pay tradesmen – we were having quite a lot of improvements done to the house and garden, and there was a conservatory being built on the back of the house as well. Many tradesmen resent having to pay for depositing cheques and much prefer cash. They probably don't like paying tax either, but that's a matter for the government; it's their problem, not ours. However, that's neither here nor there.'

'Where was this money kept, Mrs Chapman?' I asked. 'In a safe, perhaps?'

'No, Charles always left it in the top drawer of his desk. It wasn't locked up or anything like that. The fact is that we trusted Robert – after all, he was about to become family – and didn't for one moment imagine that he would go rooting about in Charles's study. Even Fiona and I would hold back from entering what we called Charles's own space, if you know what I mean. His inner sanctum, as it were. However, on that fateful day of the wedding, after Sharp failed to turn up at the church, we found that the money was missing. Charles went into his study – some sort of sixth sense, I suppose – and saw that one of his desk drawers had been left open.'

'And all of it, five thousand pounds, was missing?' I could hardly believe that people could be so stupid as to leave that amount of money more or less just lying about.

'Yes, at least Charles thought it was about that much, but that wasn't all. Later on, I found that some of my jewellery was missing. Not all of it, and I suppose he thought that by taking only some of it, I wouldn't notice until I went to look for a particular piece. And that's what happened – it must've been about a month before I realized some of it had gone.'

'What is your husband's profession, Mrs Chapman?'

'He's a property developer. He seems to have a knack for it.'

'Did you report this theft to the police?'

'When we were able to find a police station to report it to, yes,' said Mrs Chapman, with an element of irritation. 'A young man eventually turned up and took a few details, but I have to say he didn't seem very interested. I got the impression he thought that if we were stupid enough to leave that amount of cash lying around, we not only deserved to lose it, but could afford to.'

There wasn't a lot I could say about that. Since the savage cuts to the budget, the police have not been able to provide the service expected of them. There was a time when chief officers would have banged on the Home Secretary's desk and complained bitterly, but not any more. Honours are at stake, although I knew of one or two former commissioners who'd have raised merry hell about any reduction in funding.

'How long after this did your daughter take her own life, Mrs Chapman?' Dave asked.

'Three weeks and two days, Mr Poole, during which time she was utterly inconsolable. She spent most of her time in her room crying her eyes out. I do believe that she was in love with Sharp heart and soul. That wretched man had promised her the earth and he destroyed her at a stroke. There was the property he owned in the Caribbean, the exotic holidays he enjoyed on the French Riviera, the cars he owned, although we never saw any of it, and all of this was going to be Fiona's. But it was obvious to me, Mr Brock, once I'd thought it through, that he sniffed money the moment he set eyes on where we lived. And frankly, I don't think he had a brass farthing to his name.'

'Where is it you live, Mrs Chapman?' I asked.

Rebecca Chapman opened her handbag and took out a visiting card which she handed to me. The address was in a fashionable part of Belgravia. Beneath that address was another, for a country residence in Devon.

'I wonder if I might take a copy of this photograph, Mrs Chapman.'

'Why should you want a photograph of Robert Sharp, Mr Brock? He's dead, surely.'

'Yes, he is. But we're still making enquiries and we haven't seen a photograph of him until now. It would greatly assist us if we were able to show people a photo because we understand that, on several occasions, he has used other names.' I was by no means sure of that, but it seemed an odds-on bet that he did. In my experience, most confidence tricksters had several aliases.

'You can keep it, Mr Brock. It was on my daughter's bedside table and she was clasping it the day she died.'

'Thank you.' I took the photograph out of the frame.

'You can keep the frame, too,' said Rebecca Chapman. 'Throw it away if you like. For Charles and me it brings back too many unpleasant memories.'

'How did Fiona die, Mrs Chapman?' asked Dave.

'A drug overdose, Mr Poole. It seems to be the method of choice among the younger generation.' Again, there was that touch of bitterness in Rebecca Chapman's voice. 'How exactly did Robert Sharp die, Mr Brock?' she continued, turning to me. 'The newspaper reports were a little vague, other than saying it was at some sort of nudist colony.' Rebecca Chapman's bland expression suggested that she had no objection to naturism.

'It was at the Pretext Club, a naturist establishment not far from Harrow. He was shot and then his body was set on fire.'

'I hope he suffered,' said Mrs Chapman.

'Incidentally, Mrs Chapman,' I said, 'where did Fiona meet Sharp?'

'Ironically, it was at one of these nudist colonies. I've no objection to such places at all, but if Fiona hadn't decided to go to this one, she'd never have met the damned man.'

'D'you know the name of the club that Fiona joined?'

'No, I can't remember. All I can tell you is that it wasn't the one where Sharp was murdered. The Pretext Club, did you say?'

'Thank you for coming to speak to us, Mrs Chapman. I'll see you out.' I conducted her to the doors of the police station and down the steps. 'May I call you a taxi?'

'No, thank you, Mr Brock. I think I'll walk for a while.' Rebecca Chapman shook hands and I stayed on the steps watching her erect figure making its way along Agar Street towards Trafalgar Square.

'Well, that's a turn up,' said Dave, joining me at the door.

'It makes me wish that he was still alive, Dave. I'd love to see that bastard sent down for the rest of his life.'

'Funny mistake for a con man to make,' said Dave, 'giving someone a photograph of himself. He must've been very confident of not getting caught. Still, as Alexander Pope wrote: *Pride, the never-failing vice of fools.*'

'Smart-arse,' I said. 'This afternoon we'll visit Paul Harrison and rattle his bars a bit.'

I thought it would be preferable for Nina Harrison not to be at home when Dave and I called on her husband, both for her and for us. I hoped that being on his own might prompt Harrison to be more truthful than he was on the last occasion we spoke to him. I rang the mobile number Nina Harrison had given us and suggested it to her.

'I shan't be at home anyway, Mr Brock,' she said. 'I'm having tea with a friend at the Savoy this afternoon.'

'Oh, it's you, Chief Inspector.' Paul Harrison was unable to disguise his surprise – or maybe his shock – when he opened the door to us. 'Do come in.' His false bonhomie rapidly returned and he managed to sound as though he was actually pleased to see us.

We followed him into the sitting room and accepted his invitation to sit down, but refused his offer of alcohol.

'And to what do I owe the pleasure of this visit, Chief Inspector?' Paul Harrison's urbane confidence was now firmly in place.

'Where were you on Saturday the twentieth of July this year, Mr Harrison?' Dave had a habit of dispensing with the niceties in circumstances such as these and went straight to the point.

For a moment or two, Harrison stared at Dave. I could almost see the wheels turning as he tried to convince himself that the question had been posed by my sergeant rather than me and was, therefore, of lesser importance. He was not the first suspect to make that mistake.

'The twentieth of last month, you say. As it was a Saturday, I was probably playing golf.'

'So, if we make enquiries at your golf club, they will confirm that, will they?' Dave, idly tapping his pocketbook with his pen, put the question almost casually, as though he was merely going through a list of routine questions that I had given him with instructions to ask them, one by one.

'Er, hang on a moment.' The first signs of Harrison's uncertainty and an ebbing of confidence were beginning to show. 'I'll just have a look in my diary. I've a terrible memory.' He stood up and left the room, returning a few minutes later clutching an A4-sized book. 'Saturday the twentieth of July,' he mumbled, as he sat down and flicked through the pages. Finding the appropriate entry, he said, 'Oh, it seems not. No, in fact, I had a meeting.'

'A business meeting?' asked Dave, still contriving to sound as though he wasn't really interested in the answer.

'Er, no. Well, not exactly.' Harrison slammed the diary shut. He was clearly rattled. 'Might I ask why you're so interested in that date, Sergeant?'

'It's the day on which Robert Sharp was murdered at the Pretext Club,' I said. 'When we spoke to you before, you told us that you and your wife were both here all that weekend and your wife confirmed it.'

'Oh, did I say that?'

'So, where were you, Mr Harrison?'

'Look, why are you so interested in *my* movements on that day?'

'For the simple reason that the last time we spoke to you, Mr Harrison, and your wife's infidelity with Robert Sharp was discussed, you said . . .' I paused and glanced at Dave. 'What did Mr Harrison say on that occasion, Sergeant?'

Dave made a big thing of thumbing through his pocketbook. 'Detective Inspector Ebdon made a note of Mr Harrison's exact words, sir, and I have a copy. He said, "I might've been tempted to do him an injury." I suppose that could be considered as a threat of GBH.'

'Would you agree with that, Mr Harrison?' I asked.

'It's possible I might've said something like that,' said Harrison airily, at the same time making a brushing motion with his hand as though to dismiss the comment as too trivial for real comment.

'However, you have yet to answer my question.'

'I've forgotten what it was.'

'Where were you on the twentieth of July?'

Harrison let out a sigh. 'I was with a lady friend,' he finally admitted.

'And her name and address, sir?' This time Dave's pencil waggled in Harrison's direction in the menacing way I've seen him do so often in the past.

'Oh, God! This is awfully embarrassing. She's a married woman, you see.'

'And you're a married man, Mr Harrison,' I said. 'Doesn't that make things a bit tricky, given that you pretend to be holier than thou?'

'Her name's Anne Craven and she lives in Beckenham,' said Harrison reluctantly. 'You're not going to see her, surely?' There was an element of concern in his voice now.

'How else do we confirm your alibi?' asked Dave. 'Of course, if you have a mobile phone number for her, we could speak to her in the absence of her husband.'

'Yes, yes, that would save her being embarrassed.' Harrison promptly furnished the number.

'One last thing,' I said. 'I must warn you that interference with a witness is a serious offence. I would caution you against contacting Mrs Craven in an attempt to ensure that she backs you up. Were she to do so falsely, she *also* would commit the offence of perverting the course of justice.'

We left Paul Harrison a worried man and considerably less bombastic than when we'd arrived.

'Make for Beckenham, Dave,' I said, and keyed in the phone number for Anne Craven that Harrison had given us. It was answered immediately.

'Mrs Anne Craven?'

'Yes, who is this?'

'Detective Chief Inspector Brock of the Murder Investigation Team at New Scotland Yard.'

'Good heavens! What's happened?'

'We'd like to speak to you about Mr Paul Harrison, Mrs Craven.'

'Oh, Lord! He's not been murdered, has he?'

'No, but we'd like to talk to you about him.'

'All sounds very mysterious, but yes, do come and see me.' Anne Craven gave us her address and I could only presume that she was alone.

We pulled up outside her house ten minutes later.

Anne Harrison was an attractive, mature woman. Her most noticeable feature was her high cheekbones which lent her a slightly oriental appearance. She was dressed in jeans and a sweater.

'Come in,' she said, once we'd introduced ourselves, 'and tell me what ails you.'

'What ails us? Are you a doctor, Mrs Craven?' asked Dave impishly, as we all sat down in her sitting room.

Anne Craven laughed. 'Yes, I am actually, but not a medical doctor, and it's Anne. Everyone calls me that, and don't call me "doctor" either. But if you're interested, I have a PhD in town and country planning, which sounds terribly boring and most of the time it is. Now then, what is it you want to know about Paul?'

'We interviewed Mr Harrison a short while ago in Bromley, Anne. He tells me that he spent Saturday the twentieth of July with you. Is that correct?'

'Probably, but just let me check.' She crossed the room to where her handbag was lying in a chair, and took out a small Filofax. She flicked through the pages and then nodded. 'Yes, we actually spent that weekend at a naturist club.'

'May I ask which one?' I asked, trying not to sound too bored. I didn't know whether to hope it was the Pretext Club or another one.

'It's quite a distance from here,' said Anne, 'at Paul's insistence.' She took her membership card from her handbag and handed it to me. 'It's in France.'

'We seem to be running across an awful lot of naturists recently,' said Dave.

'There are about four million of us in the country altogether,' said Anne. 'It's good fun and very liberating.'

'Is your husband a member, too?' I asked, as I returned her membership card.

'I'm divorced,' she said, laughing. 'And so's Paul.'

'We spoke to his wife only this morning,' I said. 'And she was under the impression that Mr Harrison was in New York that weekend.'

'His wife?' Suddenly, Anne Craven threw back her head and laughed. '*O, what a tangled web we weave when first we practise to deceive!*' she quoted. 'But who was the poet?'

'Walter Scott,' said Dave.

We left the merry divorcée and drove back to central London.

'I think Paul Harrison, in his own way, is a sort of con artist, but he's not very good at it,' said Dave. 'I wouldn't mind betting he's promised to marry Anne Craven.'

'Funny that,' I said, 'because he's the sort of individual who'd criticize someone like Robert Sharp for playing fast and loose with women.'

Back at Belgravia, Kate Ebdon reported to me with the results of the follow-up enquiries on the ex-boyfriends of Janice Greene and Gina Page. They were disappointing.

Stephen Hall, the university employee who was Janice

Greene's ex, had indeed moved to Swindon. Kate got in touch with the Wiltshire police and arranged for an officer to inter- view him. The detailed statement, taken by a detective inspector, reported that the man's original fury at the loss of Janice had been set aside and that he now had another girl- friend. Questioned further, he was able to provide a rock-solid alibi for the weekend that had seen the death of Robert Sharp.

Kevin, Gina Page's former boyfriend, who, she had said, was hopping mad at losing her, had moved to Australia and according to the Victoria police now lived in Melbourne and was there at the time of Sharp's murder. Colin Wilberforce had spent a great deal of time and trouble to track him down, all for nothing. But that's police work for you.

DS Liz Carpenter had reported back to Kate that the follow- up enquiries she and Nicola Chance had made in response to the telephone calls received on the hotline had also come to nought. The five London-based women had met Sharp, or thought they had. Two of them claimed to have met him at the Pretext Club, but enquiries there indicated that neither woman had ever stayed there. However, none of them had had an affair with Sharp. The woman in Cornwall and the woman in Birmingham were now not sure that the man they'd met was, in fact, Sharp, and on reflection thought it might have been someone else. There are always people seeking their five minutes of fame following a well-publicized murder and these women were possibly among them. Interestingly, none of the seven women had lost any money. It came as no surprise that there was an absence of people appearing on television to say what a nice, quiet neighbour Robert Sharp had been. He'd never stayed anywhere long enough.

Thus, nine more lines of enquiry had been closed and we were no nearer to discovering Sharp's killer.

By the time I'd finished messing about with trivia – but necessary trivia all the same – it was five o'clock. I decided that nothing was likely to happen that evening and that any further developments would probably be as a result of the National Crime Agency searching Madison Bailey's make-up case on her return from Bogotá. And that was not going to happen until Sunday morning. All in all, I was thoroughly depressed and decided that an evening with Lydia would be the best antidote. I telephoned her.

'Hello, stranger. What are you doing wasting time phoning me when you should be out catching murderers?'

'I've decided to wait until they give themselves up, Lydia darling. If you can put up with me for an hour or two, I fancy a dip in your pool.'

'I'd love to see you, Harry. It's obvious that this nudist colony thing's caught on if you want to come down here and tear all your clothes off.' She laughed her deep, throaty laugh. 'But it's my food you're interested in, isn't it?'

'And not only your food,' I replied.

'One thing at a time, ducky,' she said, adopting a cockney accent. 'How long's it going to take you to get here?'

'Depends on the traffic but, all being well, I should be with you in about an hour and a half.'

I left via the incident room, gave Colin Wilberforce Lydia's address and told him that's where I'd be for the rest of the evening.

'We already have a note of Mrs Maxwell's address on file, sir.' I'm sure I detected an element of smugness in Wilberforce's comment.

The traffic wasn't too bad and I drove home to Surbiton where I left my car before taking a cab the rest of the way. I knew Lydia would produce a magnificent meal and it would be a travesty not to sample the wines that she always selects to go with her creations. The last thing I wanted was to give the Black Rats the satisfaction of arresting a CID officer who was over the limit. Apart from that, a conviction would almost certainly result in me losing my job.

The cab deposited me at Lydia's house. After some time, she opened the door.

'Sorry to keep you, Harry, darling, but you got here sooner than I expected.' She was wearing a white thigh-length towelling robe and her hair was wet.

'In the pool, were you?' I asked, as I kissed her.

'No, I was mowing the lawn. What did you think I was doing? Come on in and get your kit off.'

'Blimey, you don't mess about, do you?'

I stayed the night and had to make an early start the next morning. Lydia insisted on making breakfast for me at five o'clock. 'Can you come again tonight, darling?' she asked.

I was in the office by just after eight. As I'd anticipated there had been no developments during the night.

FIFTEEN

L
ydia and I were in her swimming pool again on Saturday
evening, as a preamble to dinner. At about half past six,
I emerged to pour us both a glass of wine when my
phone played its distinctive sound announcing a call from the
incident room.

'Oh, no!' exclaimed Lydia, as she climbed out of the pool
to join me. 'Not again.' She had learned to identify that ring
tone very soon after the start of our relationship.

'Brock. What the hell is it this time?' Unforgivably, I
snapped at the caller.

'It's Gavin Creasey, sir.'

'Sorry, Gavin.'

'I've just had a call from a Peter Sullivan, a senior customs
official of the NCA at Heathrow, sir,' said Creasey. 'He wanted
your phone number but I told him we didn't disclose officers'
phone numbers. So, he gave me his mobile number and asked
if you would call him.'

'Thanks, Gavin.' I'd given Sullivan the incident room number,
guarding the number of my mobile from anyone not needing
to know it. I got enough calls on it as it was. Presumably
Sullivan had called the Belgravia number believing I'd still be
there on a Saturday evening. Not if I could help it.

'Peter, it's Harry Brock.'

'Sorry to bother you on a Saturday evening, Harry,' said
Sullivan, 'but I've been thinking about this matter of Madison
Bailey's make-up case and I thought that, after all, you might
like to be at the airport when we searched it.'

'Yes, I would, but as I said when we met, Peter, she knows
me and if she spots me it might compromise your operation.'
I glanced at Lydia's anxious face, shook my head and mouthed,
'It's OK.'

'I understand that, Harry,' continued Sullivan, 'but I wasn't
suggesting that you took part. You could watch from our

observation room, and if you got the result of the search straight away, it would be better than me phoning an hour or two later. Anyway, it's better to see it actually unfold than to get a report. What d'you think?'

'Could speed things up, I suppose, Peter. What time does her flight touch down?'

'Estimating at zero-eight-thirty Zulu plus one.'

'What the hell does all that gobbledegook mean, Peter?'

'Half past nine local time, that is to say British Summer Time.'

'Well, at least it's a reasonably civilized hour. I'll see you there, Peter.'

'You haven't got to go out, have you?' asked Lydia, having failed to understand my earlier whispered message. There was an expression of mounting disappointment on her face. It had happened all too often in our short relationship.

'Not this time, but I have to be at Heathrow by half-nine tomorrow morning. I'll just ring the office and arrange for Dave to pick me up.'

'Why don't you stay the night?' suggested Lydia. 'Dave can pick you up from here.'

'What a lovely idea,' I said, clasping her in a tight hug.

'I'm all wet,' she said.

'Big deal! So am I.'

I dislike airports and I particularly dislike the crowds of people who wander aimlessly around, arguing with airline officials, complaining about lost luggage and querying if they really did need a passport to go to the United States because unfortunately they'd left this vital document at home in Orpington. What's more, these lost souls would buttonhole anyone who happened to be wearing a suit and was striding purposefully among them in the belief they'd found an official who could tell them what had happened to the flight from Papua New Guinea. In actual fact, the aforementioned 'suit' was probably trying to escape the madding crowd but regrettably, it's unseemly to run. Herd instinct being what it is, the crowd would panic and start running too, but without knowing the reason.

I'd arrived at Heathrow at nine o'clock, having established beforehand that Madison Bailey's flight was on time.

'As we discussed the other day, Harry,' explained Sullivan, once I'd located his airside office, 'the intention is to have a blitz on the crews of three different airlines, including Miss Bailey's, of course. It's something we do from time to time, and it won't look as though we're taking a special interest in her if we pick three separate crews apparently at random.' His personal radio buzzed and he was told that the Bogotá flight had touched down.

'Come on through, Harry. You can watch from the search room,' said Sullivan. 'You can see out, but Bailey won't be able see you. The window is one way.'

This was not the moment to tell Peter Sullivan that I was fully conversant with one-way windows.

All the crews had been asked to make formal declarations and most were allowed to pass through customs without further delay. The officers on Sullivan's team had been carefully briefed and the crews of the selected airlines were subjected to a more thorough search. One or two pieces of luggage were opened and examined and, one by one, the female members of the cabin crew had their make-up cases examined. Several of these cases were removed to a back room ostensibly to be X-rayed, including the one taken from Madison Bailey.

But her case was not X-rayed because the officials had a good idea what they were looking for. And they found it.

Peter Sullivan was called over by one of the searchers. 'How about that, guv?' The officer displayed a number of plastic-covered packages containing white powder that had been taken from a compartment at the bottom of the case.

'How much does it weigh?' asked Sullivan.

'A kilo, give or take, and it's pure cocaine.'

Sullivan nodded as he did some mental arithmetic. 'Street value of about seventy grand, I reckon. But now comes the hard part. We need to know where it's going.' He walked over to an officer in civilian clothing. 'Come over and have a look at your target, Grant.' He led the officer across the room to the window. 'That good-looking black girl in stewardess's uniform is Madison Bailey and she's your target.'

'Very tasty,' said Grant, the senior surveillance operative. 'She's a real stunner.'

'Well, never mind that. Keep your mind on the job, because we need to know where she goes and who she's meeting.'

'I do know the drill,' protested Grant. 'I've been doing this job for quite a few years now.'

'That's what worries me,' said Sullivan, who knew that spending too long in the same job sometimes leads to carelessness. 'Just make sure you don't lose her. And keep in touch all the time.' There was no love lost between the customs element of the National Crime Agency and the men and women who undertook the tailing operations.

The NCA surveillance operative took out his personal radio and gave the members of his team, who were positioned in various parts of the airport, a full description of Madison Bailey.

Sullivan glanced at the search officer. 'All set?'

'Yes, guv. The originals were photographed in situ and the substitute packages have been put in their place. We're good to go.' Madison Bailey's case now held the same number of packages, identical with the originals, but each containing an innocuous white powder of the same weight as the cocaine they replaced.

'Right, return the cases to their owners, apologize for the delay and send them on their way rejoicing.'

I stood at the window and watched as the cases were handed back. It was particularly noticeable that Madison Bailey displayed no emotion whatsoever when she took her case from the customs official. Either she had been supremely confident of her own deceit or she didn't know the cocaine was there, something that Sullivan told me happens from time to time. On the other hand, rather than being an unknowing 'mule', she may have been a consummate actress. But that requires a great deal of nerve.

The operation was under way, and with luck and professionalism on the part of the surveillance team, I might, at last, discover the identity of Robert Sharp's murderer. There again, all that we might have turned up is a drug-smuggling operation involving Madison Bailey but having nothing whatever to do with the murder of Robert Sharp.

*   *   *

I left the airport and made my way directly to my office in Belgravia. Peter Sullivan had promised to keep me informed of the progress of the surveillance operation as it unfolded. It turned out to be a running commentary as the reports, monitored at Heathrow, were passed immediately to me by one of Sullivan's men.

The first surprise was that Madison Bailey did not go home to the flat at Harlington that she shared with Jeanette Davis, but drove her distinctive white Mini convertible with its personalized number plate straight on to the M4.

Keeping strictly to the speed limit, she continued her journey for just over forty miles until she arrived at Chieveley Services at junction thirteen. She parked her car and, carrying her make-up case and a small overnight bag, went inside. Peter Sullivan had assured me that there were several women on the surveillance team and one of them had followed the target into the facilities area where Madison had shed her uniform, taken a shower and donned white linen slacks and a yellow crop top. She had undone the French roll she adopted when on duty so that her black hair now hung loose around her shoulders.

From there she went to Costa, where she had a latte and a Danish pastry before returning to her car. The watchers reported that she was now wearing a pair of wraparound sunglasses and suggested that this was an attempt to mislead the surveillance team. Although not mentioning my view to the NCA team, I thought this was an absurd observation to have made. Assuming that Madison Bailey was under the impression that she had been cleared by customs at the airport without arousing suspicion, she was continuing to drive a car registered in her name. It was surely quite natural for an attractive woman like her to want to shake off her uniformed image, apart from which the sun was shining and dark glasses were essential to safe driving. There was no reason why she should have embarked upon evasive tactics.

Leaving the service area, Madison drove back on to the M4 until she reached junction twenty, when she took the slip road to join the M5 towards Bristol. The surveillance team now speculated that Bristol was going to be her destination. But neither their intelligence sources nor ours indicated that she had any connection with that city and, as if to prove it, at junction thirty-one she swung on to the A30 towards Bodmin.

She made another stop at Cornwall Services and spent thirty-seven minutes purchasing and consuming a salad at the Cornish Kitchen before continuing her journey. But her final destination could still only be guessed at.

Madison Bailey's mystery drive continued until, 300 miles from Heathrow, she turned on to the B3306 road.

'It looks as though she's going to Penzance, Harry,' said Sullivan, calling personally for the first time since the operation began. 'Does she have any connections there that you know of?'

'It doesn't ring any bells, Peter. At a guess, if that's her destination, I'd say she was meeting the person who'll take the drugs off her hands there.'

'That was my conclusion, too. As usual, it's turned out to be a waiting game.' But then came a surprise. 'Hang on, Harry. I've got another message coming through.' There was a pause and then Sullivan came back on the line. 'She's just driven into Land's End airport, Harry.'

'There's only one place she can go from there,' I said. 'St Mary's on the Isles of Scilly.'

'Yes,' said Sullivan, 'I've just been told that. One of my blokes here knows Scilly well. He reckons it opens up quite a few possibilities apparently. If she's meeting someone it could be on St Mary's or any one of the other inhabited islands: Tresco, St Martin's, Bryher and St Agnes. Added to that there are scores of uninhabited islands, and there's nothing to stop someone camping on one of them without worrying about being spotted from the air provided they camouflage themselves. But I'm told that would mean hiring a local boat and the Scillonian boat owners want to keep on the right side of the law, so I doubt our target would chance it.'

'Have you thought that the meet, if there is to be one, might take place on a yacht moored off St Mary's?' I asked.

'We're arranging to cover that possibility, Harry. A customs vessel, Her Majesty's Cutter *Guardian*, is in the area and will be directed to Scilly if that turns out to be necessary. The surveillance team has promised to get some of their people over there as soon as possible. In addition to the fixed-wing aircraft service, there's now a helicopter service in place. To be quite honest though, we've been caught on the hop.'

'Will your cutter get there in time, Peter?'

Sullivan laughed. 'It rather depends where he is when we call him, but the skipper can get twenty-six knots out of the vessel's two Caterpillar engines.' He paused. 'So I'm told.'

It was another twenty minutes before Peter Sullivan rang again. 'The surveillance team have managed to get a couple of their people on the next helicopter after the one the target's on. Meanwhile, we've been in touch with the police on St Mary's and asked them to keep a lookout for Madison when she alights from the chopper. It's only a matter of twenty minutes between flights, so nothing can go wrong.'

'Keep in touch, Peter, and thanks for the update.' I ended the call and wondered how many times I'd heard the phrase 'nothing can go wrong', only to find that an anonymous police gremlin had struck again and, to use a familiar police term for disaster, the wheels had come off.

I rang Commander Cleaver at home, knowing that he never minded being disturbed about something important. In fact, he would be annoyed if he was *not* told something important whatever day it was or whatever time it was.

'What's the problem, Harry? You sound like you've got the weight of the world on your shoulders.'

'It's been a long day, guv'nor, and it's not over yet. I know you said you didn't want a blow-by-blow account of my enquiry, but I thought I should bring you up to date on this one. We seem to have reached a critical point.' And I went on to tell him that Madison Bailey was now in the Isles of Scilly. We assumed, I said, that she believed she was still in possession of seventy thousand pounds' worth of cocaine, and that we were waiting to see what happened next in the hope that her contact was also the man who'd murdered Robert Sharp.

'Sounds hopeful, Harry,' said Cleaver. 'I think you should get over there as soon as possible and I'd be inclined to take Kate Ebdon with you as there's a woman involved, but that's your decision, of course. You're running the show.'

'I'll do that, sir, and thank you.'

'Let me pull a few strings to see if I can get someone to take you over there, Harry. Like our people or the Royal Navy.'

I telephoned Kate's home number and told her to stand by for a move, thinking how different Cleaver was from his predecessor, who could never come to terms with the possibility that a detective chief inspector was capable of making a decision without first receiving his advice.

Even though it was a Sunday, Commander Cleaver had succeeded in bringing his influence to bear and had arranged for two helicopters to get us to the Isles of Scilly. I don't like helicopters because they have this nasty habit of stopping in mid-air in order to allow other aircraft to pass in front of them. Nevertheless, I could hardly refuse the commander's offer as he had gone to so much trouble to save us from a time-consuming train journey that might have got us there too late.

We were transported – this time by a traffic car on blues and twos – to the London base of the National Police Air Service. Its Airbus helicopter flew Kate and me as far as the outskirts of Yeovil where we touched down. We then transferred to a similar helicopter that had flown up from the NPAS base at Exeter. Just over two hours after leaving London we arrived at St Mary's airport on the Isles of Scilly.

We were met by a man who promptly produced his National Crime Agency identification. 'I'm Sandy, a member of the surveillance team.' I suppose Sandy might even have been his real name; there was no way of knowing because his ID disappeared as quickly as it had been produced. He went on to explain that the target was now under the surveillance of his colleagues.

I introduced myself and Kate Ebdon. 'Where exactly is Madison Bailey at this moment?' I asked.

'Sitting on Porthcressa Beach in a bikini, taking in the sun, admiring the view and acting like she hasn't got a care in the world. A couple of my colleagues are keeping an eye on her. We'll take a walk across there. It's only about a mile and a half.'

'I presume she's got the all-important make-up case with her, then?' I asked, as we set out from the airport.

'No, she hasn't. We think she must've left it in her room at the bed-and-breakfast she booked into when she arrived. My colleagues are searching her room as we speak.'

'Of course, it could be that she's only an innocent mule, after all,' said Kate Ebdon.

'What d'you mean, exactly?' Sandy frowned.

'Perhaps she's unaware that she's been carrying cocaine worth seventy grand all the way from Bogotá. If she knew, surely to God she wouldn't have left it in a hotel room – not that she knows it no longer contains the real stuff. But if she'd known all along that she was carrying cocaine, she'd be unlikely to leave it lying around, would she?'

Sandy nodded. 'If that's the case, what's she doing on the Isles of Scilly?'

'Well, according to the airline she works for, she's on holiday,' said Kate. 'It might be as innocent as that. But if your people do find the duff packages that were put in her case at Heathrow, you'll have a bit of a job proving possession of talcum powder if the packages are in her guesthouse room and she's down here. She'll deny all knowledge of them and might even suggest that your colleagues planted them to incriminate her.'

'Bloody hell!' exclaimed Sandy, as we reached Porthcressa Beach. 'That'll mean this whole operation will have been a complete blowout.'

'Welcome to the *real* world of crime detection, mate,' said Kate, sounding more Australian than usual. She didn't have a very high opinion of the National Crime Agency.

Sandy pointed out the man and woman surveillance team who were sitting on the beach not far from Madison Bailey. The air stewardess, distinctive in a white bikini, was sitting with her arms clasped around her knees, and peering out to sea.

'Yes, that's her,' said Kate. 'She looks as though she's expecting something or someone.'

Sure enough, further discussion was interrupted by the arrival on the beach of an inflatable dinghy with an outboard

motor. The man in the dinghy was wearing a colourful shirt
and shorts, sunglasses and a white baseball cap pulled well
down, making it difficult to identify him without binoculars,
perhaps even then. He waved at the girl.

Madison Bailey waved back and stood up. Picking up her
large beach bag – the one she'd been carrying when we saw
her at the Pretext Club – she walked casually across the sand
to the boat, splashing through the shallow water of an incoming
tide. The man who had brought the dinghy inshore helped her
aboard and gave her a hug and a kiss. She relaxed in the stern
of the vessel and her companion spun the craft before heading
back to sea.

'Ye Gods!' exclaimed Sandy. 'Now what's happening?'

'At a guess,' I said, 'they're going out to one of those yachts
that are moored out there.'

'But there are dozens of them.' Indeed, there were yachts
of all shapes and sizes ranging from the very small to the very
expensive.

'You'll just have to wait and see,' said Kate, who was rather
enjoying the spectacle of an NCA officer who seemed to have
lost the plot. 'The smart money says that the bag she's carrying
contains what she thinks is cocaine to the value of seventy
grand.'

'Oh my God!' Sandy suddenly realized that what Kate had
said was almost certain to be the truth. He pulled out his
mobile phone and, like a man possessed, started to wander
about the beach trying to get a signal. 'I've alerted *Guardian,*
one of the customs cutters,' he said, when eventually he'd
managed to make contact, 'which unfortunately is quite a
distance away. Now we'll have to wait and see what happens
next.' Taking a small telescope from his pocket, he trained it
in the direction of the disappearing inflatable. 'They're both
climbing aboard a cabin cruiser, Harry, and the inflatable is
being hooked on the stern.'

'Is there a name on the cruiser that you can see, Sandy?' I
asked.

'No, just a number, but that's good enough. Ah! He's going
southeast, at some speed, too. It looks as though he's making
for France. I hope *Guardian* gets here in time to track him.'

Within minutes, the cabin cruiser with Madison Bailey aboard had vanished over the horizon.

Sandy collapsed his telescope with a snap that betrayed his annoyance. 'I suppose I could alert the French police,' he said.

'Only if you can tell them which part of France they're making for,' said Kate.

SIXTEEN

The three of us made our way back to the police station in St Mary's and Sandy made a call to the team who were searching Madison's room at her guesthouse. 'They've found nothing, Harry,' he said dejectedly when he'd finished the call. 'The make-up case was there, obviously, but when they opened it up, the dummy packages had gone. Oh, God! The whole thing's a fucking disaster,' he said and, realizing too late that Kate was standing beside him, apologized for his bad language.

Kate laughed. 'You wait till *I* get going, mate,' she said.

There was now no alternative but to await a report from the customs cutter if, in fact, its crew had managed to catch up with the errant cabin cruiser.

The three of us adjourned to one of the few restaurants in the area and enjoyed a well-deserved meal.

It was now nearing ten o'clock in the evening of what was proving to be a very long day. I was tempted to give up and return to London. As we were leaving the restaurant, Sandy received a phone call from the skipper of Her Majesty's Cutter *Guardian*.

'It's a blowout, Harry,' said Sandy, as he finished the call. He was still as dejected as ever, if not more so. '*Guardian* couldn't find the damned cruiser anywhere.'

'Got any ideas, Sandy? Where could this guy have gone in the time available?' I asked.

Sandy did a quick calculation. 'I suppose it's possible that he'll finish up in a French port or, for that matter, on any one of the dozens of beaches and coves on the Brittany or Normandy coast where it's possible to land. It's going to take forever to track him down, and what's more, he might've got rid of the boat by now which will make it even harder to find him. Oh, to hell with it! He could be anywhere.' He paused as another thought occurred to him. 'God, even if we find him, he's bound to have disposed of the bogus cocaine by now. If the handover's taken place, that's it. Finished. Zilch!'

'I should imagine that the receivers would have tested the produce before parting with any cash, in which case the transaction probably ended in violence. For all we know, Madison and her conspirator could both be feeding the fishes by now,' said Kate, a comment that appeared to make Sandy even more dejected than before. 'But how about the Cornish coast?' she suggested. 'Who's going to query a cabin cruiser turning up there and mooring? And he could've doubled back just to fool your people. I don't think this guy is an amateur. And he might have to wait to keep his meet with whoever he's selling the cocaine to.'

'It's possible, I suppose,' said Sandy, reluctant to admit that someone from another organization might know better than he did. 'But why?'

'Because there aren't any customs officers on the Isles of Scilly,' said Kate, 'and our man probably thought that it would be risk-free. No one would be much interested in a guy in a cruiser coming into Porthcressa Beach and picking up an attractive girl in a bikini to take her for a run round the islands or for a day of sex on one of the dozens of uninhabited islands. Happens all the time,' she added dismissively.

'What time is *Guardian* expected to dock, Sandy?' I asked.

'In about half an hour's time. We'll have a chat with the skipper, but I doubt we'll learn any more than we know already.'

And indeed, that turned out to be the case. The skipper of *Guardian* reported that he had arrived off Porthcressa Beach about thirty minutes after receiving the call and started a sweep between there and the French coast but found nothing. Perhaps, after all, Madison Bailey's accomplice had been taken in by the dummy packages and had made for somewhere where he was sure of offloading them without being seen. Which left a number of unanswered questions. Who was the girl's confederate and where was he now? And who was the intended recipient of the cocaine? However, that was for the customs element of the NCA to sort out. My own concern was that if

Madison's partner was Robert Sharp's murderer, I wanted to put him in the dock at the Old Bailey. But first we had to find him.

We had more important priorities than those, however. Both Kate and I were tired out. We found a comfortable guesthouse that had two rooms vacant.

Next day, after a tortuous journey involving a twenty-minute helicopter trip from St Mary's to Land's End, a nine-mile cab ride from there to Penzance railway station, a five-hour train journey to Paddington and, finally, a taxi to Belgravia, Kate and I arrived at the office at about five thirty on the Monday evening.

'We've had a vague message from the National Crime Agency, sir,' said Wilberforce, by way of greeting. 'The cabin cruiser has been found abandoned at Penzance. Does that make any sense, sir?'

'I'm afraid it does, Colin, but I'm damned if I'm going all the way back there just to look at a bloody motor boat. Did they say anything else about it?'

'Not in the message, sir, but it contained a request for you to liaise with Mr Sullivan at Heathrow.'

I rang Peter Sullivan's extension from my office and after a short delay he came to the phone.

'I gather you had a disappointing day in the Isles of Scilly,' he began.

'You could say that, Peter. So, what have your people got?'

'It's not so much our people as the Devon and Cornwall Police. It was their officers who found the cabin cruiser and it had previously been reported stolen from Totland on the Isle of Wight on Tuesday the thirtieth of last month.'

'Interesting. If it was Brooks who nicked it, I wonder where he's been since absconding from Ford open prison on Saturday the thirteenth of July.'

'Are you going down to have a look at this boat, Harry?'

'No, there's no point. I doubt there'll be anything to find that'll be of any use in my murder investigation. I'll ask the Devon and Cornwall Police to check any fingerprints they find. If James Brooks' dabs are there it'll be a help. He's my number-one suspect for Robert Sharp's murder. But if it is him, he'll be long gone by now.'

It was at eight thirty on Tuesday morning that a phone call from Peter Sullivan informed me of an event that was to take us one step nearer finding Sharp's killer.

'I've just had a call from the headquarters of the Devon and Cornwall Police, Harry. The body of an unidentified woman has been washed up on Lamorna Cove beach. It was found by a young couple who were going for an early-morning swim.' Sullivan chuckled. 'Quite put them off their breakfast by all accounts.'

'You say unidentified, Peter. Is there any clue as to who she might be?' I wondered why Sullivan thought this would be of interest to me. But his next statement explained it.

'Oh yes,' said Sullivan. 'She is described as a very attractive twenty-five-year-old, with long black hair and light black skin. She was wearing a white bikini. Remind you of anyone?'

'Madison Bailey,' I said. 'Have they come up with a cause of death yet?'

'First indications were that she had drowned while swimming, but an initial examination showed that she'd been the victim of manual strangulation. Subject to confirmation when the post-mortem is completed, of course.'

'Is it just the woman's body that's been washed up, Peter?' I asked.

'That's all they mentioned, Harry. What makes you ask?'

'My Inspector Ebdon has a theory that both Madison and her colleague might've been murdered if the receiver believed they'd reneged on the deal when he found the dummy packages.'

'Oh, God! This job just gets worse, Harry.'

'Where's the body now, Peter?' I asked.

There was a rustling of paper as Sullivan went through his notes before he replied. 'The West Cornwall Hospital in Penzance, Harry.'

There was really no way out of it. I would have to view the body that had been found if for no better reason than to satisfy myself that it was that of Madison Bailey.

To make doubly sure, I decided that Kate Ebdon would come with me.

Colin Wilberforce was very good at travel arrangements, but even he couldn't manage to cut our journey time by much. A combination of flying from Gatwick to Newquay and taking a train from there to Penzance – which included a change – only managed to shave a few minutes off the time it would have taken to go all the way by rail.

Wilberforce had informed the Devon and Cornwall Police of our approximate time of arrival at the hospital and we were met in the entrance hall by a man of about fifty. He was a touch overweight, balding and had a greying, ragged moustache. His tweed suit had turn-ups and there were leather patches on the elbows of the jacket.

'DCI Brock, is it?' He asked, raising his pork-pie hat.

'Yes, that's me.'

'I'm DI Trevelion, sir, from Penzance. I'm looking into the matter of this dead girl who was found at Lamorna Cove this morning.' Trevelion spoke with a soft Cornish accent.

'I take it that you've not yet had a formal identification, Mr Trevelion.'

'No, sir. My name's John, by the way.'

'Mine's Harry,' I said, 'and this is DI Kate Ebdon.'

Trevelion shook hands, first with me and then with Kate. 'Pleased to meet you,' he said. 'I understand from these Crime Agency people that you've been across to the Scilly Isles.'

'Yes, we have, John,' I said, and gave Trevelion a brief rundown on what had taken Kate and me to St Mary's. I went on to describe the escape of the cabin cruiser that had first picked up Madison Bailey.

Trevelion nodded. 'I knew no good would come of removing the customs officer from St Mary's. We've got three police officers there and a police community support officer, but they can't be doing customs work as well as their own. It's the cut-backs you know. Anyway, you'll not want to stand here gossiping. I'll take you to view the body.'

The Cornishman led the way along a corridor, turning corners a few times, until we reached the mortuary. He rang the bell and the door was opened by a man in a white coat. 'All ready for you, Inspector.'

We followed Trevelion into the mortuary and the attendant withdrew the shroud that was covering the female body.

'Yes,' I said. 'That's Madison Bailey, an air stewardess. Would you agree, Kate?'

'Yes, sir,' replied Kate without hesitation.

'It would oblige me if one of you could make a formal written statement of identification, Mr Brock.'

'Of course, John.' It appeared there was no way that I was going persuade Trevelion to use my first name. He was obviously a policeman of the old school – all too rare these days, I'm sorry to say. We strolled back to the entrance hall of the hospital. 'Did you have anything to do with the cabin cruiser that was found at Penzance, John?'

'I did, sir, and from what you've been telling me, it would appear now that there's a connection.'

'There's no doubt about that. Were there any packages aboard the cruiser when you searched it? Dummy packages made to look as though they contained cocaine that had been placed there by the customs people at Heathrow.'

'No, there was nothing like that. The National Crime Agency officers who were here never mentioned anything about that.'

'That doesn't surprise me,' said Kate. 'That lot play their cards very close to their chest. You wouldn't think we were on the same side.' Kate Ebdon had this habit of saying aloud what the rest of us were thinking.

'Have you examined the cruiser for fingerprints, John?' I asked.

'Yes, but although we found quite a few on the steering wheel, they didn't find a match in the national fingerprint database. Incidentally, some were the dead woman's, but that's hardly surprising.'

That none of the prints were on record puzzled me and I said as much. 'That rather upsets my theory, John. I was convinced that the man who stole the cruiser and who picked up Madison Bailey from Porthcressa Beach in St Mary's was James Brooks, an escapee from Ford open prison. Could the other prints belong to the owner of the cruiser, d'you think?'

'That's possible,' said Trevelion. 'We're waiting on the Hampshire Constabulary to interview the owner. He's at Totland on the Isle of Wight and I'm told they're having a bit of a job getting hold of him. He's apparently off somewhere on a business meeting. If you're right about Brooks being the thief, Mr Brock, then as an escaped prisoner he's bound to have worn gloves because he'd have known his dabs were on file.'

I was impressed. Despite his homespun appearance and laid-back attitude, it was quite obvious that John Trevelion had a keen brain and didn't miss a trick. I could just imagine that a London villain – like Brooks – would think him a pushover. If that were the case, he'd get a very nasty shock.

It wasn't just police work that Trevelion was good at; he also turned out to be an excellent host. Not only had he arranged decent accommodation for us, but had also made reservations at an excellent restaurant, where he joined us for dinner, insisting that Devon and Cornwall Police would be paying the bill.

The least I could do was offer to inform Madison Bailey's flatmate and her employer of her death.

'That'd be most helpful, sir, thank you very much,' said Trevelion. 'These things are better done face-to-face, don't you think?'

'I quite agree, John, and I'll send you a formal report when that has been done.'

The following morning the Cornish DI appeared at our hotel and announced that he had a car outside that would drive us to the railway station. Kate and I decided that we would take the train for the entire journey back to London rather than mess about with changing trains and fighting our way through crowds at Newquay and Gatwick airports. We arrived at Belgravia at three o'clock in the afternoon.

My first job the following morning was to contact the Hampshire Constabulary officer who'd been tasked with inter-viewing the owner of the cabin cruiser. I was put in touch with a DI at headquarters who handled requests from other forces and he told me that the matter had been allocated to a PC on the Isle of Wight. This officer, I was told, would make the enquiry when he had the time.

I explained that the question of the cruiser and the finger-prints found on it were of vital importance in what was now a double murder enquiry.

'I wasn't told that, Mr Brock.' The Hampshire officer sounded defensive. 'A DI Trevelion from Penzance spoke to me but said nothing about any murders.'

'He didn't know anything about the murders until I gave him the details when I saw him the day before yesterday,' I said.

There was a pause before the DI spoke again, but eventually he said, 'If you want to do the enquiry yourself, Mr Brock, I'm sure my detective chief superintendent wouldn't raise any objections. Don't think I'm fobbing it off on to you, but with a murder enquiry, you might find it better to do it yourself.'

It was the answer I'd hoped for from the Hampshire officer. I could have done it myself anyway, but common courtesy demanded that I got in touch with Hampshire first as they had already received a request from the Cornwall police. 'I'll happily take it on,' I said, 'and I'll let you know the outcome. When can you give me the go-ahead?'

'If you can hang on a moment, I'll just go down the corridor and ask the boss.' A minute or so later, the DI was back. 'Yes, Mr Brock, he's quite agreeable for you to carry out that enquiry. When d'you propose to see the owner?'

'As soon as he's back from this business trip I'm told he's on. Do you have a telephone number for him?'

'It's a mobile number, Mr Brock,' said the Hampshire DI and gave me the details.

'I'll let you know the outcome.' I finished the call to Hampshire and immediately called the number the DI had given me. A male voice answered the phone, which gave me hope that it was the boat's owner.

'Mr Charles Lavender?' I asked.

'Yes. Who's this?'

'I'm a police officer, Mr Lavender. I'd like to come and see you about your cabin cruiser.'

'Ah, at last. When were you thinking of coming?'

'This afternoon if that would be convenient.'

'Yes, this afternoon would be ideal. But where are you coming from?'

'London. I understand that you live in Totland. Perhaps you'd give me your address.'

Lavender emitted a loud sigh. 'I used to live in Totland,' he said, 'but I moved to Cowes eight years ago.' He gave me his current address. 'I keep telling the authority that holds the register of boat owners that I've moved, but it would appear they still haven't updated their records. But why are you coming from London? It was the police in Cornwall who telephoned my daughter and told her that my cruiser had fetched up in Penzance and that someone from Hampshire police would call me.'

'I think it would be easier if I explained when I got there, Mr Lavender.'

'That's probably for the best. It's beginning to sound complicated.'

I glanced at my watch. There was just enough time for Dave and me to go out to Heathrow and speak to Clare Hughes, the security officer at the airline for whom Madison Bailey had worked. I was aiming to catch a train to Southampton and then cross to West Cowes by the Red Jet catamaran ferry which takes about twenty-five minutes. Overall, a more comfortable journey than our recent trips to the Isles of Scilly and the West Country.

I sent for Steve Harvey, our latest addition to the MIT, and told him to drive us to the airport and wait, in order that he could drop us at Waterloo on the way back from there. Harvey had replaced the late John Appleby who had been murdered on duty and whose name now appears on the Roll of Honour at New Scotland Yard. Not that it's much comfort to his young widow Patricia, a nursing sister.

Clare Hughes wasn't in her office. She was 'out and about', as her assistant in the outer office vaguely put it, but he would call her and tell her we were here.

Ten minutes later, Clare appeared, apologized and ushered us into her office.

'Been out putting my ear to the ground, Harry. Anyway, what can I do for you?'

'Bad news, I'm afraid, Clare,' I began. 'Madison Bailey has been murdered.'

'I'm not surprised.' Clare was ex-Job and expressed no emotion whatever, but that's what thirty years of policing does for you. 'She had a reputation for putting herself about, if you know what I mean. Rumour even had it that she was a member of the mile-high club. What happened to her?'

I told Clare the story of the drugs, the man in the cabin cruiser and the finding of her body at Lamorna Cove in Cornwall.

'Thanks for letting me know, Harry. If I hear any scuttlebutt that might help your enquiries, I'll give you a bell.'

'Thanks. I'd be grateful if you would you let Jeanette Davis know, Clare. She's cabin crew with your airline, but she shares a flat with Madison Bailey. Or did. It would save me a run out there.'

'Sure. Leave it to me, Harry. I'll let her know next time she comes on duty.'

SEVENTEEN

Charles Lavender lived in a large house not far from the coast of the Isle of Wight. He answered the door and showed us into his sitting room. I reckoned he was about fifty years of age, and he sported a neatly trimmed beard and possessed a full head of iron-grey hair.

'This is all a damned funny business, Chief Inspector,' Lavender said, after I'd introduced Dave and myself. 'When we spoke on the phone, you said something about explaining it all face-to-face.' He waved towards a couple of armchairs. 'Do sit down.'

We were about to do so when a woman appeared in the open doorway. She was dressed in jeans and a Breton sweater and although clearly quite a bit younger than Charles Lavender, I wondered if she was, in fact, his wife, but he answered that question for me.

'This is my daughter, Natalie,' he said. 'She's looked after me since my wife died a couple of years ago. These are the police officers I told you were coming about the boat, my dear.'

'Hi,' said Natalie. 'Would you like a cup of tea?'

'Thank you. That would be most welcome.' Dave and I sat down. 'We're attached to a murder investigation team at New Scotland Yard, Mr Lavender.' I began to explain why I was here rather than a Hampshire officer or even a Cornish one. 'We have reason to believe that the man who stole your cabin cruiser is responsible for a murder, maybe even two.'

Lavender looked like a man who read the newspapers and the moment I mentioned the Pretext Club, he told me that he had read all about the murder that had taken place there and found it quite intriguing, which was more than I did. I then gave him a brief rundown about Madison Bailey's body being found at Lamorna Cove in Cornwall by a couple taking an early morning swim. I told him that she was last seen climbing

aboard his stolen cabin cruiser off St Mary's in the Isles of
Scilly. I made no mention of the drugs aspect as I thought
that would confuse matters even more for Lavender, even
though he appeared to be an intelligent man.

'Good God! I'd no idea.' Charles Lavender was clearly taken
aback at the thought of a double murderer stealing his boat.
'But how did you make the connection between this murderer
and my cabin cruiser?'

'We're not exactly amateurs at this business, Mr Lavender.
We've been flat out on this enquiry for almost three weeks.'
Although Dave smiled as he said it, he had no intention of
revealing the finer points of the investigation. Like me, he was
conscious of the lure of cheque-book journalism, and the last
thing we wanted now was for Brooks, assuming he was our
man, to learn how far we'd got with our enquiries. In fact, it
had been simple. We'd taken a note of the number of Lavender's
cabin cruiser when we'd seen it at St Mary's and traced him
that way, despite the records showing him as living in Totland.

Natalie Lavender came into the room with a large tray,
pausing as she looked around for somewhere to put it. Dave
shifted an occasional table, took the tray from her and set it
down in front of her.

'Thank you, Inspector,' she said, and began to pour the tea.

'I'm only a lowly sergeant, Miss Lavender,' said Dave. 'If
I was very clever, I'd be a chief inspector.'

'Oh, come off it.' Natalie laughed and handed round the
tea. She paused as she gave Dave his. 'Were you at London
University by any chance?'

'Yes, I was, Miss Lavender. Reading English. And you?'

'The same, and for goodness' sake call me Natalie. I thought
I recognized you. But you've joined the fuzz!' The implication
was that Dave had done something quite awful, in addition to
which he'd wasted his degree.

'When will you be returning my boat?' asked Charles
Lavender, cutting sharply across this cosy little chat. Dave
later told me that as we'd entered the house, he'd seen a plaque
in the hall that bore the arms of Balliol College, Oxford, and
thought that Lavender was probably a bit sniffy about London
University, even though his daughter had graduated from there.

'It's something you'll have to discuss with the police in Cornwall, Mr Lavender. They might ask you to go down there to collect it,' I said. 'Incidentally, to clarify something: was your boat stolen from Cowes or do you keep it somewhere else?'

'No. From here in Cowes. I moor it at one of the sailing clubs. I've a golfing partner who's the secretary there, you see. I thought it would be reasonably safe, but it seems it wasn't.'

'Obviously not. However, Mr Lavender, your inflatable dinghy was not found.'

'What inflatable dinghy? There wasn't one on the boat.'

'We've established that the murdered woman was picked up in an inflatable dinghy with an outboard motor and taken out to your cabin cruiser, Mr Lavender. As I said just now, this occurred at Porthcressa Beach at St Mary's on the Isles of Scilly.'

'I'm afraid I can't help you with that. I've got an inflatable, but it's still here. Deflated and in my garage, as a matter of fact. D'you want to see it?'

'No, that won't be necessary, thank you, Mr Lavender. Now, to get to the purpose of my coming to see you. The police in Cornwall want to have a set of your fingerprints.'

'Why on earth would they want my fingerprints? Do they suspect me of some crime?'

'No, not at all. Their forensic examiners found a number of fingerprints that they've been unable to identify. Those prints were on the steering wheel of your cabin cruiser and elsewhere on the boat. I imagine that some of them will be yours and, once they've been eliminated, those that are left will belong to the man we want to speak to in connection with the two murders I mentioned. At least, I hope they will.'

'Do I have to find a police station that's open? Or even find a police station?' Lavender, in common with a lot of taxpayers, was unhappy about the number of police stations that had been shut down in an attempt to offset the swingeing cuts the government had imposed on the police. Regrettably, all that had been achieved was to alienate the very public it should be serving.

'No, Mr Lavender. My sergeant has brought the necessary equipment with him.'

'Oh, fine. Where d'you want to do it, Sergeant?' asked Lavender, addressing Dave.

'The most practical place to do it would be on, say, a kitchen table, sir.'

'Follow me,' said Natalie, and led the way to the large kitchen at the back of the house.

'I thought the police used these electronic hand-held gizmos now,' said Lavender, glancing at the inkpad, metal plate and other paraphernalia that Dave was laying out.

'They're mainly used for roadside checks by the traffic police,' said Dave, 'in order to establish if someone has a criminal record. This is the old tried and trusted method.' When he'd finished taking Charles Lavender's finger impressions, he turned to Lavender's daughter. 'I presume you've been on your father's boat, Natalie.'

'Oh, yes. Daddy and I spend as much time on the water as we can. We were bloody annoyed when we found that some rotten bastard had pinched the boat.'

'In that case, I shall need to take your prints as well.'

As he had done with Charles Lavender, Dave held Natalie's hand as he guided each finger first on to the inked plate and then rolled it on to the form to get a good impression.

'Are our fingerprints kept on record forever, now, Chief Inspector?' asked Lavender, once Dave had finished. It was a common enough question from the average upright citizen who'd had his prints taken for elimination purposes and who was concerned about his civil rights.

But it was Dave who answered. 'Good heavens, no. Once we've identified those on the boat as yours, we destroy the ones I've taken today. We've got enough villains clogging up the system without keeping those of innocent members of the public.' Dave packed his equipment and we took our leave.

We returned to London, and Dave arranged for Colin Wilberforce to forward the Lavenders' fingerprints to DI Trevelion at Penzance. I telephoned him to tell him they were on their way.

'Incidentally, Mr Brock. Our fingerprint people were able to get a print from Madison Bailey's neck.'

'Has it been identified, John?' This was exciting news indeed.

'It's only a partial, Mr Brock. What I mean is that there aren't the sixteen points we'd like to have to put before a jury, but our fingerprint lady did match it with some of those on the steering wheel.'

'I just hope your partial doesn't match Charles Lavender, the boat's loser,' I said.

'Oh God, d'you really think it might, Mr Brock?' Trevelion sounded grave, as though the thought had not occurred to him.

'No, no, John,' I said hurriedly. 'It was a joke.'

'Yes, I know,' said Trevelion, and burst out laughing, proving once again that police black humour crosses force boundaries. 'But as I told you when you were down here, none of the prints we found on the steering wheel are on record. It would appear that our murderer has no previous convictions. Scrapings taken from under the victim's fingernails showed that she'd managed to draw blood from somewhere on the killer's body, and we're waiting to see if it matches any DNA samples that are on record.'

I'd thought about this enigma ever since hearing it, but I wasn't sure whether to regard it as good news or bad news. It crossed my mind that maybe this whole drug business and the murder of Madison Bailey might have nothing whatever to do with the death of Robert Sharp at the Pretext Club. Clare Hughes had said that Madison 'put herself about' and it followed, therefore, that her murderer might not have been James Brooks after all, but some other man with whom she'd forged a relationship. Perhaps this mystery man had never been to the Pretext Club and his only interest in Madison Bailey was her usefulness in smuggling cocaine from Colombia.

It was no great comfort that, in my experience, murderers are eventually brought to book. Even if it takes twenty years. But I'd prefer to clear this one sooner rather than later.

It is probably a truism that most criminals are not very intelligent. There are, however, a few who are very intelligent and, by the same token, overconfident. Those individuals make the mistake of trying to be too clever by committing a crime that's too sophisticated, and that often finishes up trapping them. The police call it over-egging the pudding. And that's how it turned out to be with the Pretext Club and Lamorna Cove murders.

I anticipated progress being slow for a day or two while administrative matters took their course in the murder assigned to me and the one in Cornwall in which I had an interest. I had taken a chance and spent the weekend with Lydia, but it wasn't really a relaxing few days because I felt guilty at taking time off when the rest of the team were slaving away. Apart from which, I expected a phone call to come at any moment – nothing in particular, it's just that weekends with Lydia always seem to be interrupted by work.

But progress was faster than I'd anticipated. DI John Trevelion's forensic examiner had sent the fingerprints found on Charles Lavender's yacht, and the partial found on Madison's neck, to the national fingerprint database the moment they had been lifted.

It was on Monday morning, only a matter of three days later, that I got a visit from Linda Mitchell, our crime-scene manager.

'I have some good news, Harry. I think.'

'I could do with some, Linda. What have you got?'

'The senior fingerprint officer in charge of the scenes-of-crime index rang me about half an hour ago. The prints found on the steering wheel of Charles Lavender's cabin cruiser are a match for prints found on a marble-topped table at a house in Chelsea a year ago.'

'I wonder what that was all about. A burglary perhaps?'

'I've no idea, Harry. The prints belong to someone who hasn't got a conviction and, like you, the SFO thought it might have been a burglary and offered to find the entry on their database when he had a moment, but I told him that all you'd want was the address.' Linda handed me a slip of paper with the details.

It was a three-storey house in one of the streets behind Harrods. A young Filipino maid answered the door.

'Is Mrs Crosby at home?' I asked. The maid was rightly reluctant to admit us and so I showed her my warrant card, which she examined carefully. 'We're police officers, miss, but there's nothing to worry about.'

'Ah! OK.' The young woman smiled and invited us into the hall. 'I tell Mrs Crosby,' she said.

A few moments later a middle-aged woman descended the staircase. She wore a grey skirt and jumper and sensible flat shoes and her grey hair, styled so that it fell just below her ears, had a fringe. The entire ensemble presented a school-marmish image.

'Jasmine said you're from the police.' She peered at each of us in turn. I suspected that she was short-sighted but was either too vain to wear spectacles or had forgotten where she'd left them.

'Yes, ma'am. I'm Detective Chief Inspector Brock of the Murder Investigation Team at New Scotland Yard and this is Detective Sergeant Poole. It's Mrs Crosby, is it?'

'Yes, I'm Anne Crosby. Do come in.' She led us into a comfortable sitting room and invited us to take a seat.

'Would you care for coffee? I usually have mine about now.'

'That's very kind of you. Thank you.'

Mrs Crosby rang a small bell and the Filipino maid appeared promptly. Mrs Crosby issued a string of instructions in what I presume was the maid's native language.

Seeing my surprise, Mrs Crosby said, 'My late husband was in the Diplomatic Service and our last posting was in Manila. I've always had a flair for languages and enjoy learning them.'

'You certainly seem to have mastered that one,' said Dave. 'I presume it was Filipino.'

'Thank you.' Anne Crosby raised her eyebrows momentarily, presumably because Dave recognized the language, but then inclined her head, looked at me and smiled. 'I'm intrigued by your being from a murder squad or whatever it was you called it? I presume, therefore, you're here in connection with a murder.'

'Not directly, Mrs Crosby,' I said, 'but we are investigating two murders.' That wasn't strictly accurate; the murder of Madison Bailey was Devon and Cornwall's case, although I suspected that we might finish up solving it for them. 'A number of fingerprints were found on a stolen cabin cruiser that was abandoned in Cornwall. When checks were made in the records, it was found that they tallied with some found on a marble-topped table in this house about a year ago.'

'My word, that's very impressive.'

'Can you recall how those fingerprints got there? If you know, that is.'

'I remember it only too clearly, Mr Brock.' The coffee appeared and Mrs Crosby spent a few moments pouring it from a rather splendid silver coffee pot. She pointed to a matching creamer and sugar bowl and invited us to help ourselves. 'I saw this advertisement in the newspaper that had been placed there by an antiques dealer. He offered to value people's antiques for insurance purposes and, to use his own words, might be tempted to make an offer if he liked a particular item.'

'D'you recall this man's name, Mrs Crosby?' asked Dave, who had now started to take notes. He forbore from suggesting that to invite such a person into one's home was asking for trouble. In this case, it might turn out to have been helpful. To us, that is.

'Yes. It was Forbes. Norman Forbes.'

'What did he look like? Are you able to describe him?'

'He was of medium height,' began Anne Crosby. 'A full head of hair and a very suave manner. Oh, and he had what I call fleshy good looks. Does that make sense? I'm sorry I can't be more helpful than that, but it was a year ago.'

'It's perfectly all right, Mrs Crosby, it was asking a bit much,' said Dave, being his own suave self. 'I wonder if we might see the table.'

'Yes, of course. It's in the drawing room.' Anne Crosby rose from her chair and made for the door. Dave scooted ahead and opened it for her. Again, she smiled at him and murmured her thanks.

Standing in the centre of the room into which we were shown was a rather squat table with three feet, each of which was shaped like a lion's paw.

'This is it. It's what they call a French Empire *guéridon* – a pedestal table – and we picked it up in Paris, years ago, when my husband was second secretary at our embassy there.' Anne Crosby placed her hand on the table, splaying her fingers so that only the tips touched the marble top. 'That's how his fingerprints came to be on it.'

'Why were the police involved?' I asked,

'This Forbes person examined this table very carefully, even getting down on his knees at one point. Eventually, he shook his head and estimated that it was worth about a thousand pounds. Well, I knew that was nonsense. Several of our friends said that it was worth at least twice that if not more. However, to get to the point, Mr Brock, after he'd left the house, I noticed that one of my ornaments was missing from the mantelshelf.' Anne Crosby pointed. 'Right there in the centre, it was. A Chinese jade snuff bottle probably worth about four thousand pounds. But it was only two inches high and Forbes must have slipped it into his pocket when I wasn't looking. Thinking about it, he obviously recognized it and knew its worth.'

'And so you called the police.'

'Of course,' she said, rather tartly reawakening the school-marm impression. 'They came along and took a few details. I told them that the man had put his hand on the table and a fingerprint chap came along and put powder all over the place. It took Jasmine ages to get it off. But I never saw my snuff bottle again.'

Dave, like me, had come to the conclusion that Forbes' modus operandi was similar to that of Robert Sharp in that he went only for portable items of value. Much as he might have liked the French table, he could not have carried it away. That would have meant having a motor vehicle of some sort that would have had a number plate. And a number plate meant that there would be a chance of the vehicle and the con man being traced. Dave opened his briefcase and took out the photograph of Sharp that had been given to us by Rebecca Chapman, whose daughter Fiona had committed suicide after Sharp had left her pregnant and waiting at the church. And he had stolen five thousand pounds from the young woman's father.

'Would you look at this photograph, please, Mrs Crosby.'

She took it from Dave and stared at it. 'That's him!' she exclaimed. 'That's Norman Forbes.'

'Are you certain?'

'I have no doubt whatsoever. Has he been arrested?'

'We think he's dead, Mrs Crosby,' said Dave diplomatically, not wishing to admit that it looked very much as though Sharp was alive and well and had *not* been murdered at the Pretext Club. Or anywhere else.

EIGHTEEN

'What do we do now, guv'nor?' asked Dave, once we were back at Belgravia.

'Start looking for the bugger, Dave, but first I must speak to the commander.' Anne Crosby's revelation had just turned our murder enquiry on its head.

I walked down the corridor and tapped lightly on Alan Cleaver's open office door.

'What's on your mind, Harry?' The commander waved me towards a chair. As usual, he was in his shirtsleeves and his desk was clear. Folding his copy of the *Daily Telegraph*, he dropped it into the wastepaper basket. That he'd been reading a newspaper was a sure sign that he had no outstanding problems to deal with. Until now.

I brought him up to date with the investigation, finishing by recounting our interview with Anne Crosby.

'The scenes-of-crime prints taken from Lavender's boat led us to Mrs Crosby in Chelsea. Sergeant Poole showed her the photograph of Sharp that Mrs Rebecca Chapman had given us, and Mrs Crosby identified him as the guy who stole her snuff bottle, although she knew him as Norman Forbes. It looks very much as though I got it wrong, guv'nor.' There was absolutely no point in being other than completely straight with Cleaver.

'Don't beat yourself up, Harry. There was no way in which you could have thought that the victim was someone other than Robert Sharp. According to the pathologist's report there was nothing that would enable you to identify the body, and in view of the circumstantial evidence and the statements of the staff at this nudist place, the victim had to be Sharp. After all, he was found in Sharp's room at this club. I'd have come to the same conclusion. The problem now is what to do about it. What are your thoughts?'

'He'll be pretty confident that he's in the clear,' I said. 'He knows that his fingerprints aren't on record because he's never been arrested. And it's a racing certainty that he won't know that the dabs he left on the table at Mrs Crosby's place are on file. Knowing what we know about his modus operandi, I'm sure he'll think we're looking for James Brooks, the guy who escaped from Ford open prison. But now it looks as though it was Brooks' body that was found at the Pretext Club. Although we'll never know for sure unless Sharp levels with us. *If* we find the bastard.'

'I'm inclined to agree, Harry.'

'However, sir, if Sharp learns from the press and the television that we've mounted an active search to find him, he might get desperate. If my theory is right, he could be facing a life behind bars for two toppings – Brooks and Madison Bailey – and I don't doubt that if he has to kill again to escape, he won't hesitate. After all, he can only do one term of life imprisonment, no matter how many toppings he does. It's also possible that he'll try robbery because he's bound to be running short of cash. I'm sure he thought he'd hit the big time when he came up with this scheme to get Madison Bailey to smuggle drugs, and he was confidently expecting seventy grand's worth of cocaine to drop into his lap when he picked her up at St Mary's. But he must've gone ballistic when he found out that it was most likely talcum powder he was betting on.'

'He probably thought she'd had him over and had flogged the gear to someone else, Harry,' said Cleaver. 'I reckon it's a strong possibility that he strangled her in a fit of rage and chucked her body over the side. Mind you, that is a guess and from what you've said previously about Madison Bailey, she doesn't sound bright enough to have come up with a plan like that. But we've got to keep our feet on the ground, Harry. Despite all the ifs, buts and maybes, there's no firm evidence that Sharp is the killer. Speculation won't hack it at the Old Bailey and for all we know at the moment, she might have been in cahoots with some other guy over the drug smuggling.'

'I was about to say the same thing,' I said. 'My one hope is that when the scrapings from under Bailey's fingernails are compared with Sharp's DNA, we'll have a match. Then we'll have him bang to rights.'

'So, what can I do, Harry? You're the investigating officer, but my job is to give you any support you need.'

'I should like to impose a news blackout on this latest twist, guv'nor. If the public is allowed to carry on thinking that we're looking for Brooks in connection with two murders, Sharp might just start to get overconfident. But, as I said just now, once he knows he's wanted, he could become dangerous.'

'I'll speak to the Yard's director of media and communications or whatever it's called this week, Harry. The media never likes having this sort of muzzle put on them, but if we promise them full disclosure – including being honest about our first wrong turning – I think they'll go along with us on this one.'

'Thank you, sir. It wouldn't be a bad thing if they were to say something about the search for Brooks being intensified with regard to a murder in Cornwall.'

'I'll do that now and let you know that they've agreed it.'

I'd only been back in the incident room for five minutes when Cleaver rang me there. 'All set up, Harry. Now go out and find this guy.'

Cleaver's predecessor would have dithered for half a day and then consulted the deputy assistant commissioner. But then he wasn't a real detective.

That evening's TV news bulletins did us proud. They reported that we were actively hunting Brooks in connection with the death of Sharp and Bailey, and the following day's press went along with it.

It is well-known among detectives that even the most sophisticated of criminals will sometimes make the stupidest of mistakes that result in their undoing. And so it was with Robert Sharp.

We had put Sharp's description on the Police National Computer and added copies of his photograph and the fingerprints found on Mrs Crosby's table and steering wheel of Charles Lavender's boat. Finally, we emphasized that neither the media nor the public must get to know of our desire to speak to him. His one-time alias of Norman Forbes was included in the information we put in the entry. On the eighth day, the trap was sprung, not by CID officers but by our old adversaries the Black Rats.

About the only sophisticated part of Robert Sharp's scam was to steal a new car and, by dint of bribery, persuade a corrupt dealer to provide number plates that were identical with an exactly similar make, model and colour of car. The scam was made even easier now that the tax disc had been abolished and it became unnecessary to forge one. As a result, Sharp's stolen vehicle was able to assume, to the casual observer, the legitimate car's identity. Unfortunately for him, the police are not casual observers.

There are many simple errors that, in the past, have trapped the criminal mastermind, not that Sharp was in that class. Being stopped at night for having a defective rear light has, more than once, brought about an arrest for a multitude of crimes.

In Sharp's case, the stupid part was to drive too fast on that section of the A40 out of London where a speed limit of forty miles per hour had been imposed. Which, as it turned out, proved the point that it's possible to have too sophisticated a plan.

An unmarked police BMW was parked in a lay-by when a Ford Mondeo swept past at approximately seventy miles an hour.

'I think we have a customer,' said Tracy, the sergeant driver of the BMW, as she started the engine and accelerated in pursuit. To aggravate his offence the driver of the Mondeo frequently changed lanes and, on occasion, passed other vehicles on the nearside.

Waiting until he saw a suitably safe place to bring about a stop, Martin, Tracy's co-driver, illuminated the blue lights secreted behind the radiator grille and switched on the siren.

The driver of the Mondeo, believing that all that would happen was a summons – which, of course, would go to the owner of the car that legitimately held the identical number plate – dutifully pulled into a lay-by.

'Seventy-two miles an hour,' said Tracy, 'which is thirty-two miles an hour over the speed limit for this section of the carriageway.'

'Good heavens! Really? Surely not.'

'Changing lanes and passing other vehicles on the nearside on at least four occasions.'

'I don't think so, Officer.'

'It's all on our video recorder,' said Tracy. *They always say the same things*, she thought, *and always get the same answer. Why do they bother?* 'D'you have your driving licence?'

'Not on me, no.'

'What's your name?'

'Norman Forbes.'

'Do you own this vehicle, Mr Forbes?' It was like pulling teeth but Tracy wasn't bothered about that. The moment she saw the man, she realized, from the photograph on the PNC, that she'd got the man wanted for questioning in connection with two murders. And when he'd said that his name was Norman Forbes it clinched it. Apart from which, he was not shown as the registered owner on the PNC.

'Yes, it's my car.'

'Just step out of the car, Mr Forbes,' said Martin, holding a hand-held device, 'and place the forefinger of your left hand in here.'

Forbes knew that this device would check his fingerprints with the central database and this was to be avoided. Although having no previous convictions, he did not want the police to have his fingerprints as this might lead to much worse consequences than a motoring offence.

It was at this point that a routine traffic stop turned into something more sinister. Rather than doing as the traffic PC had asked, the Mondeo driver suddenly produced a gun, but Tracy's knowledge that she and Martin were now dealing with a possible double-murderer had made her wary. And prepared.

The Mondeo driver's gunslinging ability would not have secured him a part even as a walk-on non-speaking extra in a spaghetti western. Clearly unused to handling weapons with any degree of speed and efficiency, his movement was too slow to be threatening. Suddenly, he felt a crippling blow as Tracy's baton, wielded with as much force as she could muster, fractured the wrist holding the weapon. As if that were not enough, he also received a debilitating discharge of fifty thousand volts from Martin's taser gun and fell to the ground.

'Oh dear! They will do these things,' said Tracy as she donned protective gloves and retrieved the .22 pistol. It wasn't loaded.

After a visit to St Mary's Hospital in Paddington where 'Norman Forbes' had his fractured wrist put in plaster, he was escorted to Paddington police station where his fingerprints were taken. When compared with the database, it confirmed that Forbes, also believed to be Robert Sharp, was wanted by DCI Harry Brock of HMCC (West). The PNC entry stated that Forbes was wanted in connection with the theft of a snuff bottle, but also suggested that he might be able to assist police with their enquiries into two murders. The CID were called and he was handed over to them.

I returned from lunching at my favourite Italian restaurant to be greeted by a jubilant Colin Wilberforce. And it's not often that Wilberforce becomes jubilant other than on a rugby football pitch.

'What is it, Colin?'

'Sharp's been arrested, sir.'

'Where?'

'Paddington, sir. He was stopped by a traffic unit for exceeding the speed limit on the Paddington flyover and when they were about to fingerprint him, he produced a pistol.'

'Was anybody hurt?'

'Only Sharp, sir. The lady traffic sergeant broke his wrist with her baton.'

'Oh dear! It sounds as though she'd get on very well with Miss Ebdon. What's the SP?'

'An escort from Paddington nick is bringing him up to Belgravia as I speak, sir.'

The Assistant Commissioner Specialist Operations and the Chief Constable of the Devon and Cornwall Police had agreed that the Metropolitan Police should take over the investigation into the murder of Madison Bailey.

The prisoner had been delivered to Belgravia police station

and Dave and I went downstairs from our offices to interview him.

As is so often the case with murderers at first sight, he appeared to be an ordinary, almost inoffensive sort of man. His date of birth, given to the arresting officers, showed him to be thirty-seven years of age. Mrs Rebecca Chapman, whose daughter Fiona had committed suicide thanks entirely to Robert Sharp, had given us a photograph of the man. She had described him as personable and good looking which, in reality, is a matter of personal opinion. My own view was that he had the fleshy appearance of a mummy's boy who had developed into a man who always got his own way in life. But then I'm a cynical copper who's seen too much of the seamy side of life.

'Robert Sharp?' I asked, as Dave and I sat down opposite the man.

'No, I'm Norman Forbes.' The denial was made almost apologetically as if to correct someone who had made a genuine mistake. So confident was this man that he had declined a solicitor, even when we told him that if he could not afford one, the taxpayer would provide one.

'I'm Detective Chief Inspector Brock of the Murder Investigation Team. This is Detective Sergeant Poole.'

'And this is a photograph of you given to us by Mrs Rebecca Chapman,' said Dave, 'whose daughter committed suicide after you reneged on your promise to marry her. And as if that wasn't enough, you nicked five grand from her father and left her pregnant. Even so, you didn't give a damn, did you? Personally, I'll be very happy to see a scumbag like you, Sharp, go down for a full-term life sentence. I hope the screws on Dartmoor give you a hard time. And if they don't, they'll turn a blind eye when half a dozen other hairy cons come into your cell feeling a bit fruity.' He glanced at me. 'Shall I turn on the tape-recorder now, sir?'

'Yes, Sergeant,' I said, thus putting the interview on a formal footing.

'You're not obliged to say anything, Mr Sharp,' said Dave pleasantly, 'but it may harm your defence if you do not mention when questioned something that you later rely on in court. Anything you do say will be given in evidence.'

'I haven't got anything to say,' replied Sharp with what, I imagined, he thought was a disarming smile. Nevertheless, he had clearly been shaken up by Dave's comments about life in one of Her Majesty's less desirable penal establishments. But the truth was even worse than the brief picture Dave had painted.

'I don't have anything to ask you, Sharp,' I said, 'but I'll tell you why you're here. You invited James Brooks to your chalet at the Pretext Club near Harrow and shot him. The pistol taken from you by the traffic officers who arrested you has been sent to the ballistics laboratory and I have every confidence that it will prove to be the weapon you used to kill Brooks.'

'But how on earth . . . ?'

'Just listen.' I held up my hand. 'With the assistance of Madison Bailey, who brought plastic bottles of petrol into the club's premises in her beach bag, you set fire to Brooks' body and you then left the club, having given Bailey time to depart first. Having murdered James Brooks, who you thought was a loner, you assumed his identity. But unbeknown to you, Brooks had escaped from Ford open prison. Not the cleverest of moves to try passing yourself off as an escaped prisoner for whom the police were actively searching, was it?'

'I don't believe it.' If the expression on Sharp's face was anything to go by, the enormity of his crass mistake suddenly dawned on him. 'You've got to be kidding me.'

'Then, you hit on what you thought was a foolproof way of making money by getting Bailey to bring in drugs from Colombia on her next routine flight to Bogotá. To that end, you bought a make-up case at a cost of nigh-on two hundred pounds. The shop assistant remembered you clearly because you invited her out to dinner. But worse than that, Sharp, you paid for the transaction with your own credit card. That is to say, a credit card in the name of Robert Sharp. Not very bright at all, was that, considering that you were trying to convince the police that you were dead.'

'I think you must be mixing me up with someone else,' said Sharp vainly, but the expression on his face was only too clearly one of despair as he realized just how thorough our investigations – and how stupid his blunders – had been.

'Of course, the customs people are wise to the Colombia run and are always alert to drug-smuggling. Most intelligent smugglers don't bring it in direct; they lay it off through less suspicious countries. Consequently, when the cocaine was found in Madison's make-up case, it was replaced with packets of innocuous white powder. They were going to track you down, Sharp. You succeeded in establishing, from that moment on, that there was nowhere you could hide.'

'I thought Madison had swapped them over and sold them for herself,' said Sharp. 'She was a cunning little bitch.'

'Yes, that is what you thought, unfortunately for Madison Bailey. So, you strangled her and threw her body overboard from the cabin cruiser you'd stolen from Cowes on the Isle of Wight.'

'I didn't strangle her,' said Sharp pathetically. 'It was an accident. We hit a bit of rough sea and she fell overboard. She must have hit her head on the side of the boat as she went down because she sank like a stone and there was no trace of her. I dropped anchor and dived in, but I couldn't find her.'

'Your fingerprints were found on Madison Bailey's neck, Sharp,' said Dave, 'and the pathologist is adamant that they are in exactly the right place to have effected a strangulation.' Wisely, Dave didn't mention that the skin found beneath Madison Bailey's fingernails almost certainly would match Sharp's DNA when it was compared.

'And you did all this because you couldn't resist women,' I said. 'You were obsessed with sex and what better place to find attractive young women than naturist clubs, where you picked up each and every one of your victims, including Madison. You had women all over the place because you couldn't resist a naked flame. And it was a naked flame – in more ways than one – that did for you. Some of these women became pregnant by you. In another instance, you were buying a house to set up home with another of your pregnant conquests, and you promised marriage to several of the others. In order to finance your lifestyle, you set about the petty thieving of antiques. But that didn't fill the void. You were then in so much debt that the only solution was to disappear to avoid your creditors. You set about faking your own death at the expense of James Brooks' life, who you shot before setting fire to his body and stealing his identity. Then you tried drug-smuggling, but that didn't work either, and you murdered Madison Bailey. As a result, Robert Sharp, you will now be charged with the murders of James Brooks and Madison Bailey.'

'I told you, Madison's death was an accident.' Sharp's hands were clenched, one around the other, as he made his pathetic and implausible denial. 'Honestly! And I don't know anything about a fire at the Pretext Club.'

'No doubt the Crown Prosecution Service will consider charging you with the theft of five thousand pounds from the Chapman residence and, as you've acknowledged being Norman Forbes, with the theft of Mrs Anne Crosby's jade snuff bottle from her house in Chelsea.'

'I've never heard of the woman,' said Sharp desperately.

'You obligingly left your fingerprints on her French Empire *guéridon*, Sharp.'

'Oh!' said Sharp.

NINETEEN

The next problem that had to be dealt with was one of jurisdiction. Happily, that was one problem that didn't fall to the police. For once, we were able to sit back and watch the lawyers fight it out.

Madison Bailey's body had been washed up at Lamorna Cove in the county of Cornwall and the Crown Court at Truro was the obvious venue for a trial. For purely personal reasons, I didn't fancy spending a couple of weeks or more in darkest Cornwall. On the other hand, if the murder of Madison Bailey had occurred in international waters, what the lawyer's describe as murder on the high seas, it is almost certain that the trial would be held at the Old Bailey.

The Crown Prosecution Service pondered this enigma for some time, the arguments going backwards and forwards between the head office in London and the area office in Bristol. Finally, someone with backbone made a decision: the trial of Robert Sharp was to be held at the Old Bailey where he would face two counts of murder.

'Oyez! Oyez! Oyez! All persons having business before this court of oyer and terminer and general gaol delivery pray draw near.'

The centuries-old proclamation opened the trial of the Crown against Sharp, who appeared in the dock with his right wrist still in plaster. He pleaded not guilty to murdering James Brooks and Madison Bailey.

The prosecution didn't have too difficult a task, added to which the jury consisted of eight women and four men. It was not the best balance for a man whose character would be assassinated by counsel for the Crown as he listed Sharp's transgressions against women.

Some of the women in the jury box appeared to be in their twenties and I could imagine that defence counsel would be worried that they might find Sharp guilty whatever the evidence. Consequently, it was obvious from the outset that Sharp's counsel, a strikingly handsome lady of Indian descent, was going to have a hard task defending him.

I was the first to give evidence for the prosecution by testifying to those parts of the long and complex investigation that were relevant. Defence counsel gave me a hard time during my day and a half in the witness box, but never once gave me the pleasure of correcting suggestions designed to prove her client's innocence. Because she didn't make any. She even ensured that she used my correct rank on every occasion. But only the slipshod ignorance of scriptwriters has a chief inspector being addressed as 'inspector'. This lady barrister carefully avoided affording me that discourtesy.

The next witness was Kate Ebdon who stepped into the witness box to corroborate my testimony. Gone were the white shirt and jeans and in their place a smart black suit, the skirt at an appropriate length, a white blouse and high-heeled shoes. Her hair was swept back into a ponytail allowing her gold earrings to be displayed to advantage. She called it her 'Old Bailey kit'.

Henry Mortlock followed Kate into the witness box. His portly figure, his pince-nez, his bow tie and his pedantry lent him a theatrical air and two or three actors who could play him on TV immediately sprang to mind. However, as always, his evidence was far from theatrical – it was precise, factual and indisputable. There were no cracks through which defence counsel could force an opening.

Similarly, Martina Dawson, the fire investigator, had given evidence so often that she was unlikely to be caught wrong-footed, and she wasn't. Her lucid evidence left no doubt that the fire had been started deliberately.

Linda Mitchell, our crime-scene manager, was always very professional in the witness box. On this occasion, the only evidence that really counted, and shaped the verdict, was that the scrapings from beneath Madison Bailey's fingernails – which surprisingly had survived immersion in sea water – proved to be a match for Robert Sharp's DNA.

The ballistics expert testified that the pistol taken from Sharp at the time of his arrest was the weapon that fired the round found in Brooks' body by Dr Mortlock. Once again, it was incontrovertible evidence and was not disputed by the defence.

As the ballistics expert left the witness box, Dave whispered: 'Game, set and match, guv'nor.'

Detective Inspector John Trevelion had travelled from Penzance for the day to give evidence, which he did in a slow but confident manner, his tweed suit and Cornish accent paradoxically underlining the authenticity of what he was saying. Once released by the judge, Trevelion made his farewells to us in the echoing lobby of the Old Bailey and expressed his dislike of London, couldn't understand why we worked in such a lawless and polluted city, and couldn't wait to get back to his native Cornwall. On reflection, I think he probably has the right idea.

Tracy, the traffic unit sergeant who had broken Sharp's wrist, afforded the trial a little light relief.

'Why did you consider it necessary to assault my client with such force that he suffered a fractured wrist, Sergeant?' asked Sharp's counsel with the intention of showing the officer to be a callous, albeit female, thug. This despite Tracy being the most feminine of officers.

'When your client produced a firearm, madam,' began Tracy, 'I concluded that he did not intend to abide by the Queensberry Rules. Therefore, I also abandoned them.'

A ripple of laughter had followed this spirited response, but once it had died down, the judge, directing his mild observation to Sharp's counsel, said, 'The officer seems to have answered your question, madam.' And another few laughs followed.

When the defence case opened, Sharp's counsel called a few expert witnesses, but to no avail.

Finally, despite the uphill struggle she was facing, she put Sharp in the witness box to deny the charges against him. It was a bad tactical mistake because it left her client open to cross-examination. Predictably, the Crown's counsel clinically destroyed every one of his vain excuses until he was reduced to a sobbing, pitiable figure as he protested his innocence. It was a sad and pathetically lacklustre performance.

On the twelfth day of the trial, the jury retired and its four men and eight women deliberated for a total of four hours before returning to deliver a verdict of guilty on both counts of the indictment.

Although trial by jury is a bastion of the English legal system, it's difficult to detect the hidden prejudices of its members until it's too late. Women, generally speaking, don't like womanizing men, particularly those who steal from their conquests or promise marriage or leave them pregnant. In the case of Fiona Chapman who had committed suicide, Sharp had been responsible for all three elements. When that evidence was given, it was obvious from the expressions on the faces of the jury that the young woman's demise did more damage to Sharp's case than all the other evidence put together.

After delivering a little homily about 'having lived the dissolute life of a wastrel' which, no doubt, the judge thought was a pretty smart remark, he sentenced Sharp to life imprisonment with the caveat that he was not to be considered for parole for at least thirty years. As Sharp was escorted downstairs from the dock he was probably working out that he would be sixty-seven years of age before he even stood a chance of experiencing freedom again. If he lived that long.

I glanced up at the public gallery as I turned to leave the court and noticed, for the first time, that Rebecca Chapman was seated in the front row. I assumed that she had been there for the whole trial, although I hadn't noticed her until today. She was smiling a distant smile of satisfaction and I decided not to break her reverie by going upstairs and talking to her.

On the Friday evening following the end of the trial, I gathered my team together in a nearby pub and bought them all a drink. It was not a celebration of securing a sentence that condemned a man to thirty years in prison; that was never something to be celebrated. It was, instead, a way of marking the end of a difficult and lengthy investigation and inadequately thanking them for their efforts.

Leaving my team to enjoy the rest of the evening and wasting my breath telling them not to get drunk, I caught a train to Esher. I had determined to spend the weekend relaxing with

Lydia without wondering if a phone call would summon me back to work. At least, that was my fervent hope.

Lydia had obviously been watching for my arrival and opened the door as I was about to ring the bell. She was wearing a long black velvet dress that I'd not seen before.

Taking hold of my hand, she said, 'Come in, darling. I've got a surprise for you.'

I just hoped she hadn't arranged a dinner party – surprise parties I can do without – apart from which, I didn't want anyone else intruding on our evening. But I needn't have worried, nobody did. Which, in view of the surprise Lydia had arranged, was probably just as well.